SACRIFICE

Rosalind Fox

a78l5-377 0638

BRN NO: 2042784

To all my family, with love.

HR

PROLOGUE

Tuesday 22nd June 1557

'The white wings of Angels! Look above us.'

She looked up into the intense blue of a summer sky, squinting as the sun came out from behind the circle of white, banked clouds, bathing the market place in golden light.'

'He comes! Our Saviour comes for the righteous.'

She recognised the voice of the bald man with the black eye and bloodied nose who, like her, had spent the night confined in the cellars of the Star Inn.

The man's voice, hoarse and rough, gained strength. 'And straight way there was with the angel a multitude of heavenly soldiers, lauding God, and saying: Glory—'

As the words rang out across the crowd, a low hiss of condemnation came from a group of bystanders, each holding up a cross, each craning forward to stare at the ten prisoners, who were tied around the stake in a grim echo of a country maypole dance.

A tall man dressed all in black, stepped forward with a lighted torch and thrust it into the faggots at her feet. She closed her eyes, her bound hands clenched into two helpless fists. The high keen of terror from the woman tied on her right rose in a crescendo and she smelled the sickly odour of voided bowels before the blessed smoke billowed around her, filling her nostrils and bringing oblivion.

1

Summer 1555

Katherine sat by the window in the vicarage and watched the rivulets of rain slide down the thick glass, hesitate on the lead strip, then tip over and cascade down onto the next pane. She rubbed away the condensation that her warm breath was making on the inside and narrowed her eyes to peer out. She could just make out the shape of George, as he tramped doggedly across the field towards her, an old piece of sacking wrapped around his shoulders.

The long, wet grass on each side of the path slapped against his legs and, as he came closer, she could see his face screwed up against the rain pouring steadily down, straight and silvery like a hail of sword blades. His dark hair was slicked, wet and shining close to his head and droplets ran down his cheeks and dripped from his chin and nose. His mouth was moving and she knew he would be counting his steps out loud. It must not be more than one thousand, eight hundred and forty from his house to hers. If it was, something bad would happen. She had overheard him telling this to Harry, although she knew that her three-year-old son would have no idea what George was talking about. Nor did she.

When George lengthened his stride, she knew he must be nearing his deadline and Katherine caught her breath as he overreached himself and nearly slipped on the wet path. The boy was a strong, sturdy lad of about eleven summers and she was fond of him, but he was certainly strange. Why on earth should the number of steps matter?

Now he was at the door. She heard the latch rattle and the stamp of his feet in their small hallway followed by a giggle as her small son rushed out of the gloom and clasped him around the knees.

'Dord, Dord! Come play Dord.'

'Leave off Harry, let me get inside. Let's find your mother, eh?'

With his skirts lifted high, showing short, chubby legs with dimpled knees, Harry appeared in the doorway, towing George behind him.

Despite the fact that he looked as if he had been swimming in the river, George blinked the wet from his eyes and looked kindly down at Harry and Katherine was pleased with the thought that George liked coming here. Certainly her house was much more spacious than his, which must feel cramped when all the family were at home. Here there were three rooms, a small entrance hall and an attic for storage. The main room where they ate and Katherine did her sewing was pleasant and usually full of light, for there were glazed windows on two sides – a real luxury.

The settle where she sat, was placed to catch the light and was padded with cushions and strewn with material and bright embroidery threads, while a large trestle table occupied the centre of the floor with a bench on either side and a chair at the head. Under each window was a chest, one of which had carvings of oak leaves and acorns and three squirrels decorating the front. The carvings fascinated young Harry who would happily sit for ages tracing his fingers over the raised, shiny wood.

Katherine smiled at George and he looked away. She laid her sewing to one side of her and beckoned to her son. 'Harry, leave George alone.'

'Dord play now.'

His mother looked at him affectionately, 'Soon, Harry, soon, but I need George to do some things for me first.'

She looked up at the dripping boy, still standing awkwardly in the doorway. 'Good morrow, George,' she said. 'I see it still seems to be raining as hard as ever. I heard it in the night and thought it would wake Harry and my husband as it rattled on the shutters, but, as usual, they slept like babes.' She chuckled. 'They didn't even hear the thunder though 'twas enough to wake the dead.'

George gave no answer, but stared at the floor while picking at his shirt. Katherine, however, carried on talking in a normal, friendly voice. 'We need some more logs out of the store, so if you could bring those in first and stack them over there, and then draw some water from the well. Afterwards you must dry yourself – you may use that old cloth there on the stool. If the rain eases a bit later the vegetables need weeding again. All this wet weather makes them grow apace.'

George nodded his head, scattering raindrops like a wet dog. Gently he set the child out of his way and headed back towards the door.

'Dord! Dord!'

'Hush Harry. George will likely play later. Come, sit with me and I'll tell you a story.'

Harry stood where he was; his small feet planted firmly apart and shook his head deliberately from side to side. Eyes large and round he put his thumb in his mouth.

'You don't want a story?' said his mother, raising her eyebrows invitingly. 'Not even the one with the knight on the big white horse who—?'

'Yesh, horsey,' said Harry and launched himself into a staggering run. He grabbed Katherine's skirts and heaved himself onto her lap.

'Good boy.'

Katherine settled him on one knee and picked up her sewing, winding the material carefully over her left hand and anchoring it against the child's leg. Over the months since her illness she had found ways of coping with a weak hand and arm, but, nevertheless, it was awkward with her son on her lap.

'No,' said Harry and tried to push the material from her hands.

'Careful, you'll prick yourself on the needle. Mother must sew as I have to finish this, but I can still tell you about the white horse.' With a sigh the child snuggled against her and replaced his thumb in his mouth. 'Once upon a time there was a king who was very bad. He had dark, dark hair and mean, mean eyes and on his back he had a big hump. Now this king wanted—'

The door slammed and George came in carrying a basket of logs. He brought the smell of damp earth with him and left wet footprints on the flags as he stumbled across to the big open hearth and began to stack the logs against the sidewall where they would dry further before being used on the fire.

'Not too many at once, George, you'll strain yourself.'

He certainly was a willing worker, she thought. She didn't know how she would have managed without him for these last two years. He helped with all the heavy chores while her husband, William, was out in the Parish.

She had told Harry the story of bad King Richard so often, she barely had to think about what she was saying, so, as she spoke and sewed, her mind wandered to the world outside - a world that she was now no longer able to roam. For almost three years, she had been confined within the house or, with much effort, to their patch of land just outside.

She paused in her story and sighed, her needle poised in the air as she stared into space. Harry looked up into her face and frowned at the hesitation. He patted her hand gently. As though waking from sleep she gave a start, dropped a kiss on his fair hair and continued her tale.

George had finished stacking wood and Katherine could hear the squeak of the handle as he raised the bucket from the well. She glanced out of the window and was pleased to see that at last the rain had eased and a watery sun was making the drops on the trees glisten in a thousand tiny rainbows. She finished the story and Harry slid off her knees and ran to find George. Harry loved the boy, who, despite his awkwardness with adults was gentle and caring with the toddler. She smiled as their shapes passed the window – Harry riding on George's back and shouting 'Gee up' with great glee. She was so grateful to George who supplied the action that an active little boy needed and which she was unable to provide.

William had often told her that Harry's birth had been an answer to a secret prayer; one which for many years he had not dared to utter aloud. As priest of St Denys' Church in Rotherfield he had, under old King Henry, been forbidden to marry, but then the sickly boy-king, Edward, had changed the country's religion to Protestant and it had become lawful for a priest to have both wife and family.

Katherine smiled to herself as she remembered how William had lost no time in courting her. As a young widow she worked as needlewoman at the manor house and William had visited often. She had always thought that he was merely showing the deference due to My Lady, but William later confessed to her that he had invented many excuses in order to visit the manor and catch a glimpse of her. He was, he declared, enchanted by her calm, gentle manner and fair complexion.

For the young couple their marriage was a joyful celebration. She had been deeply in love for the first time in her life, but not only that - William had given her the security and confidence that she'd always craved.

Just over eighteen months later, Katherine had given birth to Harry, attended by George's mother Ann, who had helped to deliver many of the children in the village. The birth had not proved difficult and William and Katherine thanked God for the blessing of their child. But their joy was short-lived. A month after the boy was born Katherine had a terrifying seizure, and it left her unable to use either her left leg or her left arm.

A doctor visited once, bled the already weak Katherine and pronounced her humours out of order due to her recent delivery. It was Ann who had been most help to her – had become her friend - visiting daily, tempting her with nourishing food, massaging her arm and leg and insisting that Katherine try to exercise and move her useless limbs. Gradually she had recovered her strength and, despite her disability, she muddled through the first year of Harry's life until Ann had suggested that perhaps her youngest son, George, should help Katherine each day in return for a few pence. He had been only nine then, but was tall for his age and a strong lad, and even though many thought him simple because he shied away from people and often didn't answer, he was quick to learn and had proved to be a blessing.

Katherine continued sewing for another hour, smiling at the constant babble of Harry's voice as he trailed around the garden after George and then, grabbing for her crutch, she heaved herself up and hobbled about the room slowly preparing the meal. Using her good arm she swung the pot over the fire. Likely William would be home soon, hungry after a morning about the parish and she did not want to keep him waiting. She was just setting the pewter platters on the table, when she heard excited shouts from

Harry and the sound of a horse's hoof beats. Unconsciously her hand went to her coif and she tucked in the stray curls of fair hair that always refused to be confined for long. She smoothed down her apron and stood a little straighter, smiling as the door burst open and her husband bounded in.

Often when she looked at him she thought how very unpriest-like he looked. Most of the clergy she had known in the past seemed to be a little portly with thinning hair and a pious expression. William, however, was a tall, lean man with black hair, dark eyes and seemingly boundless energy. He had a wide mouth, strong, white teeth and a loud, uninhibited laugh which always made her want to smile too.

She was smiling up at him now and saw with relief that the frown which had appeared recently between his eyes was, today, replaced by an answering smile of affection. She caught her breath. William was a good priest and a very good husband and he was all hers!

She put her good arm around him and hugged him to her and he in turn lifted her off her feet and kissed her soundly. She giggled like a girl and pushed him away indicating the two boys who stood grinning in the doorway. George was almost as dark as her husband and, standing there, could be mistaken for his son, were it not for his startling blue eyes. Harry, on the other hand was all her – delicate features, fine, fair hair curling around his face and chubby, rosy cheeks that gave him the look of a cherub. Strange how humans could be so different, she thought, especially when the Bible said that God had created man in his own image. Was God dark or—

'—so have you?' William was speaking to her, looking down at her with one eyebrow raised quizzically.

'I'm sorry, my love, I am distracted this morning. What did you say?'

'I asked if you had finished the sewing for the manor, as I have to ride there this afternoon and could take it for you if you wish.'

'Oh, almost. Another half an hour would see it done and I would be very grateful if you could take it today, as My Lady was keen to have it before her visitors from London arrive and she won't be best pleased if it's late.'

'I've said before, Katherine that there really is no need for you to do all this sewing. I'm sure My Lady does not expect it and—'

'I know, William, but I would be loath to stop. With my... my... infirmity, the sewing gives me something to do instead of just sitting with nothing to occupy me and I enjoy it. If you are willing I will finish while you and the boys eat your meal.'

'No, no. No need to miss your meal. I have some reading to do after dinner so will happily wait while you finish and will ride to the Manor this afternoon.'

'Thank you William. That would be good.' She took her place at the table and nodded to Harry who obediently put his hands in his lap and bowed his head, though continued to peer up through his eyelashes with eyes as wide as possible. 'Eyes, Harry,' she said as William waited to say Grace.

As William prayed, Katherine thought of all her blessings. They had a fine house, a garden, a horse and even a small library of six books of which William was very proud. Her husband was a good man and he loved her. She was, indeed a most fortunate woman.

2

Lizzie lay back exhausted as Ann wiped the baby with a piece of cloth from her basket.

'It don't get easier despite what they say.' The voice was barely a whisper.

'Often not,' Ann agreed gently. 'Though some are lucky and birth with ease.'

She looked down at the red, wrinkled baby in her arms and with her thumb, smoothed away a smear of blood from its cheek, before wrapping the child in a thin cloth and handing it to its mother. Eyes still tightly shut, the baby immediately started rooting at Lizzie's breast and, despite her exhaustion, the young woman smiled and a dimple appeared in her right cheek.

She was a small woman with clear blue eyes and a full, sensuous mouth. Wisps of ash-blonde hair, now darkened with sweat and plastered to her forehead, had escaped from braided plaits, which hung like ropes over her shoulders. Her breasts were full and heavy, the nipples jutting like red, ripe raspberries. As her new daughter nuzzled and took one in her mouth she nodded in satisfaction and when she spoke her voice was stronger.

'She knows what she wants, don't she?'

Ann smiled down at the woman remembering the tug of a small mouth at her own breast a decade ago. 'Seems she does, though she was reluctant enough to enter the world. She gave you a hard time Lizzie.'

'Who could blame her? I wouldn't want my time over a . . .' Lizzie gasped as pain gripped her belly once more and with a groan she pushed the bloody disc of afterbirth from her tired body.

The warm air was so foetid with the smell of stale sweat, blood and the dirty rushes on the floor, that Ann felt she only wanted to take shallow breaths; didn't want to trap that sour stench deep in her lungs. She longed to fling open the shutters to let in the cool breeze. The drear gloominess of the room was emphasised even more by a single, thin shaft of golden light that gleamed through a small crack in the wall and spoke of fresh air and sunshine. It had seemed such a long, hot afternoon and Ann was glad that she was nearly finished here and could soon escape out into the cool freshness of a summer evening.

Rising from her knees, she bundled up the soiled cloths and rinsed her hands in a pail of water that stood by the bed. A tall, strong, some would say handsome woman, she moved with a practised authority that engendered trust and confidence in the women she helped.

On the thin mattress, Lizzie eased herself into a more comfortable position so that the babe could suckle more effectively. She gazed down at her small daughter whose rosy red lips were making satisfied smacking noises. Suddenly Lizzie's expression clouded and she looked up into Ann's face with a worried frown. 'She's strong, but he won't be pleased, God help me. Another mouth to feed and another girl at that.'

'Well, girl or no, surely Matthew will be glad you've been blessed with a healthy babe? And as to adding to his family, it's not as though you were entirely responsible is it?' Ann felt a familiar ruffle of indignation at the unjust way women were blamed for becoming pregnant. Although Lizzie had not yet reached her majority, she already had two little girls – both of whom Ann had delivered safely.

Lizzie wiped the back of her hand across her nose. 'There certainly wouldn't be any more if it was up to me. Can't keep him off though, especially when he's had a few jugs of ale.'

'Tsk! Men!' Ann shook her head. 'Sometimes I despair of them,' she said, although at the same time thinking that in this case she wasn't really surprised. With her voluptuous figure and creamy skin, Lizzie was the sort of young woman that any man would find hard to resist.

She took a jar of dried leaves from her basket and tipped a few of them into a small twist of cloth, which she laid it on the table. 'Brew these leaves in some hot water and drink some morning and evening. It will help your strength and your milk.'

Lizzie looked up into the older woman's face, her expression a mixture of embarrassment and worry. 'I can't pay.'

'I know my dear; I don't expect it. Those that can do and those that can't – well. . .' She shrugged and started to gather her things together, packing them into her basket and covering all with a clean, blue and white striped cloth that had once been part of a shawl. 'I must be getting home or John will think I'm lost.'

Ann opened the door and light streamed into the room as she turned for a last glance at Lizzie who was already looking drowsy and would probably sleep now. The sun had moved slightly and mother and baby were lit with a golden light that made Ann think of the old statue of the Virgin and child that had only recently been returned to the church. She closed the door quietly. Stepping out from the close humidity of the darkened room into the freshness of the evening air, it almost felt as though she herself was being reborn and she raised her hand and called a cheery greeting to a neighbour who was struggling to lift a recalcitrant toddler.

'A healthy girl, praise be. She's feeding, so with God's help will survive.'

As she turned her face to the evening sun, Ann felt the elation of a job well done. When she handed a healthy infant to a young mother it still, after twenty years of delivering babies, felt like a miracle in which she had played a part. So many children and mothers died in childbirth that it gave her enormous satisfaction when all went well.

With a contented sigh she hoisted her basket onto her hip and, glad to be moving after several hours in the cramped room, took big, appreciative, gulps of air, savouring the scents of summer. She noted the long shadows made by the trees edging the path. It was getting late; John and the boys would be home and wanting food. She lengthened her stride, even though it was a steep climb up the hill from Lizzie's house, and she felt her calf muscles protest.

The air was still and, for the moment at least, it was a beautiful evening, but large, blue-black clouds were gathering in the east. There could well be a storm later, she thought, but for now she enjoyed the feel of the sun on her face.

As she neared the edge of the village, several people nodded to her as she passed, for she had lived all her life in Rotherfield and many of her neighbours had had occasion to bless her knowledge of herbs and cures when they, or one of their family, fell sick.

Reaching the track, she skirted the deep ruts made by the carts and hummed a tune as she mused on the events of the day. She had to admit that she would not want the ordeal of childbirth, herself, again. She was grateful for her three fine sons and had been lucky to have her own mother to attend her, but in Lizzie's case there had been no-one but Ann to ease her through the last hours of childbirth. The young woman was an orphan and those friends she might have, were busy coping as best they could with their own families and had no time to attend a lying in.

Ann had heard tell of gentlewomen spending the last weeks of pregnancy confined to bed, closeted in a darkened room being waited on by friends and relatives, but none in the village had time for such indulgence. Despite the prospering iron trade, the small Sussex village on the high Weald was not wealthy, for recent harvests had not been good and some of the best land that had once been used for crops and grazing, was now being mined for ore.

When she reached the main street of the village she turned right, past the Three Guns Inn where a small, black dog was rooting through a pile of refuse tipped outside the back entrance. As she drew level, the dog extracted a large bone almost as long as itself and ran past her, the bone triumphantly held aloft. She smiled at the sight even as she caught the whiff of rotten meat and wrinkled her nose. The dog continued ahead of her along the centre of the street and a group of seven or eight children who had been idling on a patch of grass gave chase, whooping with delight at the diversion and kicking up the dust as they tore after the animal. Despite its short legs and heavy burden the dog seemed to have no trouble in keeping ahead of them.

As Ann watched, smiling, the smallest child, a lad of about five, tripped on the rutted track, tumbled onto the ground and started to wail. Hoisting her basket she hastened towards him, but before she had gone more than a few paces, one boy from the group wearing a battered, black hat that was too big for him, dropped out of the chase and ran back to the child. As she drew closer she saw it was Simon Catt and wasn't surprised by his concern. He was a nice boy, she thought; kind and gentle like his mother. She watched approvingly as he hauled the younger child to his feet and put a consoling arm around him. The small boy was grizzling and as she drew level, he wiped his arm across his face – a long string of snot glistening on his sleeve.

'You alright lad?' She addressed the small boy, but it was Simon who answered.

'He's fine, Goodwife. Tripped over his own feet. Aint that right, Luke?'

The whooping of the group of boys became fainter as they disappeared from view and the small child sniffed abjectly and nodded.

'I'll walk him home, see he's alright,' Simon said.

Ann patted his shoulder, noticing as she did so how thin the boy was.

'Well done Simon. You're a good lad. That's kind of you. Sure you're alright Luke?' Bending down she lifted the child's hair off his forehead. 'I think you're going to have a bruise to be proud of there, but I don't think there's much damage done.'

She watched as the two boys, hand in hand, set off slowly down the road. They made a strange pair; the younger one holding his head and limping in exaggerated fashion and Simon looking like a scarecrow with his big hat perched on his sticking out ears, and skinny, bandy legs showing beneath his short tunic.

Leaving the boys to make their way home Ann turned right again, off the main street and raised her hand in greeting to Mother Birdy. As usual, the old woman was sitting on a three legged stool outside the door of a small, dilapidated, cottage which was almost completely covered in ivy. Ann sighed inwardly when the old woman beckoned with a thin and claw-like hand that was marked with brown age-spots. She was late enough already, but couldn't refuse a neighbour a few moments company and chat. Mother Birdy was a lonely soul with no family of her own now that her husband was dead and her only son, on an unlucky visit to Hastings, had been pressed into the Navy.

Ann set down her basket putting her hand to her back to ease the stiffness. Suddenly she felt very weary. These days bending over a birthing mother seemed to take its toll on her too, but she smiled and agreed with Mother Birdy that a storm was probably coming and added pleasantly that it would be a good thing as it might clear the air. Then, as soon as she decently could, she patted the woman on the shoulder, promised to pop in again for a chat in the coming week and hoisted the basket, which seemed to have grown heavier, onto her hip once more, before continuing her way homeward.

She passed the last of a row of thatched cottages and the sight of her own neat house on the outskirts of the village gave her fresh energy. She hurried her steps and noticed with relief that there was still a red glow and the sound of hammering from the forge next door. Her husband, John, was working late.

In the still air the scent of hedge roses hung heavy and sweet, while the smell of thyme was sharp and pungent as she opened the gate and walked quickly up the path. With a contented sigh she looked around her small garden, bending to pick a head of lavender and tucking it down the front of her bodice. She glanced across to the beeskep and felt herself relax as she paused for a moment to watch the small, brown creatures, all making their way in a steady stream towards the small dark hole in the woven skep.

'I was right then, my lovelies,' she said, half to herself. 'You all think it's going to rain too do you? That's right, you hurry home now.'

3

The past month had seemed more like April than June with the threat of heavy showers always on the horizon, but July had dawned clear and bright with not a cloud in the sky. The air was alive with the drone of bees systematically working their way up and down the heads of lavender bordering the herb garden at the back of the Ashdowns' cottage and a yellowhammer kept up its incessant call of "little bit of bread and no cheeeese," from the top of the oak tree behind the forge.

Ann stood on her doorstep enjoying the warmth of the sun and beaming with self-satisfaction. She had been right in her prediction of a fine day and congratulated herself. Yesterday morning she had put the family's soiled linens in the big wooden tub and had started soaking them in lye and, as she had hoped, today would be the perfect day to rinse and dry the newly washed clothes. She turned, humming a cheerful jig under her breath as she crossed to the corner and stirred the cloth around in the water. Earlier in the season John had burned an old, diseased apple tree from the orchard and she had saved the ash and mixed it into some animal fat. Her mother had always said that apple was excellent for bleaching the clothes and far superior to oak ash, which, as she knew from bitter experience, had a tendency to discolour the cloth if you weren't careful.

Soon she was splashed and damp, both from her exertions pummeling and wringing and from the water as it slopped out of the tub. As she drew more water from the well for rinsing, she thought ruefully that it would have been good to have a daughter to help her. Washing was women's work and she could expect no assistance from her boys. Anyway, her eldest son, Dickon was away on one of the carts transporting the iron down to the coast and John and Nick had made an early start at the forge, for there were plenty of travelers on the road and they had been very busy for the last three weeks. But then, she mused, she was, praise be, fit and healthy and what could be more satisfying to a housewife than the sight and smell of freshly laundered linens?

She laid the cleansed clothes into a rush basket, catching her breath when she felt a twinge in her back as she carried it into the small orchard that lay behind the herb garden. The early morning dew had dried in the summer sun and the grass smelled fresh and clean. She was so absorbed in her task of spreading her clean washing over the grass to dry, avoiding the shade of the tree branches and the possibility of a perching bird soiling it, that the sight of her youngest son striding purposefully down the lane gave her quite a start.

'Hello George, you're back early. All well?' she called as he stomped into the house. He didn't answer; just disappeared indoors. Setting down her basket and drying her damp hands on her apron Ann hurried after him. After the bright sunlight outside, it took a few moments for her eyes to adjust to the gloom of the cottage, but she saw that George was sitting on his stool in the corner, leaning forward with his arms around his knees.

She frowned and a wave of anxiety washed over her as she watched him rock himself backwards and forwards, the stool legs banging on the uneven floor. Ever since he was little he'd always rocked when he was upset, but he hadn't done it for a while and she wondered what had caused his distress this time. She went over and squatted on the floor in front of him. Although it was a mother's natural instinct to hold or hug him, she knew better than to try to touch him and placed her hands on her knees. Even as a young toddler he had shied away from physical contact with people – especially adults. The only person whom he seemed to tolerate was young Harry.

'What's up Georgie,' she said softly. 'What's the matter, love?'

George shook his head and rocked faster.

'Come on, tell me Georgie. What's upset you? Perhaps I can help.'

'Steps,' he whispered. 'I don't know the steps.'

'Steps? What do you mean? What steps? What don't you know?'

'How many steps to the cottage. I don't know how many to the cottage.'

'What cottage? Georgie, love, you're going to have to explain, I don't know what you're talking about.'

'Goodwife Collyer at the new cottage. I don't know how many steps it is. Something bad . . .' His voice tailed off and he put his head down, still rocking and refused to say any more.

Ann stood up and looked down at her son. Sometimes she despaired of him and sometimes she just wanted to shake him. Why did he have this obsession about the number of steps it took to get to places and what was all this about a new cottage? Katherine Collyer lived at the house that went with William's living, so what was the boy talking about?

'I'm going to see if I can make sense of this,' she said. 'Stay here George and don't stray while I'm gone. I won't be long.'

As she made her way across the field to the priest's house she worried about George. Her heart ached for him and she wished so much that she could solve all the problems that seemed part of his life. She frowned, trying to puzzle out what George had been talking about with all this nonsense about a cottage. She barely noticed that the air was soft and smelled of grass and summer as her skirts swished through the meadow and swifts skimmed past her like small, black darts.

When she reached the priest's house, she walked through the garden where the vegetables were growing well and the rows were free of weeds. George did have a way with plants; Katherine's family would not lack for food in the coming season.

She tapped on the door and waited. From inside there was a sudden bang and then silence once more. She looked over towards the church and could see a glimmer of light through the window, but she couldn't imagine Katherine would leave Harry alone and limp to the church on her own.

She knocked again louder. 'Katherine?' she called. There was still no answer. With a growing sense of alarm she stepped to one side and, shading the light with her hand, peered through the thick glass of a small window pane. She could see no one in the living room and, feeling rather self-conscious, moved along the wall to look in the next window. Dimly she could see the still form of Katherine on the bed with her stick lying at an angle on the floor. That must have been the bang.

With a sharp intake of breath Ann returned to the door and, concern overcoming her natural reticence, lifted the latch and let herself into the hallway. Once inside she could hear the quiet sobs coming from behind the door on her left. She felt embarrassed and worried at the same time. Should she intrude? But how could she leave the woman in such distress with no words of comfort? 'Katherine?' she called again and the sobbing ceased abruptly.

'Who's there?' The voice was choked and frightened.

'It's me. Ann. I'm sorry to intrude, but are you alright Katherine? You look . . .sound . . .upset. Can I help?'

There was the sound of nose blowing and then, in a voice still shuddering with lingering sobs, Katherine bade her come in. Slowly, Ann pushed open the door which creaked loudly and remained standing uncertainly in the doorway.

She saw that the younger woman, usually so neat, was indeed distressed and dishevelled in a way she had never seen her before. Her skirt was rumpled, her coif was awry and her hair was tumbled and knotted as though she had been running her fingers through it. Ann hurried to her side. 'Katherine, whatever is the matter? Are you ill?'

Katherine wiped her good hand across her face and pushed her hair back from her wet cheeks. She opened her mouth to speak, but shook her head as tears once more overwhelmed her.

Ann looked around for Harry but couldn't see the child anywhere and fear gripped her. 'It's not . . .Mother of God, it's not Harry? Nothing's happened to Harry has it? Katherine tell me.' Surely, she thought, God wouldn't have let anything happen to that laughing, happy, golden child. Unconsciously she crossed herself.

Pushing herself into a sitting position Katherine took a deep shuddering breath and shook her head. 'No,' she said, 'No, praise be, Harry is fine. He's out with W . . .W . . .William.' As she spoke her husband's name her eyes filled with tears again and her lip quivered.

Gently Ann sat on the side of the bed and put her hand on Katherine's shoulder. 'Steady now,' she said gently. 'Do you want to tell me? I don't want to pry on matters between husband and wife, but I don't like to leave you so distressed. I came over because George, too, seemed upset and I could get no sense out of him – only something about a cottage.'

Katherine bit her lips together trying to control herself and sat for a moment, head bowed, her breathing still ragged. 'I've got to leave,' she whispered finally. 'William says I have to go. We can't live as man and wife anymore.' Again her tears overcame her as Ann sat back incredulous.

'You've got to leave?' she repeated. 'Why Katherine? Have you had such a serious disagreement that . . . that—'

'No. You don't understand. We never argue. We love each other, but, well, I understand that it's his calling, but after all we've had - and Harry . . .' She lapsed into miserable silence while Ann sat stunned.

Quietly, more controlled now, Katherine started to speak again.

'When King Edward permitted priests to marry and William asked me to be his wife I knew he had examined his conscience long and hard and found no impediment in his faith to our union. I too prayed and felt that God's answer was that true love should not be denied, so with joy we married and our union was blessed with Harry.'

Ann nodded, wondering where all this was leading.

'Then when I had this terrible affliction I wondered if we had indeed done wrong, but again we prayed and William was sure that it was not a judgement against us, but just some awful misfortune such as might happen to anyone.'

As Ann listened she was struck by the dignity of Katherine and her desire to do the right thing before God. Ann doubted that she knew that there were those in the village who had been against her marriage to their priest and had seen the seizure as proof of God's displeasure. She was sure Katherine would be horrified if she knew that there had even been mutterings against William continuing as priest from those who, in their hearts still held to the Catholic faith. She certainly wasn't going to tell

Katherine about any of this now as, in time, most people had accepted the ways things were and generally William was well liked in the village.

Her voice still choked with emotion, Katherine went on. 'When Edward died and Mary became queen we all guessed what that would mean – a return to Rome, but I never thought, never imagined—'

'What, my dear? Whatever do you mean?'

'William has been told . . . that is, he's been ordered–' Katherine's breath caught, '–that he can no longer be a husband and a priest. If he is to continue with his calling I have to, I have to . . .' Such was her distress that Katherine was unable to speak further and just sat silently biting her lip.

'Oh Jesus help us. You mean you and William are no longer married? But how can you undo a marriage? Where will you go? What will you do? How can that be God's will? What about your child? What about Harry?' The questions tumbled out of Ann as she contemplated the horror of what her friend had told her.

As if talking to herself, Katherine continued speaking, her voice barely above a whisper. 'For some weeks I have thought something was wrong, you know. William sometimes had a closed, sad look that was not there before. He often seemed to frown and I'd thought that it was me – that he was overburdened with having a cripple for a wife. But he knew, you see. He'd been waiting. He knew what was coming.'

Ann covered Katherine's hand with her own as she listened aghast.

'I'd been afraid it was me, but oh, this is worse. It can't be right. I can't bear to be alone in the world again. William is my rock. How can I live without him? After all those years alone I thought that finally I'd found someone to love me. He does still love me - I'm sure he does - and I love him. But if we stay together he says it would mean excommunication. He couldn't live with that and I couldn't ask it of him.' Her voice rose to an agonized wail, 'Why would God want us to be apart?'

Ann sat silent, unable to answer.

Katherine took a deep shuddering breath. 'William has rented a cottage that belongs to a farm just outside Buxted. The farmer is a distant relative and William says the man will be discreet and make sure that all is well with me. I'm to go and live there on my own with Harry. He says he will try to visit me.' She brought her hand up to her mouth, and looked up at Ann, her eyes wide with fright. 'Oh, but I shouldn't have said. He said no one must know. It must be a secret. We must no longer live as man and wife and I can't . . . I can't bear it.' With an anguished wail Katherine subsided onto the bed again.

Ann sprang up and started to pace about the room twisting her hands together in distress. So that's what George had meant about the cottage. Presumably he'd heard, or been told, that Katherine and Harry would now be living at the cottage and he had assumed he would go there to help her.

No wonder he was upset. He hated change and the idea of leaving this house and garden and working in a strange place would have filled him with terror. Ann glanced across at Katherine now lying listlessly on the bed, her eyes closed. How could it be right to ruin this woman's life? She'd done no wrong. And what of Harry? Would he now be a bastard, an outcaste? Ann didn't know what to do. She didn't want to leave Katherine distressed as she was, but there was George to think of too. She had told him she would not be long.

She went back to the bed and put her hand gently on the woman's arm. 'Katherine,' she said. 'Katherine, I don't know yet how to help you, but help you I will, I can promise you that. However, I must go back to George now. Will you be alright? Is William coming back here? When is he saying you have to leave?'

With an effort Katherine sat up, sniffing as she tried to compose herself. 'I'm alright, Ann, really. I'm sorry to have burdened you with my troubles, but it is all so new. I . . . I haven't got used to the idea yet and I'm not . . .' She hesitated, then taking a deep breath she continued. 'I have to leave by the end of the week so have three days yet to prepare. William took Harry out as he didn't want the child to see my distress.' She looked out of the window at the slant of the sun. 'They will be back soon. I must bathe my face and prepare some food. They will both be hungry.'

'Here, let me help you.'

'No, really, I'm alright now. I can manage.' She looked up at Ann, her eyes like puddles reflecting the sky. 'I have no choice now but to manage do I?' Her voice had a bleakness about it that tore at Ann's heart.

She put her arm around Katherine's shoulders. 'You are very brave,' she said. 'I don't think I would be. But be assured, you will not be alone. I will help you all I can.'

4

Her mind in a whirl, Ann hurried home and found John was there before her, standing in the middle of the room staring at George in bewilderment. He looked up at her as she came in, a worried frown creasing his face.

'Oh there you are! I wondered what had happened to you. Where have you been? Is something amiss?' he asked her. 'What has upset the lad? He hasn't said a word to me, but something is obviously wrong.'

George was where she had left him, still rocking on his stool, his face stiff and shuttered.

'Come into the garden.' She took John's arm and steered him outside. 'I've just come from Katherine and there is such trouble, you can't imagine. And George – he doesn't understand, poor lad.'

'And neither do I, woman. What are you saying?'

'Oh, I'm sorry; I'm that distracted I can't think straight. How can it be right?'

'Ann!'

'I'm sorry, yes, let me explain. George came home in great distress, saying something about Katherine moving to a cottage. He didn't make sense, so I went over to the vicarage and when I arrived Katherine was sorely upset. She was crying and—'

'So it has happened at last?'

'Happened? What do you mean?' She looked at him through narrowed eyes. 'You know about this dreadful thing and you didn't tell me?'

'I didn't know, no, but it's no great surprise. I presume the bishop has told William to put aside his wife.' He drove his big fist into his hand. 'God rot these damn Catholics, where will it end?'

Ann looked around fearfully. 'Hush, John. What are you saying? Do you want to get us arrested?' Automatically she lowered her voice. 'You knew?

You knew that this was going to happen? How John? How did you know? Who told you?'

'I didn't know exactly – least not about William and Katherine, but I've heard talk from travellers. There was a man last week. His cob had cast a shoe and he was on his way to London. Stopped at the forge and was talking while I worked. He was going to see his sister. She too was married to a priest and had been cast out on the orders of the bishops. He was on his way to help her as it seemed no provision had been made and she was penniless. After all, what position does she hold now – married and yet not? Poor Katherine! I'd have thought better of William.'

'But what choice did he have if the Bishop—?'

'He could have refused couldn't he?' He put an arm around her shoulders and hugged her to him. 'I'd not give you up for God or the Devil.'

Tall as she was, she still had to stand on tip toe as she reached up and kissed him. 'You're a good man and I love you, but William's faith is very strong and it must have been an agonising decision for him. Do not judge him, my love.'

John frowned and then shrugged. 'Well he must answer to his own conscience. But what is to happen to Katherine? You said something about a cottage?'

'Yes, that's why George was upset. William has rented a cottage outside Buxted and Katherine and Harry are to move there.'

'Well that's something at least. He's not just cast her out without provision.'

'Of course not, no, but he's not allowed to visit – not openly at least. They can't see each other as man and wife any more. It's what is to become of young Harry I can't get my head around. Is he to be branded a bastard now? It's not right. It can't be.'

'How will she manage on her own? I know you said she's better than she was, but she can't manage all on her own can she?'

'She would find it difficult. I think she's hoping . . . She needs . . .' Ann broke off and frowned. 'Do you think . . .?' she began slowly, pausing between her words as she formed her thoughts. 'Do you think . . . if we could make it right with him . . . do you think that George should move to the cottage with her? So that he was to hand all the time I mean. I know it's strange and he's afeared now, but he's been helping her for nigh on two years now, so once he was used to the new place and . . . well, he's going on twelve and big and strong enough to be useful and he's got to do something,' she burst out. She twisted her hands together as she often did when worried and John put a calming hand on her back. 'I did promise we would help and John, I do worry so about our boy. How will he make his way in the world? This would perhaps be a chance for him to do something useful.'

John frowned. 'Leave home you mean? Not live with us anymore? But—'

'I know. It's a big thing, but think about it John. Lots of youngsters of his age are away from home as apprentices and the like. We've been lucky to have our three boys with us as long as we have. But we have to face it. The lad . . . our lad is, well . . . different. He's not like Dickon and Nick and I've racked my brains trying to think what the future holds for him. He can't work with you – not afeared of fire the way he is and well . . . what other master would put up with his strange ways? He would be doing a useful job – a man's job at Katherine's – and he'd be learning, perhaps enough so that one day . . .' She trailed off and put her hand to her mouth before continuing. 'He could tend the garden and do the heavy chores in return for his board and lodging. He'd not be far – it's only a few miles and not so far from where Dickon is working. We wouldn't be losing him and—'

'I don't know, Ann. It's a lot for a boy to do. And how do you think he'd cope? You say he's upset about the cottage.'

'Yes, he is now, because it's new. You know he doesn't like new things, but once he's used to it – oh leave that to me – I know how to handle him. He'll be awkward at first, but he'll be fine. We must speak to Katherine—'

'Now hold on. I haven't agreed to this yet. I need to think what's right.'

'But—'

'No, Ann, leave it now. Is there to be no food for your husband today, wife? It must be nearly midday and I'm hungry and so will the lads be. We will talk about this again later.'

'You're right. I'm sorry John. Dinner won't be long.'

'Right. I'll just finish off then.'

Going back into the cottage she bustled about the room, hanging up her shawl and quickly setting the room to rights, while at the same time keeping an eye on George, who still sat hunched in the corner. Eventually, when she could see that he was looking calmer, she went over to him. 'It's alright, George. I've spoken to Goodwife Collyer and everything will be alright, my son. We'll sort it out – you'll see – so no need to worry about the cottage now.' She smiled down at him. 'Come now and eat with us. I'm sure you're ready for a good bowl of Mother's hot pottage after a morning's work, aren't you now? Off you go and fetch me some water like a good lad.'

George didn't answer, but took the proffered pail from her hand. This wasn't going to be easy, but she was sure that the best thing for now was to make things seem as normal as possible. Soon the boy was back from the well and set the bucket down in the corner by the door, slopping water onto the floor. He stood watching his mother, but backed away into the corner and put up his arm against the glare as she blew the fire into life with the bellows.

Aware that dinner was going to be late, Ann looked into the big iron pot that always hung ready to be swung over the fire. She pressed her lips together in dismay. There wasn't much left from yesterday and no time to make more. She'd have to eke out the food somehow. She reached up and took an onion and a bunch of small turnips from the shelf which, after chopping them roughly to speed their cooking, she transferred to a large iron pot. She pulled off a few stems from a bunch of thyme that hung drying from a peg in the low ceiling before crumbling the crisp leaves into the pot. Turning round she saw George leaning against the wall watching her. She flapped her hand at him 'Don't just stand and gawp lad. Fetch the bread down and cut us some slices. Mind the knife now,' she added automatically.

She ladled water from the pail into the cooking pot to thin the pottage. Meanwhile, George carefully lifted down the bread, unwrapped it from its cloth and cut it into untidy ragged slices. He frowned with concentration and Ann sighed. Much as she loved him, she wished he could be more like his two elder brothers.

As if summoned by her thoughts, the door burst open and the small room suddenly felt full as two well-built lads exploded into the room. The tall, dark one punched George affectionately on the arm, 'How you doing little brother?'

George cringed and put his hands over his face.

'Leave him be, Dickon,' Ann said irritably. 'You know he doesn't like to be touched.'

'Touchy bugger!' Dickon grinned and then came across to her and put his arm around her waist and gave her a squeeze. Her first born had always been affectionate; had always wanted to hold her hand, long after most little boys were running free of their mothers. She looked up at him, now almost a man, tall and straight as a forest birch with a shock of dark hair that was forever flopping into his eyes.

'Brought you some eggs Ma.'

She turned at the sound of her second son's voice and smiled when he passed her his hat in which she could see the greeny-brown gleam of half a dozen pheasant eggs. 'Oh good lad, Nick!' She raised her eyebrows in mock severity.' I hope you didn't go into Hosmer's for these.'

His face was a picture of innocence. 'Me Ma? As if I would! I was just taking Old Jed back to his stable and happened to see these just the other side of the ditch, so all I had to do was simply to lean across. No trespass at all.'

Shaking her head at his cheek Ann took down a skillet from the shelf. 'Well, it looks as if, from no dinner at all, your Father is in for quite a feast. Eggs will certainly perk up this thin pottage, so thank you son, but just be careful, we don't want trouble.'

She was just thinking that the turnips would be about ready when she heard the click of the gate to the back yard and she hurried to set the skillet on the fire, carefully breaking the eggs into it, their golden yolks thick and luscious. Pheasant eggs were always richer than hens' and she felt her mouth water at the sight, reminding her that it was a long time since she too had eaten.

She ladled the pottage into wooden bowls and was just slipping an egg on top of each one when her husband came in.

'My that smells good.' He put a hand on his belly. 'I'm so hungry I could eat a horse!'

George was instantly on his feet. 'No, Father. Don't say that. That's wrong; you mustn't. Please.'

John shook his head. 'Don't worry George,' he said gently. 'It's alright; I'm only joking. I just mean I could . . . well, that I'm really hungry. I reckon every horse here abouts has cast a shoe this morning and I've worked up a fair old appetite.

Ann felt a lump in her throat as she looked across at her husband. He was so big – like a bear she'd seen once, dancing at a fair – but he was always so gentle and loving, especially to his youngest son.

'Yea. I wouldn't mind a great, juicy slice off Old Jed,' said Nick emphasising each word and looking sideways at George.

'Nick you couldn't. That would —' George started up again from the bench.

'Stop it Nick.' Ann said severely. Why did Nick always have to stir things with George? Because they were close in age she supposed. 'Hold your peace. There's no cause to tease your brother. You know you love horses just as much as he does. Nobody's eating horse either today or any other day. It's pottage as usual, so be quiet.'

Nick lowered his eyes and his body jerked slightly as he kicked George under the table.

'Enough' John's voice was sharp now and all three boys bent their heads and concentrated on wiping the last of the egg yolk from their platters with their bread.

Finally John sat back from the table. 'Those turnips were good Ann. First of the season aren't they?' John turned to her, raised eyebrows marking his question.

She nodded with satisfaction. 'Yes, indeed. They're just the thinnings, but they don't seem to have been attacked by slugs as much as last year.' Her smile encompassed all her family around the table. It was good to have them together and, after hearing of poor Katherine's troubles earlier today, it made her appreciate her family even more. She realised, however, that she couldn't keep them with her always and sooner or later change would come.

It was later that same evening that Ann slipped quietly into the church. The draught from the door set the dust motes dancing in a shimmering haze in the late evening sunlight. It was very quiet and, glancing about her, Ann was relieved that she was alone. She made her way to where the statue of the Virgin stood, her lips curved in a gentle smile. Crossing herself, Ann knelt and gazed up at Mary.

Many people had been horrified when the bright pictures on the walls had been painted over and the embroidered altar cloths had been swept away by the wave of Protestantism that the young Edward had brought to the land, but those things had not upset Ann. She had not minded that the services were said in English; that had not seemed important to her. After all, she reasoned, presumably God heard and understood all languages. Hadn't Jesus spoken the language of the Jews? And William, himself had told her that the Bible had first been written in something called Greek.

No, none of that had been important to Ann. The one thing she had missed was the statue of Mary to whom she had always confided her innermost thoughts. Admittedly, coming into the Church on that first morning and seeing it stark and bare had been a shock, but it was the empty space where the Virgin had stood that had filled Ann with a sense of loss; she felt sick and hollow inside.

Close as she was to John and the boys, Ann had a deep need for someone to confide in; someone to whom she could tell her troubles and share her joys and who would not judge her or worry about her. For Ann, speaking to Mary was a comfort and a reassurance that gave her a sense of calmness and security.

She was well liked in the village but, perhaps because she had some skill in cures, she was treated with a respect and a certain amount of distance by the other women that precluded the confidences and friendship that many shared. In an exclusively male household she sometimes longed for the closeness she had enjoyed with her own mother and which she had, for so long, hoped she would share with a daughter.

Ann knew nothing of the merits of one king or queen over another but, sorry as she was for the young king, when young Edward died, she had been so grateful to the new queen for allowing the statue of the Virgin to return to its rightful place in the shadow by the pillar. Now, bowing her head, Ann put her hands together and her lips moved soundlessly. She wasn't exactly praying; praying was what you did to God. No, she was confiding in the Blessed Virgin; telling her all the problems of her family; of George and his strangeness, the awful betrayal of Katherine and the decisions that had to be made. It felt, to Ann, the same as telling her own Mother her troubles as a child, sure in the knowledge that somehow she would help put things right. At last her lips were still and she looked up again at the serene face above. Mary was the mother of a son too; she would understand - Ann felt sure of that. She remained on her knees for a few more moments; then, with a slight nod, she got to her feet, wincing slightly at the stiffness in her joints.

"Thank you," she whispered and, as quietly as she had entered, she let herself out of the church into the still warm air of a summer's evening.

5

By the time William came back with Harry, Katherine had washed her face, combed her hair and put on a fresh coif and had readied the food on the table. Harry burst in through the doorway, his cheeks rosy and flushed with excitement.

'Been to the river. Saw an 'ish, Muvver. Big 'ish. This big.' And he stretched his arms wide.

Ann smiled a wan smile at the enthusiasm of her small son and said quietly, 'That sounds more like a monster than a fish, Harry. Are you sure it was that big?'

'Es. It was Farver, wasn't it?'

'It was indeed a very big fish, my son.'

William stood awkwardly inside the door trying not to look at Katherine. Finally, sensing the odd atmosphere between his parents the child fell silent and looked from one to the other. A shaft of sunlight from the window cut across the room like a sword separating the two adults.

Harry frowned as if puzzling over something. 'No tiss,' he said, touching his fingers to his lips. He toddled across to his father, took Willam's hand and tried to pull him across the room, but William didn't move. 'No tiss,' the child said again. He looked at Katherine standing still and erect, one hand resting on the table and his lip began to quiver. 'Muvver sad?' He let go of William's hand and ran across to his mother, putting his arms around her legs, hugging them and looking up into her face. 'Tiss Farver,' and he pursed his rosy lips and made a kissing sound.

Katherine dropped her hand onto his blonde head. 'Not now Harry,' she said abruptly and then felt remorseful as his small face start to crumple. She made a huge effort to make her voice sound normal. 'It's time for supper, child. Come, all this hanging about and it will grow cold. Here, let me wipe your hands.' She fetched a cloth and set about cleaning the child, then helped him onto his stool, all the while taking care not to look at William.

It was a strained meal, both Katherine and William talking to Harry and keeping up a flow of conversation without ever actually addressing each other. It was something of a relief when finally the boy was in his bed and they were alone and yet now they could no longer avoid what was happening to them and Katherine had to turn away to hide her tears as she thought of how their evenings had been spent in the past.

Usually, when Harry was in bed, William would read to her from the English Bible or the lives of the Saints, while she sewed until her eyes could focus no more on the tiny whirls and flowers that decorated her cloth. As the firelight died she would put aside her embroidery and they would talk about what he had read and she would be amazed and proud at his knowledge and understanding. They would then retire for the night and, before climbing into bed with her husband, she would peep at her young son, peacefully asleep in his cradle, arms flung above his head, his curls golden on the sheet.

Tonight, though, as the light faded, the silence between them lengthened, each with so much to say, but neither having the courage to start. Fearful, perhaps, that if speech brought them closer, neither would be able to endure the pain that was to come.

The last three days had passed in a fog of unhappiness and bewilderment and Katherine felt as if she was wading through a never ending patch of deep mud. No matter how she tried, she could not seem to clear her mind as she struggled to come to terms with the idea of living apart from William and, whenever she started to make sense of the situation, she felt dragged down by the uncertainty and worry of a future on her own.

How would she cope with a lively, three year old child in a place far away from neighbours and friends? How trustworthy was William's relative? Was he risking his immortal soul in order to provide her with shelter? Would he betray her and would she be dragged away to an uncertain fate? What would happen to her if she was found out? Did being married to a priest now make her a heretic? Especially as, in her heart, she still adhered to the Protestant faith. She had heard of heretics being burned – a fate too awful to contemplate. These questions went around and around in her head as outwardly she tried desperately to appear calm and smiling for Harry. Sometimes, at the thought of being alone, her pulse quickened and her breath came in shuddering gasps so that she felt she would choke.

William, too, seemed sunk into himself and would not meet her eyes when he came home for supper after visiting in the parish. Like her, he tried to put on a brave face for Harry but, as he galloped around the garden with the small boy shrieking with delight on his back, she could see the hard set of his mouth and the paleness of his brow. When the child had been put to bed he obviously found it difficult to talk to her and for the last two nights had read his Bible while the light lasted, before retiring to lie stiff and unyielding in the bed beside her. She knew it was his way of coping with what she thought of as the end of their marriage, but she was, nonetheless, hurt by his coldness.

Now, as she lay in the darkness beside him, her thoughts drifted back through the years and she remembered how she had met William and the joy and happiness he had brought her.

Her parents had died of plague when she was still a child and My Lady had taken her into her household at the Manor House. She was sensible of the kindness her Ladyship had shown in taking in an orphan child, albeit one distantly related, but her position – not quite servant, yet not an equal - meant that she grew up shy and diffident; fearful of displeasing and doing the wrong thing. As she grew into womanhood, she had proved to be an able needlewoman and it had pleased her to take her place in the household doing fine embroideries, which earned her the smiles and gentle words she so craved.

She had never been especially interested in boys, for there were no other girls of her age to encourage her to giggle and whisper in corners and she had been quite taken aback when My Lady had called her into the solar one morning to tell her that Luke Davenport had asked for her hand. She barely knew the man, although he visited frequently, as he lived but a short ride from the big house. With no family to consult she looked, as always, to her Ladyship for guidance and when told that it was a good match for her, she had willingly acquiesced.

Luke was much older than she – a man in his early fifties - but he was good, kind and gentle and was charmed by her youthful freshness. He was looking for no more than a loving nurse, for he was not a well man and had no immediate family to tend him, so their marriage had not been one of passion, but rather one of quiet contentment. The marriage bed had not proved a place of delight, but nor had it filled her with horror. Her husband did his duty but rarely and when he did, he was gentle and undemanding and she had submitted willingly as she knew a good wife should. She had felt safe with Luke and had tended him faithfully. He seemed almost to take the place of the father she hardly remembered and then, only two years after their wedding, he died.

Next to her in the darkness, William stirred and Katherine turned carefully on her side so as not to wake him. She wanted him to sleep; couldn't bear lying next to him knowing he was awake, but separated from her by a wall of misery that neither seemed able to scale. She lay rigid and tense until she heard his breathing deepen again. Only then did she allow her thoughts to whirl back again to happier times.

After Luke died she returned to live at the manor house and reluctantly took up her position as needlewoman again. She was still very young; too young, according to My Lady, to live independently and, although she now had a little money of her own and a few small pieces of jewellery, Luke's house had not passed to her. So she had returned to her old position, but she had missed the affection and attention of her elderly husband and felt even more lonely and unwanted than before her marriage.

Then one day she had come into the big hall to find her Ladyship talking to a young man in priestly garb whom she had never seen before. He was dark haired and, when he looked up at her entrance, she was immediately struck by the intensity of his gaze. Unexpectedly, she felt herself blush and she started to retreat, but her Ladyship had beckoned to her and she came forward into the room to be introduced to William Collyer, who was newly appointed to St Denys' Church in Rotherfield.

From that moment, Katherine's life had changed. She no longer lived the quiet, insular life of a widow but, like a giddy girl, found herself taking walks where she had never walked before, just because she knew she might see William. She became a devout member of his congregation just so that she could listen to his voice and she spent her nights dreaming of a dark young man lifting the latch to her door. But, despite her dreams she knew that, in reality, she and William could never be together – he was a priest and priests could not marry and she tried hard to resist her sinful thoughts.

But then came an event that changed the world. King Henry – that larger than life, irascible monster of a king, who had been on the throne for all of her life – finally died. For a while it felt as if the country was adrift, rudderless on an unknown sea. Even far from London, people found it hard to contemplate a future without bluff King Harry.

His heir was Edward, the sickly son born to Jane Seymour who had died so tragically in childbirth after giving the King his heart's desire. As Katherine heard her Ladyship discussing the new reign with a visitor from London, she had, as yet, no idea that the change of king would bring about such an enormous change in her own life.

In the darkness Katherine smiled as she remembered her bewilderment when, at last, her furtive glances at the young priest were suddenly returned with a radiant smile and his visits to the manor house became more frequent, so that she always seemed to be bumping into him. She sighed a deep, shuddering sigh and clenched her hands as she recalled one particular afternoon in late Autumn. She had been strolling in the garden and, hearing footsteps behind her, turned to find William approaching. His answering smile was dazzling and made her feel aglow with a happiness tinged, as always, with regret that their friendship could never go further. But when he drew level with her William took her hands and, feeling her pull away from him said quietly, "All is well, Katherine, all is well."

What he had meant, she did not know then, but she heard the sincerity in his voice, had believed and trusted him and been reassured. And all had been well.

Katherine and William had been joined in holy matrimony and now…... now, at the whim of another royal person all was no longer well. All was destroyed and she would never again know what it was to be cherished and adored. She would never again feel safe.

Harry was over excited and boisterous as they set out from the vicarage on a grey drizzly evening; Katherine riding her docile white pony, its paniers behind her stuffed with her most precious belongings and William leading the way with Harry bouncing on the saddle between his arms.

William had told her that she would not be able to take much with her to the cottage other than bare necessities like a few clothes and, of course, her sewing box. He did not want her departure to be the subject of gossip in the village, but hoped that they could slip away one evening unnoticed. Obviously, her absence, especially from church on Sunday, would be remarked upon, but William planned to say that she and Harry had gone on an extended stay with a relative. Strictly speaking it was a lie, but one for which he would ask forgiveness and, in the circumstances what else could he say?

She could not prevent herself glancing back when they reached the curve of the lane and pulled the hood of her cloak over her face to conceal her tears before urging the pony into a laboured trot. Would she ever see her home again? Was she to spend the rest of her life hiding in shame for something that was not her fault?

6

A year later – June 1556

Ann could hear the screaming long before she reached the house. Despite the door and shutters being firmly closed, there was no denying the sound of a woman in distress. Poor Nell. Her labour had obviously started and she was having a bad time again. Not surprising the way he made her work – and probably knocked her about as well.

Ann's steps faltered and she found herself holding her breath with each scream. She hesitated as she drew level with the door. Should she knock? She raised her hand then let it drop again. She wouldn't be welcome, she knew that. James Catt liked to keep his family to himself and didn't welcome interference from what he called the 'nosey bitches' in the village. The screaming had stopped and was replaced by a low moaning and the sound of a sharp slap. Ann started to move away, but the moans were somehow worse than the screams. After all, she thought, she had known Nell all her life. What harm could come of an offer to help?

Setting her basket on the step, Ann straightened her apron and rapped loudly on the door. Slow footsteps sounded on the other side and finally the door opened to reveal a coarse, mottled face, fringed with grey hair which escaped in wisps from beneath a dirty white coif and small, black eyes that squinted at her in the bright sunlight. The room behind was in semidarkness lit only by firelight.

'Yes?' Ann recognised the sharp, unfriendly voice of Goodwife Catt - Nell's mother-in-law.

Ann felt a catch in her throat at the forbidding stare and she hesitated, suddenly strangely nervous.

'Well? Do you want something?'

'I . . . I wondered if you, that is–' Ann gathered her thoughts and drew herself up to her full height, '–I wondered if I could be of any help. Nell is obviously in travail and, by the sound of it, having a hard time.'

'We want none of your witchcraft here. Nell's fine; just making a fuss, as usual.'

From inside the room Ann could hear a feeble voice calling out to her.

Goodwife Catt turned her head sharply and uttered one short word. 'No.' Then, without another word, slammed the door shut with such force that Ann took an involuntary step backwards.

For a moment Ann remained outside the door, her heart beating rapidly, stunned by the vitriol in the woman's voice and by the word 'witch'. Witch was a word that instilled a sense of horror and dread in anyone so accused - and with good reason. Fear of witches had stalked the countryside for centuries and sudden death, freakish weather or natural misfortune could all be explained away by accusing someone of witchcraft. Anyone who used herbs or 'potions', anyone who had knowledge beyond the ordinary, anyone who seemed to interfere with God's gift of life or death - all invited accusation from the ignorant and the bigoted. The punishment for witchcraft was death by hanging or even, worst of all, by burning and the 'trials' by which guilt was established were almost as horrifying. Ann remembered her grandmother telling her of a poor woman in Crawley who drowned in a pond while being tested; sinking proved she was innocent, while floating would have proved her guilt.

What kind of test was that, Ann thought as she imagined the horror of the water closing over her head? She took a deep breath. What was she thinking? She knew that some ignorant people viewed her knowledge of herbs and potions with suspicion, but she was being ridiculous taking notice of the ranting of a nasty old woman. Picking up her basket of wild strawberries, she hurried on down the lane, as the sky darkened ahead of her.

She did not tell John about the incident. Why, she was not quite sure. In any case, he was full of some new work from young Squire Hosmer – something about new wrought iron gates that would be worth at least two weeks of regular shoeing, and she did not want to spoil his good humour, so the evening passed as normal, the two eldest boys bickering good-naturedly as they ate their supper.

Just as they were finishing their meal it started to rain heavily, a real summer cloudburst starting with huge drops that soon became a torrent, coursing down the thatch and pounding at the shutters so that she had had to draw them closed to keep out the wet. Then, as suddenly as it had started, the rain stopped, the clouds cleared and the late evening sun turned the raindrops quivering on the long grass into sparkling diamonds.

Ann breathed in the warm, damp smell of the earth and felt a housewife's satisfaction that she'd gathered the strawberries this afternoon.

After all this rain the slugs would be out in force tonight and by tomorrow many of the juicy berries would have been damaged.

It had been a long and busy day and they didn't linger long after their meal, but soon went to their beds. Despite her earlier disquiet about Nell, Ann was tired and fell asleep quickly, so that it seemed as if the candle hadn't long been snuffed, when there was the sound of footsteps outside and a pounding on the door.

'God's teeth! What in hell's name . . .?' John rarely blasphemed, but he had clearly been woken suddenly from the exhausted, first sleep of the night and was fuddled and disorientated. He tumbled from the bed and, not stopping for a light, fumbled for the door. The pounding continued until John lifted the bar and someone nearly fell into the room.

'Goodwife Ann. Goodwife Ann, be she here?'

'Where else would she be at this time of night?' John grumbled. 'Simon? Is it you?' John peered at the figure silhouetted against the last glimmer of the darkening, twilight, summer sky. 'Si Catt?'

'Aye Master Ashdown, it's me. Goodwife Ashdown is please to come quickly. It's me Ma. She's in a bad way.'

In a moment Ann was out of bed. She pulled on her skirt, gathered her shawl around her and picked up the lantern from the chest. So, they needed her 'witchcraft' after all! Well, she would not deny a woman in travail. She never had, and was not about to do so now.

'It's alright John. You go back to bed.' She turned to Simon. 'Fetch up that basket from the corner lad, while I put a light to the lantern. Mind you take it careful now.'

John put a hand on her arm. 'Are you sure, Ann? It's very late; I don't like you going there at this time of night.'

'It's not far and all will be well, John. Nell is in need and I'll be as quick as I can.' She touched his cheek and spoke reassuringly, more to calm the beating of her own heart, than to lessen the concern of her husband.

The sudden chill of the night air made her shiver after the cosy warmth of her bed. She hurried after Simon. He was such a skinny lad, a bit older than her George, but he was speeding along on his thin legs as if the demons of hell were after him.

She quickened her pace and as she did so, reckoned up in her head – this would be Nell's sixth, or was it seventh babe? She was unsure. There was, however, no time to dwell on that now with Simon, racing ahead of her, obviously afraid for his mother, and not without reason. Nell was not strong, nor was she a young woman.

The earlier rain clouds had completely cleared away and a weak moon was rising through a haze of mist. She tried to keep up with the boy, who seemed to have owl vision and she was glad that she had the lantern, so that she could, at least, avoid the worst patches of mud. Overhanging bushes, weighed down with the earlier rain, slapped at her face and hampered her skirts. She dodged this way and that trying to side-step them and as she did so, nearly took a tumble on the slippery path. It had certainly been a wet, drear summer, she thought, with precious few of the golden, shimmering days when the whole countryside seemed to slumber in the heat and the only sound was the low droning of the ever busy bees.

As they descended the hill the trees closed overhead in a tunnel so that the dark enfolded them like a bat's wings. Ann cursed silently as her foot caught on a tree root and she almost fell again. She put out her hand to save herself and grasped a branch of holly that pricked her fingers and made her gasp.

By the time they reached the Catts' cottage Ann was panting from her efforts to keep up with the boy and her skirt was muddied and damp. Simon stopped outside the door and, handing her the basket, stood back.

'I'm not to go in Goodwife.' He looked anxiously up into her face. 'Please help her.'

'I'll do my best Si, I promise. You say a prayer for her now.' Nell was, she knew, a devout woman and perhaps the familiar words of a prayer to the Virgin would bring comfort to the lad. At the very least it would give the boy something to do and make him feel he was helping his mother.

Muttering a quick prayer herself, she pushed open the door and involuntarily put her hand up to cover her mouth and nose, as she was hit by what seemed to be a wall of hot, stale air that stank of smoke, urine and excrement. Goodwife Catt lounged on a stool by the fire that was stoked and blazing well. A pot of ale stood on the floor by her side.

On the far side of the room, away from the fire, a single candle, set next to a figure on the floor, gave off a smoky glimmer. Nell lay half naked on a sodden, straw pallet, her belly huge and white like a fat maggot above pale, thin legs that reminded Ann of twigs peeled of their bark. The woman rolled her head from side to side, her eyes tightly closed. Her breathing was shallow and fast. As the fire flared it revealed a yellowing bruise on one cheek and several more on her thin arms. Ann drew a breath, almost gagging as the smell hit the back of her throat. It was as she feared; Catt did beat his wife then.

Goodwife Catt half turned as Ann entered. 'Who sent for you? That bleedin' boy, I suppose. I told you we want none of your witchcraft here. Girl's fine. Just restin' a bit thash all.' She turned back to the fire, mumbling incoherently to herself.

Ann didn't reply to the drunken troll, but dropped to her knees next to Nell. Her face was covered with a thin film of sweat and had an unhealthy, bluish tinge, but as Ann put her hand on the woman's forehead, the eyelids fluttered open.

'Help me.' The words were so soft that they were barely audible, and

Ann had to bend low to catch them.

'That's what I'm here for, my dear.' Quickly she mixed some rosemary leaves and shepherd's purse into some fresh, clean water from a flask in her basket and, lifting Nell's head gently, held it to her lips. 'Drink this. It will give you some strength and help with the contractions.'

''Ere, what you givin' her? She don't need your potions. We're not paying for potions . . .' The voice in the corner sank to a low muttering as Nell thirstily gulped the cool liquid.

'Slowly Nell, Just small sips.'

Putting a hand on the bulging belly Ann could feel that the contractions were weak and irregular. With the mother so exhausted, she doubted that this babe was going to be born at all, but she would do what she could. She laid her hand on the taught skin and gently felt her way around the belly. Straightway she could feel what the problem was; the baby was not in the right position for birthing. It was lying crossways and no amount of pushing was going to force it into the world. She feared it wasn't to time and, judging by the bruises on the side of Nell's face and arms, a beating had brought on labour early before the babe had turned. Silently Ann gave a sad shake of her head and stroked the limp, mouse coloured hair back from the pale face. Although Nell seemed to have rallied slightly after the drinking the infusion, Ann knew there was nothing more she could do.

For what seemed like an age the three women sat in the close, claustrophobic atmosphere, the only sound the crackling of the fire and the incoherent muttering of the old woman.

Then, just as Ann was feeling her own head droop with weariness, despite the suffocating heat of the room and the blazing fire, Nell began to shiver and her teeth chattered.

'So cold,' she whispered. Ann looked around for something to cover the woman who had been weakened by hours of fruitless pushing and, as she rose to gather up a ragged cover discarded on the floor, Nell gave a sudden cry and blood gushed between her legs. Ann stared in horror. What was happening? Bleeding after birth was not uncommon and often fatal, but Nell's baby had not yet been born. What should she do? Had the womb had finally torn? She wasn't sure.

At the cry, Goodwife Catt straightened up. 'What you done to her? I saw you, you witch.' She pointed a gnarled finger at Ann. 'Gived her a potion you did and brought forth blood.' She struggled to her feet and crossed herself with wild, exaggerated movements. 'Killed her you have. Killed our Nell with your spells.'

Shutting her ears to the ranting crone, Ann tried to stem the flow of blood by pushing the cloth in her hand against the woman's vagina, but she knew it was hopeless and soon the material was soaked and warm blood was dripping through her fingers. Nell arched her back and her legs twitched before she finally fell back onto the straw and was still.

Ann felt shaky and near to tears. She had attended many births, and not all had gone well, but she and Nell had been friends for many years and to see her die like this and be unable to help was dreadful. However, as she looked up at the old woman, she forced her voice to be strong and firm. 'It is not I who have killed her. It is you with your neglect and your son with his beatings who have caused the death of this poor woman.'

Goodwife Catt ignored her and lurched to the door, flinging it wide and screaming into the black night. 'She's done for her! It's witchcraft! The witch has killed our Nell!'

'Be quiet woman, I've done no such thing. Have some respect for the dead - even if you had none for the living.' The last part of the sentence she muttered to herself as she looked round for something to cover the dead woman and make her decent.

Goodwife Catt turned. 'Don't you touch her,' she screamed. 'Get out. Go on. Out. I'll have the law on you, I will.'

Shaking, Ann gathered her shawl around her and, as the old woman lurched towards her, picked up her basket and stumbled into the darkness, not stopping to light her lantern. For the first few yards her way was lit by the faint glow from the cottage, but as the door was slammed behind her the path plunged into darkness and she jumped and cried out as she felt a cold hand on her arm.

'Is she dead, Goodwife? Is me Ma dead?'

Thankfully she recognised the voice and taking a deep breath to calm herself, replied gently. 'Yes, Simon, I'm so sorry, but she is. There was nothing I could do for her. The babe was the wrong way round to be born. Go in now and say your farewells.'

'No Goodwife. I don't want . . . I don't want . . . ' a sob caught in the boy's throat and she felt in the darkness for his hand. 'I'll walk with you Goodwife. I can see in the dark I can. I'll guide you. I can't go back in there yet.'

John and the boys were snoring gently as she softly opened the door. John flinched slightly when her cold arm touched him as she slid into bed beside him, then he turned on his side and flung an arm across her as he was wont to do, unconsciously pinning her to the mattress. She didn't disturb him. She knew she wouldn't sleep.

She lay on her back listening to the regular breathing of her husband, his arm heavy across her breasts and she couldn't get the images of the night out of her mind – the pitiful body lying on the sodden straw, the vicious look in Goodwife Catt's eyes as she swept her out of the door and the feel of Si's thin body against her arm as he guided her home through the dark. Poor lad. With his mother gone, he had no one to protect him from the violence of his father. What had she calculated? Would this have been Nell's sixth or seventh child? Seventh, she thought? The eldest girl was away serving at the manor she remembered, but they'd want her back now to look to the little ones.

John turned away from her in his sleep, mumbling before settling again to a gentle snore. Released from the weight of his arm she too turned on her side, feeling the solid warmth of his back against hers, but still she did not sleep as Nell's cry of 'Help me, help me,' and the word 'witch, witch,' seemed to echo around the room with each breath she took.

7

Next morning as they broke their fast John had asked Ann about Nell and expressed sympathy for the family over her death, but his mind was obviously on his new work for young Hosmer and he was plainly eager to get off to the forge, so she had not detained him. Alone in the house, as she went about her tasks, she couldn't help herself listening for the sound of footsteps on the path.

She both expected and dreaded a visit from James Catt. She felt sure that neither his mother, nor he, would accept any responsibility for Nell's death and she would be a ready scapegoat. He was known as a violent, vindictive man and she was sure that, egged on by his mother, he would try to say that Nell's death was her fault. It would be convenient for him to have someone else to take the blame. She wasn't frightened of him. Well, to be honest, she was, but she knew he would never dare hurt her physically and risk John's anger, but still she dreaded a confrontation with him.

There were, she knew, those in the village who would go along with his accusations. Unfortunately, she couldn't help in all cases and that was where the problem lay. Sometimes she was called too late and sometimes people were just too sick and it was then that relatives would point an accusing finger and seek to blame her for what was not her fault.

Ann had learned most of what she knew of illnesses and birthing from her own mother, who had brought a good few of the villagers into the world. She too had sometimes been looked at askance when her patients had died, but it had never stopped her offering succour to the needy and Ann was determined that she wouldn't be intimidated either. But determination didn't stop her stomach churning at the word "witch".

With John working as a blacksmith and hearing the news from passing travellers, Ann was only too aware that witch hunts were not entirely a thing of the past. There had been a woman only recently who had been accused of witchcraft. What she had done Ann did not know, but the poor woman had been tortured and hanged. Perhaps she had been a witch. But perhaps too, she had been like her - simply blessed with the knowledge to heal if God willed it.

There were many people like Catt, who were ignorant and vindictive and frightened of the unknown. It was all too easy for them to accuse a poor lone woman of witchcraft and a pact with the Devil if a loved one died or a precious cow failed to calve. But, Ann told herself, I am different. I am not alone. I have a husband and a family of fine sons to protect me against the Catts of the world.

So, talking softly to herself, Ann took herself to task as she went about her morning chores. She would weather this storm and all would be well. Brooding on what had happened and might yet happen was of no use at all. She must get on with her day and stop these dark thoughts. She looked around the room and wrinkled her nose. The warmer, damp weather was making the rushes on the floor stink and she was glad of a job that would help to take her mind off poor Nell. Taking her broom from the corner she set about sweeping them into a pile, working with a will until she was quite out of breath.

It was a relief to go out into the sunshine and tip them onto the heap beyond the vegetable garden. Then, taking up a large flat basket and a short scythe that John had fashioned for the purpose, she set out for the brook where, at this time of year, the rushes grew along the bank in thick, green swathes. Catching up her skirt between her legs, she tucked the end into her belt and waded into the cool, shallow water swinging her scythe and harvesting the spear like leaves. At first the sunshine and the rhythm of her work calmed her, but thoughts of Nell, her poor swollen body with its vivid bruises and the venomous accusations of Goodwife Catt, kept intruding and gripping at her stomach. Returning to the house she spread the rushes on the cleanly swept floor, her ear still tuned for the sound of footsteps on the path outside as she tried to stave off her growing dread of a meeting with James Catt.

But when the sound of steps came at last, it was only Dickon, home from the ironworks, hungry as always. He went straight to the shelf and took down one of the loaves of bread. It was still warm and fragrant with yeast as she'd fetched it from the bakery only that morning. He beamed at her when she frowned in mock disapproval, as he hacked himself a large slice and she felt a rush of love for her first-born.

'No wonder you're so tall, lad,' she said. You eat enough for two. I don't envy any girl foolish enough to marry you – she'll never be done cooking for you.'

He grinned, crossed the room in two strides and picked her up and swung her round.

'Well you seem to manage with three men in your house and I won't marry anyone who isn't as good a cook as you.'

'Put me down, you great fool, you're covered in grime.' Shaking her head she brushed the front of her apron and straightened her coif. She watched him as he gobbled down the bread with obvious relish. He was so like John, tall and broad – easy going and always cheerful. How was it, she wondered, that two people could produce three such different sons?

Dickon had arrived in this world a big, bouncing baby with an abundance of dark hair. He had suckled well and slept contentedly. From a toddler he'd been interested in everything around him and was always dragging something indoors shouting, 'What's this Mother?'

He'd been happy to help John in the forge when he was younger and she knew John had felt that he would make a fine blacksmith and had hoped that he'd take over the business in time, but, as he got older, it became obvious that his early curiosity extended beyond the confines of the house and village. Dickon wanted to experience the world. With the iron works on their doorstep, expanding every year, it soon attracted her son's attention.

He would disappear for hours at a time and come home full of stories from the waggon drivers who brought in supplies to the works and took out the smelted iron. His face glowed as he told of the canons that, in earlier times, had been made for King Henry's ships and soon he was talking of getting himself a job on the waggons that set out across the countryside from Hugget's Furnace. He'd been happy then and had travelled as far as the coast and seen the sea. Sometimes, as now, he worked in the diggings, hacking the ore from the ground. The work was hard and she wondered why he'd choose that over the blacksmith's forge, but he liked the outdoor life, was happy and popular with the men and that was all she wanted.

Nick was altogether different. A small, pale sickly babe, reluctant to suckle, he'd worried her near to death as he screwed up his little face and howled, tucking his legs up and squirming. Dickon would look in bewilderment at his tiny brother and pat him, none too gently, on the head. They had never understood each other and to this day they bickered and fought.

She loved all her children, but that didn't mean that she could not view them realistically. Nick was not as clever as Dickon and not as tall either - something she knew irritated him immensely. He was always looking for approval; always sure he was being compared to his elder brother and taking every opportunity to pick a quarrel with his big, easy-going sibling.

As a young child, he had seemed an unlikely blacksmith, but he now had broad shoulders and was a strong lad, but still, she knew, he envied Dickon and John their height. He was a good, steady worker and was proving an increasing help to John in the forge. Unlike his brother he enjoyed the settled, steady work of the smithy and his father was happy with his work and hopeful that there would, after all, be a son who could carry on the business after him. Certainly it seemed that Nick had no wish to travel and was often somewhat shy with strangers.

And then there was George.

Despite herself Ann sighed and Dickon looked across at her. 'Mother?' he said.

'Just thinking about your brother.'

'Which one? Trouble or Touchy.' He grinned. 'No wonder you sigh with those two as sons! Why didn't you get yourself three like me?'

Ignoring him, Ann spoke half to herself. 'I hope we did the right thing letting George stay with Katherine. He seems happy enough when we see him, but it's not been easy this last year with him gone. I do miss him.'

'Gone? Why he's only a few miles away and you can see him whenever you want to. Georgie's alright. Do him good to be away on his own. Might teach him to appreciate us and not be so touchy all the time.' Without being asked he took the heavy pan out of her hand and lifted it easily onto the hook over the fire.

She smiled her thanks and sat down on the stool by the hearth. 'I don't know, Dickon, it's so difficult to know what he thinks about things and you have to admit it's a bit of a strange life for a young lad with just Katherine and young Harry for company. At least here he had you and Nick – and his father.'

'Not that he ever seemed to appreciate us.' Dickon grimaced ruefully. 'Always in a world of his own, our George. Always got something that he must do or "something bad will happen." Where he get these weird ideas I don't know?'

'Well he's mine and I love him dearly as I do you all, but I have to admit that I don't understand all that goes on in his head. He's a difficult person to know that's for sure.'

Dickon looked serious at her concern and, squatting down in front of her, put a hand on her knee. 'You're not really worried about him are you? He seemed happy enough last time I stopped by. Do you want me to go over tomorrow and see him? I could go on my way home from work – it's not much out of my way and if it would—'

'Oh you're a good lad, Dick.' She touched his cheek. 'Would you mind? Not that he'll tell you anything, but just go and see how he seems to you. It's an awkward age for a lad. He's no longer a child, but he's not quite a man either and—'

'I know, and you worry about him. Just like that old brown hen when she has her chicks you are. Cluck, cluck—'

'Mind your cheek boy! You're not too big for a good thrashing.' Ann punched her fist against his arm feeling the bulge of hard muscle which made a mockery of her threat, but he laughed and pretended it was enough to overbalance him and he rolled onto the floor.

The door banged and Nick and John entered. Dickon turned from where he sat at her feet and held up his arms in mock defence. 'Help me, Father,' he laughed. 'My Mother's attacking me.'

'Is she indeed! And if so, I'm sure it's with good reason son, so don't expect aid from me.'

Ann smiled up at her husband. How fortunate she was compared with poor Katherine. John came across and kissed Ann on the cheek leaving a slight smudge of dirt on her face.

'You two look cheerful,' she said. 'Have you had a good day?'

'We have indeed Ma,' said Nick. 'Squire Hosmer came over and he's right pleased with the gates. They'll be very grand and Father's going to—'

'That's good Nick. I'm sure you've been a great help to your Father." She turned back to John. 'Dickon says he'll go across to Katherine's tomorrow and see our George. Just to check he's alright.'

Nick scowled at the mention of his younger brother. 'Of course he's alright. He's having a great time I should say. Not exactly hard work he's doing is it? Just a bit of light gardening and women's work.'

'That's enough Nick. You know your brother has problems and—'

'Don't we all,' Nick muttered under his breath.

'And I for one am very glad that he can be of use to poor Katherine. God knows she's had it hard these last few years.'

John noticed the sharp edge to his wife's voice and looked sideways at her. There was a frown between her eyes and a thinning of her lips that he knew did not bode well. Something had upset her. Was it just worry about George? He knew how protective she was of their youngest son, but somehow he had the feeling there was more to it than that. He would wait until after supper and perhaps then she would tell him what was troubling her.

8

George loved this part of the day. His chores were done, Harry was in bed and he was sitting in his favourite place on a small bench where he could look out of the open shutters across the fields.

Beyond the rather broken fence - which he noted guiltily, as he should have mended it by now - the meadow, spattered with water avens, ox eye daisy, knapweed, buttercups and many flowers he didn't know the name of, sloped gently down to a line of small trees that he knew marked the bank of the river. Earlier in the day he and Harry had watched as a kingfisher had dived again and again from an overhanging alder branch catching small minnows for its brood in a hole in the bank. To the left, almost out of his view, the river disappeared into the dark smudge of the forest, its edges fringed with graceful silver birch trees, their white bark making them stand out from the dark depths behind like tall, elongated ghosts.

At last the weather seemed to have changed. The day had been hot and his face and arms glowed where he had caught the sun. Katherine was sitting across the room from him at the other window. The sun was getting low, but still lit the small room with a golden glow in which the dust motes danced in the welcome, cool breeze of evening. She was sewing as always - an intricate blackwork design with curlicues and stylised leaves and flowers that flowed out from her needle like ink from a quill; making the most of the remaining sunlight as she said that the black was difficult to see by candlelight.

George sat with his knees drawn up to his chest and his arms wrapped round his legs. He was aware of Katherine out of the corner of his eye, but his attention was focussed outdoors, as he kept watch for the fox that often skirted the edge of the field at this time, intent on sniffing around the hen house. He had shut the hens up earlier, but wasn't at all certain that the house he'd made for them in the spring was totally fox-proof. He was good at making things, a talent perhaps inherited from his father, but the hen house had been quite a challenge to his skills.

Katherine sneezed and then sniffed delicately. 'I do believe I might be coming down with a summer cold. It's probably all this damp weather we've had recently. Though at least today has been more like summer.'

There was no reply from George, but she was quite used to that and went on thinking aloud. 'Poor little man, he took a long time to shake off the cough he had in April, so I wouldn't want him to sicken again. If it hadn't been for your Mother's linctus I don't think his chest would ever have cleared. It was a blessing that you and I did not have it too.'

It didn't occur to George to answer Katherine. He rarely saw the need to reply and couldn't understand people who chattered about everything and nothing. That was one thing he liked about her – and Harry – neither of them expected him to keep up a conversation with them, so he had time for his own thoughts. Harry talked a lot, but didn't mind if he didn't get an answer.

He let his thoughts wander now, as he scanned the edge of the meadow. He hoped that Katherine would never have to go back to Rotherfield. He was happy here. It was quiet and Katherine let him get on with doing things without interfering. He'd planned the vegetable garden and then marked it out using a stick as a measure- twenty sticks by twenty. He liked the number twenty – a swan with the moon behind it was the way he thought of it. A magic number that always brought him luck. He liked it when the number of steps he had to take could be divided up into twenties; it made him feel safe. Two lots of twenty from the well to the door; three lots of twenty to the end of their plot. Sometimes he had to take large or small steps to be sure to make it fit, but he didn't think that would matter. The thing that worried him was he still wasn't sure how many steps it was to take him all the way home. The three or four times he'd been back to visit in the year he'd been here, Dickon had given him a lift on the waggon. On the way back he'd had to make a diversion to pick up something Katherine needed. How many steps would it be if he went straight from door to door? A lot, he thought, and he wasn't at all sure that he could count that far.

He liked not having his family fussing around him and wanting to know what he was up to. Liked the house here too – all on its own, a good distance outside the village. It wasn't as big or as grand as the parsonage, but George thought it was far nicer. It was set amid the fields away from the main route from Rotherfield to Buxted and few people had cause to come this way so there were no unexpected visitors. Once they'd seen a pedlar who had missed his way, but George had hidden in the hen house as he didn't much like strangers. Katherine, though, had talked to the man for some time and given him a mug of ale before giving him directions and sending him on his way.

She was sneezing again and George sneaked a glance at her as she delicately dabbed at her nose with a kerchief. She had never told him about William's visits and George understood instinctively that he wasn't supposed to know about them, but he was aware that the priest had been to the cottage on more than one occasion. For several weeks after they moved he had not come and Katherine had been listless and unhappy. Harry too had missed his father and would sometimes tug at his mother's skirts and ask plaintively 'When's Farver come?'

Then one night after George had gone to bed, the priest had slipped in after dark and George had gone to sleep lulled by the murmur of their voices, only to be woken at what he guessed to be around midnight, by hoof beats as William left. He did not return for many weeks and then one day Katherine had sent the boy on an unexpected errand. How she knew her husband was coming he didn't know, but he'd come back early and seen William's horse tied up by the gate and waited behind the hen house until he'd ridden off.

Keeping his head still, George made his eyes into slits and slid them right and left, glancing around the room and through the door to the bedroom. The cottage was small, but there were two rooms – one where they cooked and ate and where he slept on a straw pallet by the fire and one where Katherine and Harry slept. Yes, it was a comfortable place and George was contented with life here. The well was good and reliable and the soil was dark and rich and the garden was growing well. But most of all there was the book. That was the most important thing in his life now; the thing that gave him a frisson of excitement in his stomach when he thought about it on waking.

A movement in the grass interrupted his thoughts and he slid off his seat, walked quietly to the door and went out. He picked up a large stick which he'd left propped against the wall outside and trod quietly round the side of the house.

'What the hell?'

As he turned the corner a roar from a large figure nearly frightened the life out of him and, dropping the stick, he ran back into the house and slammed the door behind him, leaning on it with a wild and frightened look on his face.

Katherine started to her feet, nearly stumbling in her haste as a knock came at the door and a voice shouted.

'George? Georgie? What's the matter with 'ee? It's me you darn fool – Dickon. Open the door.'

Katherine put her hand to her mouth and giggled like a girl. 'You look as if you've seen a ghost, George. Did he give you a fright? Open the door lad. It's your brother.'

Frowning, George opened the door and looked up at Dickon.

'What were you doing lad, creeping round the house with a great club in your hand? I thought you were about to brain me.'

George hung his head. 'Fox,' he mumbled and shuffled back to his seat.

Katherine limped forward, after carefully laying aside her cloth. 'Come in Dickon. I trust you are well. I'm sorry for the reception your brother gave you, but he's been worried about the fox getting to the hens.'

Dickon laughed and dipped his head respectfully at Goodwife Collyer, then turned to his brother. 'Well I don't envy old foxy if he meets you and that stick George.'

'Take a seat, do,' said Katherine, for all the world as though a gentleman had come calling. 'George, fetch your brother a drink. Where are your manners child?'

George pulled a face as he crossed the room to the jug which stood on the table and Dickon ruffled his hair affectionately as he passed.

'Don't.' Instinctively George shied away from his brother.

'Oh sorry, I know. Don't touch you.' Dickon grinned at Katherine with a conspiratorial air. 'Doesn't change, our Georgie, does he?'

At this point the door to the second room creaked slowly open and a tousled Harry, flushed from sleep, stood on the step squinting at the light and rubbing his eyes. 'Farver?' he murmered.

Katherine flushed. 'Oh Harry what are you doing out of bed you bad boy? You should be fast asleep.' Katherine shook her head with exasperation.

'I'm sorry, it's my fault for making so much noise and waking the lad.' Dickon scooped up the child and carried him across to his mother, dumping him in her lap. Harry clung with chubby pink arms around her neck and yawned widely.

'Farver?' he mouthed again, barely awake.

'Hush now. It's only Dickon come to see George, Harry.' She stroked her son's cheek. 'Hush now, go back to sleep.' She turned to Dickon. 'Don't worry he'll go off again soon. He and George have had a busy day, so he must be worn out.' She glanced across at where George stood carefully pouring small beer into a mug for his brother. 'George is a great help to me,' she said rather primly. 'Your mother would be proud of the way he's sorted the garden and gathered the—'

'Well I'm glad to hear he's not just a nuisance!'

George narrowed his eyes at his brother as he held out a beaker to him, taking care that their fingers didn't touch.

Dickon smiled at George. 'Come for a walk with me brother?' he asked more gently. 'If Goodwife Collyer can spare you for half an hour that is.'

Katherine nodded her assent and settled the child more comfortably on her lap. 'Go along with Dickon, George. You've been sitting there this last hour watching for that fox. A walk will do you good and I'm sure your mother will want to know from Dickon how you are faring.'

Giving the funny little bob of his head that was his favoured way of communicating, George made for the door and Dickon, gulping the last of his drink followed him.

'I'll not keep him long, Goodwife, but yes, you are right, our Mother frets about him even though she knows he's fine really.'

'It's a hazard of motherhood Dickon,' Katherine said and smiled down at the now sleeping child on her lap. 'Remember me to Ann and ask her when she is going to visit. She's always been a good friend and it's a while since we saw her.'

'Aye, I'll tell her. She's been busy of late, but I'm sure she'll come to see you soon.' And nodding his head in what seemed to her a grown up version of George's head bob, he went out, closing the door gently behind him.

Outside, George was waiting by the path across the meadow. He was running his hand up the long stems of grass, collecting handfuls of seed and hurling them into the air so that they fell like rain.

'Alright George?' Dickon looked sideways at his brother who nodded. 'Mother sends her love. She wanted to come herself, but as you can guess she's busy with the garden and harvesting and drying her herbs and well, whatever else it is that women do!' George nodded. 'The garden looks good. You've done a good job there lad. And I don't reckon Mr Fox will get a look in at those hens either. Looks like you've built a castle keep rather than a hen house.'

'No it doesn't, Dickon. A castle has a wall round it and we've only got—
'

'No I didn't mean it was a castle. Just that it was strong like one; difficult for anything to break in. Well done.'

'I've never built a hen house before. But it's not a castle.'

'No, I know that George. You've done a good job.'

For the first time since his brother arrived, George smiled.

They walked in silence, side by side, George's pace nearly matching that of his brother's long legs. Dickon was used to his brother not initiating conversation, but finally he felt the silence had gone on long enough.

'Sorry I've not come by for a while, but I've been on the waggons for a couple of weeks. Had a right to do last Thursday as we were taking a load of sows to Parrock and a wheel broke. Tipped the lot in the ditch and—'

'Oh no!' George looked stricken. 'Were they hurt?'

'Hurt? Oh I see! No George, not live sows. Sows are what we call the iron bars. Pig iron – sows – do you see?'

George frowned. 'So why are they called sows if they're not pigs, they're iron. That's silly. I don't understand.'

'The hot metal is tipped into a channel called a sow because off it there are lots of smaller sections that look like piglets suckling. We were taking a load of sows to be—'

'So nothing was hurt?'

'George will you shut up and listen! You and your animals! As is happens something – or rather someone was hurt. Kit Muddle was at the side of the cart and as it tipped his leg got trapped. You should have heard him yell. By the time they got him out he was as white as a sheet and his leg was just hanging off and they had to cut it—'

'Is he dead?' George asked, his eyes wide.

'Not yet he isn't, but I can't see him getting over that, poor chap. I never liked the bastard – mean fellow, steal anything he could lay hands on, but I wouldn't wish what happened to him on anyone.'

'And what happened to the sows?'

'Well we finally got another waggon and then had to get them onto that but it was—'

'How many sows did you have?'

'How many? George, I don't know. Just don't tell Mother what happened. She worries enough without thinking I'm going under the wheels of a waggon.'

George nodded. 'I won't, Dickon.'

'Good lad. Now tell me, what else you been up to? I mean, are you happy here? Mother worries about you as well, you know. You can come home if you—'

'No!' George looked agitated. 'No, I don't want to come home.'

Dickon looked in surprise at his brother's agitated face. 'It's alright; I'm not saying you have to, just that if you want to you can always—'

'No, I need to stay here.'

'Well, yes, I know it would be difficult for Goodwife Collyer to manage without you but I dare say that—'

'No, I haven't finished learning yet. I can't go home till I know all the words. Don't make me, Dickon.'

Dickon frowned, unsure what his brother was rambling about. Conversations with George were often odd, but what was this about knowing the words?

'What words, George? What do you mean?'

George stopped beneath a silver birch tree and kicked at a root that ran across the path. He stared at his feet. 'The words in the book. Goodwife Collyer is teaching me and Harry the words in the book. Harry only knows some of them 'cos he's little, but I know nearly all of them now, but there are still some of the long ones I don't know yet and I don't want to go home not knowing them.'

Dickon scratched his head, not sure he understood his brother correctly. 'Are you telling me that she's teaching you to read? That you can read? But you don't know your letters.'

'I do. I know the A, B C, D, E, F—'

'Well I'll be - so you do. But reading? What are you reading? How come you can do that? It's beyond me. I tried once, but all those little squiggles . . . Made no sense at all.'

'Oh but they do, Dickon and I told you, Goodwife Collyer is teaching me. We read the big Bible every morning and I can do most all of it myself now. She says I am a good student and I'm clever. I like it more than anything and if you make me go home I can't do it anymore.'

George frowned and breathed heavily through his nose in a way that Dickon knew meant he was fighting back tears. It wasn't often George showed such emotion, or talked so much and Dickon realised that learning to read was obviously very important to him. 'Can you write too?' he asked.

George shook his head. 'No, not yet, but I might do one day. I'm clever you see.' George said this without a trace of pride. He was just stating a fact in the same way as he might say, 'Yes, I have a hand.'

Dickon, though, was amused by this innocent boastfulness and went to punch the younger boy affectionately on the arm. Just in time he stopped himself and let his hand drop. 'You are that, brother. Wait till I tell Mother – she'll be so proud.'

'She won't stop me will she? Are you sure Dick?'

'I'm sure, George. She'll be pleased that you have your letters. I'm sure it's a great thing to be able to read.'

George smiled to himself. 'I'd better go back now,' he said. 'The fox—'

'Yes we can't have Mr Fox prowling around can we? Off you go then. I'm sure Mother will be over to see you soon. Goodwife Collyer was asking if she'd visit. Farewell, brother.' And with a wave of his hand Dickon strode off across the field.

George stood for a moment watching until his brother disappeared into the trees and then he turned and ran back the way they had come, leaping in the air every ten paces like a young deer.

By the time George returned to the cottage the sun had already dipped behind the trees leaving a red glow like the furnace at his father's forge and tinting the high, thin clouds with flames of pale orange – it would be a fine day tomorrow the boy thought as he made one last check on the hens. An owl called from the direction of the river; hunting over the meadow for voles no doubt. Opening the door quietly he realised that Katherine had already retired for the night and apart from the eerie sound of the bird, all was silent, the room full of shadows.

George tiptoed across the room to the chest and raised the lid cautiously. There was a slight creak, but not enough to penetrate the thick oak door between the two rooms. Propping the lid against the wall George needed both hands to lift the heavy book wrapped in blue cloth that was the only thing inside. Reverently he carried it across to the window, laid it on the wide sill and unwrapped it from the cloth. The cover was dark brown leather with five raised bands across the spine. George ran his hand gently across the surface before putting his face down and sniffing. He loved the feel and the musty smell of the leather and the paper. Carefully he opened the Bible.

It was almost dark now. Too dark to make out the close printed lettering, but the illuminated initial letters, some scribed with bright colours, stood out in the gloom and he could just make out the tiny figures in the woodcuts that decorated some of the pages. He would have loved to have fetched a light and spent the night practising his new found skill of reading, but he didn't dare. Katherine never allowed a light anywhere near the precious book – she was not willing to risk damage from wax or flame.

George remembered a time when the Bible had been in their church at Rotherfield. It had always been chained to the wall, but anyone was free to read it if they could. William, of course, read from it regularly during services, but few others in the village were capable of deciphering the closely printed text.

It had become too dark to make out anything on the pages, but George still stood by the window, one hand on the warm, smooth, leather cover of the book. He frowned as he recalled the Sunday when there had been a lot of angry voices in the church. He had been quite small and had been so frightened by the loud noise that he had hidden behind Ann's skirts, as people had shouted and waved their arms. The church had looked very different on that day, he remembered; the brightly coloured paintings on the walls had been whitewashed over, the statue of the Blessed Virgin had gone, as had the altar with its shining cross. Instead there was a plain wooden table. William had looked anxious and tried to calm the people.

His mother had hugged him to her while Nick had kept hopping from foot to foot saying 'Where's she gone? Has she been stolen?' over and over until Dickon had clouted him and told him to shut up.

Later, his mother had explained to him that Edward – the boy-king – wanted the church to be much plainer and that's why everything had changed. She had told him that he should feel sorry for Edward, as had been only nine - younger than George was now - when his father died.

Now poor Edward, too, was dead and there was a queen instead – Edward's half-sister, Mary. Goodwife Collyer had explained that she too had changed their religion again – back to Catholic this time. George frowned. He felt very confused; it was all such a muddle. He didn't really understand about Catholic and Protestant, but he was pleased that the virgin was back in her niche. He liked her and he knew that his mother liked her too; she had a nice, kind face and was dressed in his favourite colour blue.

He didn't think that Katherine approved of the Catholics. Her lips went all tight when she spoke of them; she called them Papists and said they were misguided. But surely, George reasoned, William must be a catholic now if he had the Virgin back in his church. Perhaps, he thought, that was why Katherine had moved away to the cottage - because she didn't like William now he was a Catholic. But they were still married and William still visited - even if it was in secret. It was all very bewildering.

In the darkness he shrugged, then picked up the book and hugged it to him. The Bible from the church was here now and that meant that he could read it. That was good. That was the best thing in his life.

9

Ann swung her feet off the bed and sat on the edge, rubbing the sleep from her eyes and pushing back the stray wisps of hair that had escaped from the plait snaking across her shoulder. She had always been proud of her hair – the colour of ripe corn, her father had said. She twisted a strand across her fingers and noticed a few threads of grey. With a wry grimace she stretched her arms above her head, then padded across the floor to the window, her feet rustling the fresh rushes and releasing a sweet smell from the meadowsweet and mint that she had strewn over them.

Appreciatively she breathed in the fragrance of summer. She loved this time of year with its sunlit mornings and long twilight evenings when she could sit with the shutters open and listen to the birds, while her hands were busy with sewing or spinning. Yesterday's glorious red sunset had promised more good summer weather today and by the look of the streaks of sun showing through chinks in the shutters, the old weather rhyme of "Red sky at night, shepherd's delight" had proved correct. Quietly so as not to disturb John who was still snoring gently, she pushed open the shutter and leaned out into the sunshine, resting her arms on the warm sill.

Dickon had gone to see George yesterday and she had slept well, reassured by Dickon that her youngest son was happy and contented. And reading too! Now that was a surprise. He was the only one in the family who was able to and she was glad for him as the more skills he learned, the easier things might be for him in the future.

The early morning air smelled of damp earth and rose blossom and she could hear the dull drone of the bees already at work in her herb garden. It really was the most beautiful morning and she felt far too wide awake to go back to bed so, catching up her shawl, she put it around her shoulders and quietly unlatched the door, glancing over her shoulder at the still sleeping John as she did so. Not looking where she was going, she stepped out of the door and felt something soft and furry brush her face. She jumped back and then screamed. Silhouetted against the bright morning sky, gently twirling where she had bumped into it, was her black cat, Puss, hanging with a cord around its neck. Instinctively, her hands shaking, she reached towards it stopping the movement and supporting its weight even as she knew it was too late.

At the sound of her cry John, leaping out of bed, came stumbling to the door. "Od rabbit it woman, what the . . .' He broke off as he saw the cat hanging in the doorway. 'Here, Love move back . . . let me.' Moving her gently to one side he reached up and broke the cord before lowering the cat. 'Who on earth would be so—'

'Catt,' she whispered. 'It's Catt. I know it is.'

John looked at her strangely. 'Ann? Are you alright Love? Of course it's a cat. We can see that. It's poor Puss. Who would have—?'

'I tell you it's Catt. Nell's husband – James Catt. He's done it. He's killed poor Puss. I know it's him, John.'

'Catt? But why, Ann?'

Ann's voice was low and she didn't look at him. 'The other night, when Nell died, his mother called me a witch and said that it was all my fault that Nell had died. She said I'd killed poor Nell with my herbs, while all I'd done was try to save her.' A huge sob seemed to come up from her belly and she bit her top lip to stop it from escaping. 'How could anyone think I'd harm Nell – she was my friend?'

'Come here.' Still holding the dead cat at arm's length with one hand, John put the other around Ann and pulled her to him. 'Why on earth didn't you tell me? That little shit of a man. I'll kill him. Good for nothing—'

'No John, leave it. I've been waiting; expecting him to come here. I knew he'd not let it rest. Don't you see? She called me a witch. And poor Puss was black! Oh God, what if people believe it?' Ann's voice was tinged with panic. 'You know what happens to witches, John; you told me about that poor woman who was tortured and then....' She buried her face in her hands and was silent for a moment. 'Don't cause trouble, John,' she begged. 'It will only make things worse and draw attention to me.'

'Me cause trouble! I'm not the one hanging people's cats and frightening them half to death.'

Dickon emerged from the other room frowning, his eyes mere slits against the sunlight. 'Was' going on?' His voice was slurred with sleep. 'Wha' you shouting about Father?'

Ann buried her head in John's chest as he held out poor Puss towards Dickon. 'Some bastard has killed your mother's cat and hung it in the doorway.'

Dickon stretched out his hand and gently rubbed the cat's head. 'Poor Puss. Who the hell—'

'Your Mother reckons its James Catt. Apparently that poxy mother of his accused Ann of killing Nell.'

'Mother? Killing Nell? That's ridiculous!' Dickon flushed with indignation.

'It's because of the herbs.' Still Ann didn't raise either her eyes or her voice. 'Goodwife Catt saw me give Nell a herbal drink and then almost immediately . . .' Ann broke off and swallowed hard before she could continue. 'There was nothing I could do. The baby was the wrong way round. Catt had obviously beaten her and the babe was too early. She just bled to death. There was nothing I could do,' she repeated in a bleak voice.

'We need to get round there Father.' Dickon's sleepiness had vanished and he was now rigid with anger. 'We need to teach that whoreson a lesson. It wasn't Mother's fault at all and he knows it. He's just trying to shift the blame onto—'

'No Dickon.' Ann spoke urgently. 'That's what he wants. He wants to stir up trouble against me. Let it lie. In time he will calm down and forget his accusations.'

'But Mother—'

'No Dickon.' She pulled away from John's embrace. 'And you too John. Promise me you won't do anything. We'll just bury poor Puss and say nothing to anyone.'

'But, Ann, his accusations are rubbish and he shouldn't get away with it.'

'No John. No. Do you hear me? If you make a fuss it will just make things worse. Let it die down - please.' She put her hand on her husband's arm and looked pleadingly up into his face. 'Please John. Promise me.'

Shaking his head John gently put his big, rough hand on her cheek. 'Well it don't seem right to me, but if it means so much to you. But if he ever—'

'You too Dickon. Promise me. Say nothing, do nothing.'

Slowly Dickon nodded his head. 'As you wish Mother. But I don't think it's right,' he added with a frown.

For the rest of the day Ann felt taut and rigid. She couldn't relax and she was constantly glancing around as if . . . Well, she didn't know what she expected, but she felt sure that James Catt had not finished with her yet. It was late afternoon and she was out in the garden hoeing between the neat rows of vegetables when a shadow fell across the earth and made her jump and cry out. She looked up into the bruised face of young Simon who was hovering uncertainly by the honeysuckle.

'I'm sorry Goodwife. Didn't mean for to frighten you.'

'Oh Si you did give me a start! Why lad what's happened to you? Your face—?'

'It were Father.' Si's voice was low and scared.

'Your Father? He did that to you? But why?'

'I wouldn't . . . I wouldn't . . .' Simon paused and then blurted the words out in a rush. 'I know'd you loved the cat and I wouldn't . . . I'm sorry Goodwife, but I couldn't stop him.'

'My cat. You know what he did to my cat?'

'He told me to do it, but I wouldn't, so he 'it me.' The boy hung his head. 'Then 'e strung the cat up 'imself. Said you was to be taught a lesson for killing Ma.'

'I didn't kill your Mother, Simon. I did all that I—'

'I know. It were 'im, 'itting her. He 'its everyone, but he wants to blame you so people won't know it were him. I can't stand it anymore. I'm leaving. Going far away where 'e can't get me. But you watch out for Father, Goodwife. He's bad and he's got it in for you.'

'What do you mean you're leaving? Where are you going? You're too young to—'

'I ain't staying anymore. I'd have run away before if it weren't for Ma. But I'm finished here now. He ain't hitting me again.'

'Oh Simon, I really don't think that's such a good idea. Where would you go? You don't have any money do you? You can't go wandering about on your own. Do you have relatives you could go to?'

Mutely the boy shook his head. 'He's sent for our Mary to come back from the big house and look after the little 'uns. They don't need me and I won't stay, Goodwife - I won't.'

Ann didn't know what to think. It was plain that the boy couldn't go home to be abused by his father, but nor could she bear to see him wandering off on his own.

'I'll be fine. Don't you worry about me.' It was as if now that he had come to it, the boy had to keep talking to convince himself. 'I knows how to catch rabbits and fish. I'll get a job and I'd work hard.'

Ann made up her mind. 'Well you can't set out now – although really, lad, I don't think you should be going at all – not at your age. Still, I can't stop you.' She raised her hand in a hopeless gesture. 'But perhaps I can help a little. Stay and have some food with us and sleep in the dry and then, if you must, you can set out at first light tomorrow.

'I d'know. You're kind Goodwife Ashdown, but what if Father were to come round? If 'e found me it'd be bad for you and I'd not have the chance to go.'

'But why would he come here?'

'I d'know, but he just might. He knows we was friends.' He looked up at her under his ragged fringe and smiled shyly. 'You used to give me a bit of 'oneycomb when I was little.'

Ann smiled back at him and put a hand on his boney shoulder. She stood for a moment thinking, then seemed to make up her mind. 'I know what we'll do,' she said. 'Keep out of sight until John and Nick have finished at the forge, then go round the back. I shouldn't really tell you this, but I know the latch on the shutter is broken and I doubt John has had time to mend it - I've heard a fair number of horses passing today. If you climb in you can spend the night there and get yourself off early before anyone's about. Will your Father miss you tonight?'

'Doubt it. Most nights he's drunk.'

'Well that's settled then. Come in with me now and I'll see what food I can find for you.'

Simon shuffled his feet and looked embarrassed. 'Thank you,' he said quietly. 'Me Ma said you was a good woman. I think she were right.'

It was Ann's turn to look embarrassed and she spun round sharply and headed for the house. While Simon hovered in the doorway she busied herself finding food that she could spare – a chunk of bread, an onion, some cheese and some salt fish. She dare not take too much, or her own family would go short and John would wonder why. Although she knew that her husband would have every sympathy with the boy, after the trouble over her cat, she felt sure that John would not want to risk her antagonising Simon's father any further.

Having assembled the food she looked around for something to put it in. Her eye fell on the blue and white striped cloth that she used to cover her basket. She could think of nothing else to use, and the boy couldn't walk far carrying provisions in his hands. Quickly she placed the food on the cloth and gathered the corners together and tied them to make a bundle.

'Here lad take this and' – she put her arm around him and gave him a quick hug – 'God keep you safe, for your poor mother's sake. She always did her best for you children. Make sure you remember her for that.'

'I will Goodwife. And thank you. I'll be back one day when I'm growd a man and Father can't hurt me anymore. You'll see how well I've done. I'll work hard and make Ma proud – God rest her soul,' he added reverently making the sign of the cross.

Feeling quite tearful Ann gave him a little push. 'Go on then, and remember what I told you. Wait 'til all's quiet and mind you get off early.'

He gave a nod and, tucking his bundle under his arm, he headed down the path, across the lane and disappeared from view behind the hedge.

10

'Get up now – Simon'. The rhythmic, demanding call was repeated again and again as slowly the boy fought his way up from the thick, dark, comfortable depths of his sleep. He lay on some old sacks, warm and relaxed, one arm flung above his head, the other across his chest, his limbs weightless in slumber. As if from a great distance the insistent calling continued until, suddenly, with a snap he was awake. He opened his eyes and sat up in alarm, his head reeling. It was dawn already; he had slept too long. The sound he'd mistaken for a voice, was the call of a wood pigeon on the gable of the forge. He should have been on his way long ago.

Scrambling to his feet he grabbed up the food Ann had given him and, cramming his battered hat on his head, he peered out from the shutters. Outside all was soft shadowed and still. The sky overhead a pale, luminescent grey, the trees black silhouettes against a horizon stained with palest yellow. He heaved a sigh. It was not as late as he had feared.

Silently he climbed out into the fresh, morning air and instantly felt the skin on his arms rise in goose bumps and he shivered. The sun had not yet warmed the earth and it was chill after the snug warmth inside the forge. He glanced towards Ann's house. The shutters were still tightly fastened, reminding him of a face with closed eyes. All was quiet.

Swiftly he ran across the lane and, skirting the edge of the trees, made his way south towards the rise of Cottage Hill. He avoided the drove road that snaked over the hill, sunk between high banks clothed in tall trees festooned with long ropes of ivy.

'Don't want to meet no one,' he muttered to himself. It was just possible that even at this early hour, there may be someone about who would know him. Instead, he left the road and swinging right, plunged into the lane that wound its way through a close tunnel of holly and blackthorn, skirting the hill to the west. Just once, he paused and looked back and, through a gap in the trees, saw that he was almost level with the spire of St Denys church on its mound in the middle of the village. Piously he crossed himself and said a swift prayer for his mother who, only yesterday, had been laid to rest in the church yard. Then turning once more he scuttled off like a frightened rabbit.

In the distance a fox, no doubt on its way home after a night's hunting, barked its characteristic three, short, sharp calls. Simon hurried as fast as he could, the cawing of rooks seeming to follow him and taunt him for his slowness. He wanted to be well clear of the village before people were up and about. His stomach rumbled and he thought of the cheese that Goodwife Ann had placed in the blue, striped cloth that swung from his left hand. A rush of saliva to his mouth made him swallow, but he daren't stop yet to relieve his hunger. He jumped as a blackbird flew up from the hedge on his left, shrieking its alarm call and he looked back nervously over his shoulder. There was nobody about and already the roofs of the houses were out of sight. He walked on whistling quietly and tunelessly through his teeth to bolster his courage.

He dropped down the far side of Cottage Hill and could see that the sky was now much lighter but, as he skirted around the western side of Castle Hill, the shadows were denser, as the sun was not yet high enough to rise over the slope. On the mound above him the tall trees loomed black against the pearly sky, seeming to wave their long arms at him like malevolent giants. He shivered and pressed on. The long grass was wet with dew and soon the bottom of his short tunic was soaked and flapped wetly around his knees. Brambles thrived on the lush green slopes and tore at him like claws as he pushed past. He didn't want to risk a path just yet – not while he was near enough to Rotherfield to be recognised.

Soon he was panting and sweat ran down his back. He stopped for a few moments, his hands on his knees, bending over to relieve the stitch in his side as he caught his breath before heading out from the shadow of the hill. He could see now that the sun had properly risen – a great golden ball soaring rapidly in the sky. In the distance, the white mist of early morning hung like a shroud over the distant trees, adding to the fear of the unknown that clutched at Simon's throat and made him gasp and occasionally whimper like a lost dog.

He tried not to think about where he was going, but sought comfort in memories of the familiar. The children would be awake by now and see he wasn't there, but probably, for a while at least, they would think he'd gone out for wood or to try for a rabbit. His father wouldn't wake yet as he snored off last night's drink. He felt bad that he'd left the little'uns, but Mary should arrive today and she would look after them. It's not what Ma would have wanted, he thought, but whether he'd stayed or not, Father would have sent for Mary to come home. As the eldest girl he had said it was her place now that Ma was gone, but he knew that his mother had been keen for Mary to get away from his father and make a better life for herself as a servant with a good family.

His Grandmother was constantly interfering and she had always been ready to criticise his poor mother, but he knew she wouldn't willingly look after the children herself and his father certainly wouldn't have the courage to ask her. Like many violent men, James Catt was basically a coward and was, in fact, scared of his mother and her vicious tongue. No, he thought, Mary would not have an easy time caught between the two of them and he was truly sorry to be leaving it all to her, but on the other hand his sense of self-preservation was strong and he felt sure that if he stayed his father would do him real harm.

He'd been walking quickly now for a good hour and was feeling quite exhausted. His legs shook and he felt light headed from lack of food and drink. He came out of a small patch of woodland onto a path that wound its way not far from a small river. He'd never been this far from home before, but he kept the sun on his left, so thought he must be headed in the right direction. It was good to be on a path – much easier to walk than through the long, clinging grass and the tangle of the woodland undergrowth. He looked cautiously around. All was still and quiet except for the gentle gurgle where the river ran shallow over stones. Just past a bend in the path a large oak tree spread its branches over a patch of bright green, fine bladed grass that looked soft and inviting. Simon hesitated. He was tired and he was very hungry.

Checking again that there was no one about he flung himself down onto the soft grass and leaned gratefully against the tree trunk. Taking off his hat he put it down beside him and wiped the sweat from his forehead with his arm. Picking up his bundle, his fingers shook with fatigue as he struggled to undo the knot on Ann's cloth, but at last the contents were revealed and he tore off a hunk of bread and stuffed it into his mouth. He'd had nothing to eat since early yesterday morning and he was ravenous.

As he'd been walking he'd been making plans and had decided that he should eat just a small portion of the food at his first stop and keep the rest for later in the day. However, faced with such unaccustomed bounty, he found it impossible to stop and crammed the bread, the cheese and finally the salt fish into his mouth, barely taking time to chew before swallowing.

After a short while all he had left was the onion, round, smooth and golden in its papery skin. Now his need was for a drink. At home, like all the villagers, they drank small beer as Ma always said water made you ill, but here he had none. He could not go on for much longer without a drink so, with a shrug, he made his way down to the river, tossing and catching the onion like a ball as he went. He found a small pool where the river eddied around a rock and bending down cupped his hand and slurped the water gratefully. It was cool and tasted like the earth smelled when it had been raining. He hoped it wouldn't poison him. He lingered by the water watching the sunlight dancing on the ripples that spread out from where he'd plunged his hand under the surface. As he straightened he felt, rather than heard, the sound of hoof beats.

For an instant he froze, then ran for cover, ducking down behind an alder bush that grew close to the river. It was only when he reached his sanctuary that he realised he had left both his hat and the bright, blue, striped cloth on the grass under the tree. He dare not go back for them now and his face crumpled in dismay as a white horse ridden by a tall man dressed all in black came into view. Holding his breath Simon willed the man to ride on and indeed it looked as if all would be well. The horse drew level with the oak and then passed it. Slowly Simon let out his breath, but then the hoof beats ceased and there was the chink of harness.

From his hiding place he watched, horrified as the man appeared around the bulk of the tree, leading his horse. The man stopped, looked down at the hat and the cloth and then looked around him. As he did so, Simon's stomach lurched, as he realised that he knew the man. It was the priest, William Collyer. He knew Simon and he knew his family. If he saw him all would be lost and he would be taken back to his father. Simon quailed at the thought of his father's anger and he made himself as small as possible behind the tree.

'Hello!' The priest's voice rang out with sermon clarity. 'Hello! Is anybody there?'

Leading his horse behind him William walked slowly down to the river looking about him as he went. Simon cowered behind the tree, sure that the priest would hear as his stomach, reacting to the sudden intake of food and water, gave a loud gurgle. He squeezed his eyes tight shut as if by restricting his own vision, he could stop himself being visible, but the tension was too much for him and he opened them again.

Reaching the bank the man allowed the horse to take in a few deep, sucking draughts of water before pulling him around and leading him back to the tree. He stood for a moment looking down at the hat and the cloth and he frowned, then bent and picked them up and stuffed them into a bag hanging from his saddle. With one final look round he swung himself easily into the saddle and, kicking his heels into the horse's sides, set off at a trot in the same direction as Simon had been heading.

Coming out of his hiding place the boy felt shaky and slightly sick and it was some time before he felt able to continue on his way leaving the path and once more heading across country.

When Ann awoke it was with an undefined sense that something was afoot. All was not as it normally was. She lay for a moment, her mind still drifting from sleep, trying to pinpoint what was hovering just out of reach and then she remembered and the memory was like a slap across the face. Simon Catt had spent the night hiding in their forge prior to running away and, as if she didn't have enough issues with the Catt family already, she was complicit in his plan. All thoughts of sleep were banished as she slid out of bed.

She froze, barely breathing as John rolled over and yawned widely. I'm too late she thought. Her husband stretched his arms above his head before propping himself on his elbows and squinting across at her. No chance then for her to check the forge before he went across to start work. She just had to hope that the boy had not overslept and that he was now well away from the village.

Silently she sent up a prayer for his safety. She had found it difficult to fall asleep last night thinking of Simon and worrying that she had done the wrong thing in helping him. He was so young, and was a kind and gentle soul. She wondered how he would fare on his own. Her only consolation was that with his lack of any bag and his poor clothes and battered hat, he was hardly going to be a target for robbers. He did, however, run the risk of being arrested as a vagabond, but hopefully he would find someone willing to give him work and a bed for the night. He would have few skills, but his ready, open smile might encourage someone to take him on. Soon it would be harvest time and extra hands were always welcome. Or perhaps he might even make it to the coast where he could well find work on a ship.'

'It is, don't you think?'

She was pulled out of her reverie by John's voice and realised she had been standing by the bed, one hand out in front of her as she stared into space and had no idea what he was talking about.

'I'm sorry, what did you say?'

'What's wrong with you woman? You haven't heard a word I've said have you?' She shook her head ruefully. 'I was saying that it seems from what Dickon was saying, that our George is doing alright for himself. It sounds as if Katherine is content with him and also that he is bettering himself. Who'd have thought that our Georgie would learn to read?' John yawned again, scratched his chest and then ran his hand through his hair making it stand on end so that he looked like a wild man from the forest. 'And easily too from what Dickon was saying. My mother tried to teach me my letters, but they never did stick in my head and anyway I was always wanting to be off out into the fresh air and wouldn't concentrate for more than a minute or two.'

'I didn't know your mother could read, John.'

'Well I don't think she could, much - not big words anyhow, but she did know her letters.'

'Well I'll be. Fancy that. I didn't know.' Glad to be diverted from gloomy thoughts as to what could befall a young lad wandering across the country on his own, she pulled on her clothes over her shift and went to the door, thinking, as she often did how glad she was that her house had two rooms so that at least she and John could sleep separately from the boys. In the main room her sons were still breathing heavily and only stirred when she went across and opened the shutters. 'Come on you lazy lumps, move yourselves, your father's already astir.' Another day had started and she would just have to take things as they came.

11

Katherine smiled as she watched her young son bounding across the meadow in great leaps, trying to keep up with George. He adored the older boy who, although taciturn with adults, was as gentle and patient with the youngster as he was with animals. She would always be grateful to George. Young as he was he had, in this last year, done much to fill the male role that William had left vacant in young Harry's life.

She had sent the boys to the mill as she needed flour and it would take them a good couple of hours there and back and keep them away from the house. She knew that William liked to see Harry when he came, but part of her felt it was unfair on the child who did not understand why his father could not stay, and a part of her - of which she was rather ashamed - just wanted William all to herself. She saw him so rarely and her heart yearned for him.

She continued to stand staring across the meadow, but as thoughts crowded her brain, her eyes glazed over and she no longer saw the bright day. As always, in moments of quiet, the turmoil of her life came crowding in as she desperately tried to see a way forward in their shattered lives. Sometimes, as she lay alone in the darkest hours of the night, it felt as if she was walking a familiar well-trodden path, but a path that seemed to have no end and spiralled around and around in ever decreasing circles. Now, as she stood by the window she went over the well-rehearsed arguments yet again. It was a recurring theme that she could never put aside for long, no matter how hard she tried.

When she had first left the vicarage and moved to the cottage she hadn't seen William for weeks and had felt wretched and betrayed. She knew that he'd vowed to follow his Bishop and put her aside, but, by marrying her, hadn't he also made a solemn vow to her too? She never doubted that he loved her, but he also loved God and by becoming a priest, had promised his life to the Church. Was she a very wicked person to want him to put love for her before his love of God? She thought she undoubtedly was, but she couldn't deny her feelings. She pressed her hand to her forehead. It was all such a muddle and she couldn't see a way out for them.

He had told her that as a young priest he had been content and had not found a life of celibacy as hard as many priests did. He was still a young man – barely thirty three - when he had met her and when they had married they had been husband and wife in the full sense. Harry was the proof of that. And now husband and wife had been ripped apart. On the whim of a Queen, her life was in ruins - married yet not a wife.

It was far worse, she thought, than when she had been widowed when Luke died. She had mourned for him, yes, but she had not felt this gut wrenching sorrow that seemed to make every breath an effort and dulled the sunlight until she felt as if she was moving in a world of shadows. As a young widow she had not suspected that it was possible for a man to make her feel as William did and now she felt like a widow all over again. But the difference was that her husband wasn't dead; he was living not far away.

Absently she chewed on her knuckle as dark thoughts flitted through her mind. It was the arbitrariness of the decree that she could not accept. If it was fitting for priests to be married when young Edward was king, why should it be different under Mary? Had God changed his mind? She didn't think so. Mary Tudor and that Spanish husband of hers were wrong – of that she was sure. There, she thought, now I am guilty of treason.

Every day she read both the English Bible and prayer book that William had brought to her from the church at Rotherfield and there was much in the Protestant faith that Katherine felt was right. Yes, Katherine mused and that makes me a heretic too. She had to admit that she felt far more sympathy with the plain form of worship that Edward had introduced than she did with all the trappings of Catholicism.

According to the new laws the Catholic mass and the saints were restored, Latin was again the language of the Church and no English translations were to be used in services. Even before William had told her that they must separate, they had heard of Protestant books being burned. William loved books and he had been horrified at the thought of them being destroyed so, despite the rulings from the Bishop, he had brought the books to her. It was probably dangerous to have them in her keeping now but, solitary as she was, they brought her comfort and William knew how much she enjoyed reading the word of God in her own language. Yes, she thought cynically, and perhaps the gift salved William's conscience just a little too. She shook her head. She must not think ill of William. He was still her husband.

Katherine stirred herself, coming back from the maze of her thoughts. She blinked, bringing herself to an awareness of where she was. He would be here soon. Now was not the time for brooding.

Having tidied away her sewing she fetched wooden platters and cups from the shelf and set then on the table. To say that she didn't miss the grander furnishings of the vicarage would be a lie, and she chastised herself for her worldliness and thanked God that she had a good roof over her head and William saw that she and Harry lacked for nothing. Even so it was sometimes hard to cope with the solitariness of her existence.

She straightened her shoulders and put these carping thoughts from her mind. What was wrong with her? Today was a happy day; William was coming.

Within a few minutes she heard hoof beats and, with a last pat to her coif and shake of her apron, she hurried as best as she could to the door. As she opened it he stood before her, hand level with her face as he raised it to the latch. Laughing, he opened out his hand and laid it on her cheek.

'My love,' he murmured and lowered his face to kiss her.

Holding the front of his coat to steady herself she drew him into the room. Much as she loved these visits she was always filled with terror that he would be seen; that someone would report him to the church authorities. There had always been that word – excommunication - hovering above their meetings, but these days there could be worse. From a passing pedlar she had heard talk of heretics and burnings and the thought of William facing such a death haunted her dreams. She also feared for herself. Would such dreadful punishments also apply to the priest's wife? Would she be deemed as guilty as her husband? Perhaps more so, as women were believed to lead men astray, just as Eve had tempted Adam. She trembled at the thought of the flames licking around her body. And what would happen to Harry if his parents were punished for their love?

She pushed these thoughts away to the back of her mind as, kicking the door closed behind him, William wrapped her in an embrace and effortlessly lifted her off her feet, carried her to the settle and put her gently down.

'Oh William it is so good to see you. It has been so long, but I worry so.'

He placed a finger on her lips, then took her hand and stroked it gently. 'Hush, my love. Today is not a day for worry. We have but a short time and I would not spend it in worry. Tell me how you are and young Harry.' He looked around. 'He is not here?'

She flushed at the half lie she was intending to tell, 'No William, he is not. I am fearful that as he grows he may speak of your visits and that—'

'But what are you saying? To whom would he speak? Am I never to see my son?' William's face was anguished.

Katherine bowed her head and for a few moments was silent. 'I don't know William. I don't know what we should do for the best. I have heard such tales that sometimes in the night my blood runs cold when I think of what could befall us if you were to be found out. But I cannot live without seeing you and you should not have to deny your son. What is to become of us, husband?'

There was silence as they sat side by side both overcome by the horror of their situation. How could any man make such a choice – his God or his family? Katherine was the first to come to her senses. 'We will find a way,' she said, forcing strength into her voice. 'We will pray together and God will show us the way. But first, come eat with me.' Despite herself her voice faltered. 'We have so little time. The boys will be home soon and you must be gone.'

As Willam rode back to Rotherfield his mind was in turmoil. Katherine's words about young Harry had shocked him and brought home to him the impossibility of his family situation. How could he go on like this, denying his wife and child in public and seeing them in secret? He had been deluding himself if he had ever thought that this arrangement would work. Deluding himself, betraying his calling and putting himself and probably Katherine, too, in great danger, for Catholic Mary would brook no backsliding in her priests. Many in the Church, including William, had been shocked and horrified when, in February of last year, John Hooper had been burned at the stake in Gloucester, charged under the revival of the heresy acts at the end of 1554.

He too was a married priest. William had met him once while a student at Oxford - a kindly, learned man who was one time Bishop of Gloucester. But his rank had not saved him from Catholic vengeance and the poor man had been martyred for his beliefs in the most savage of ways. What did William think he was doing? What if he was found out? At best it would certainly be the end of all his ambitions to rise in the Church hierarchy and in these dangerous times could lead to imprisonment or worse. He shuddered at the thought. He was not the stuff of martyrs, of that he was sure.

Thoughts tumbled in William's mind as he rode, unaware of the countryside around him. Assuredly God knew of his deceit, so where did that leave him as a priest of God's Holy Catholic Church? On the other hand, did he really believe that repudiating his wife and child was God's will? Was it worth putting his desire for advancement in the Church above his love for Katherine – for he did love her. That it should come to this, he thought. When he started out he had had such ambition and had fought against all odds for his position. How was it that it should all come to nought?

He had been brought up in Ample, a small country village near to Winchester in Hampshire. His father was a simple farm worker and William was the youngest of six children. William's earliest memories were of his mother's worried face and red, work-worn hands as she carefully broke a loaf into smaller and smaller pieces to make it go around her large family. There was never enough to eat and in winter he was always cold, as the hand-me-down clothes he wore were threadbare and thin. Even now he had a horror of the cold and dreaded the wintertime. He still remembered how he had envied the priest who had come to the house when his second sister died.

It was in the middle of winter and William seemed to have been cold for ever. The portly priest had entered their small, meagre cottage wrapped in a warm, woollen cloak and to William's amazement had obviously felt warm enough to actually take it off as he knelt to pray by Mary's bed. Although he was only seven William had decided then that he too wanted to be warm and well fed and to his child's mind it seemed obvious that the way to achieve this was to emulate the priest and enter the Church.

His father, although uneducated, was a devout man and was happy that from the age of nine his son had served as an altar boy at the local church of St Winifred and William had enjoyed being part of the ritual and ceremonial of the church services. The local priest was impressed by both his intelligence and his devotion and it was his recommendation that enabled William to get a place at a chantry school in Winchester. Although discipline was harsh, the teaching was excellent and he soon proved himself to be an able scholar. The family were so poor, though, that there was no question of him being able to fulfil his ambition and continue his studies at university until chance – or the devil, he was never sure which - showed him the way.

It was the custom that if a boy from the school proved especially scholarly, he would be sponsored by the local church to go to university and it was William's secret hope that in this way he would be able to go up to Oxford – an almost unheard of dream for a boy of his class. However, there was another boy, Joshua, in his class who, it seemed to William, was always favoured by the priest and it appeared likely that it would be Joshua and not William who would be sent up to Corpus Christi in Oxford. Likely, that is, until William happened to walk into the vestry one day and see something which changed the course of his future.

To be honest, at the time, he wasn't quite sure what he had witnessed. When he came into the vestry and saw Joshua kneeling in front of the priest, the man's hand on the boy's head, he had thought that Joshua was receiving a blessing, but from the guilty way the priest had flicked his robe and turned away, yelling at William to get out, it was obvious that here was something he had not been meant to see. Something which the priest could not risk reaching the bishop's ears. When the man stopped him one day after Mass and indicated that, provided he agreed to keep quiet, there would be a place for him at university, William had readily agreed. Still scarcely understanding what was happening he had, unexpectedly, been given the power to ensure that his ambition was fulfilled. Who knew where a bright boy could end up? Priest, bishop even – his ambition soared and the thought was dizzying.

So, Joshua had been passed over and William found himself entering the small college of Corpus Christi in Oxford. A college which had been founded in 1517 by Richard Foxe, the Bishop of Winchester and dedicated to the study of classics and had, at that time, what some said was the best library in Europe, with books in all three classical languages - Latin, Greek and Hebrew.

In the dark panelled room of the Corpus library, William discovered a world of scholarship far beyond his wildest dreams. It was the library which excited William more than anything he'd known before and he had immersed himself in books when, perhaps, he should have been ingratiating himself with the Bishop. So his first appointment had not been, as he hoped, to a prestigious living with dazzling promise for the future, but instead he found himself a parish priest in a small Sussex village. But in his heart he knew that he had much more to offer the Church and all the time he had served the good people of Rotherfield he had dreamed of an appointment in a cathedral city – Canterbury or back in Winchester perhaps – where his scholarly talents would be recognised.

He had been happy in the village, but still he had studied and read all he could and hoped for advancement. Admittedly his ambitions were confused by the great changes in the religious practices of the county, but he had tried to seek guidance from his bishop and fulfil his duties faithfully and to the best of his ability. It had, therefore, come as a terrible shock when he had first read the edict that precluded priests from marriage and he understood he had to make a choice. He would never forget that terrible morning when his world had turned upside down; he had been horrified. He and Katherine had made a life together, but now it was impossible that he continue as a priest and still keep his wife and child. On the other hand, could he abandon his calling – for, as the years had passed, he had become certain that God wanted him as a priest – and put his own desires before God?

After making the decision to move Katherine and Harry to the cottage, thereby fulfilling the letter of the law, he had soon come to the realisation that the idea was unworkable. But he had been half crazed – out of his mind with worry. His first thoughts had been that all would be well provided that no word of his circumstances reached the bishop's ear but, as the weeks and months passed by, reality had pierced his consciousness and the hopelessness of his situation had become all too apparent. Now it seemed, despite all he had been through, he was not even to see his young son. Was this God's way of punishing him for his duplicity? Or was this

God testing him in the way he had tested Abraham? Did he really want him to repudiate his wife and child altogether? How could he compare this small sacrifice on his part with the sacrifice and suffering of our Lord? I am nothing but a poor sinner, William thought piously and, as he rode, lost in thought, he came to a decision. Out of duty he would continue to provide materially for Katherine and Harry, but he must try to stop thinking of them as his wife and son and would give himself back to God and the Church.

William's horse was well used to the tracks and lanes around Rotherfield and despite very little guidance from the abstracted priest had no difficulty finding its own way back to the stable at the back of the vicarage. As it reached the rutted street that ran through the village it broke into a trot, sensing home and a feed. Jolted by the unexpected change of pace, William came out of his reverie and looked about him. Outside the Inn were a number of villagers grouped around a man that William couldn't see, but could identify from the high whining tone of his voice – James Catt.

'He's gone, the little shit. Just upped and left, unless of course he were taked by—'

There were loud murmurs from the group and William drew rein to see what the fuss was about.

Benjamin Watt, who was at the back of the crowd was the first to become aware of the tall priest looming behind them on his horse and tugged at the sleeve of his neighbour, at the same time calling a respectful greeting to William. The crowd turned towards William, several of them bobbing their heads deferentially and finally James Catt ceased his ranting, cutting off in mid-sentence.

'Good day to you all,' said William. 'James, is something amiss, you sound distressed?'

'Aye, you could say that. It's our Simon, the little sh … beggin' your pardon. He's gone. Run off. No thought for his family now his poor mother –' Catt piously crossed himself in exaggerated fashion, '–God rest her soul, has been called by Christ.'

'Simon, run off? That doesn't sound like him. He's such a caring boy. I'd have thought . . .' William paused mid-sentence as a thought struck him. He'd been so deep in his own troubles, that he'd given no further thought to the hat and cloth that he'd picked up on his way to see Katherine earlier that morning. Now, thinking about young Simon he had a sudden, vivid picture of the boy, his comical battered hat a little too large, resting on his sticking out ears. 'Wait a moment,.' He turned in his saddle and reached behind him to feel in his saddle bag, drawing out the hat with the blue cloth stuffed inside where he had put it. 'Is this . . .? It looks rather like . . .'

'Aye, that's his.' There were nods of agreement from several in the crowd. 'That's our Simon's hat that is. Know it anywhere. Where did you find it Father?'

William frowned. Much of the morning was just a blurr, obscured by his distress at not seeing Harry and his problems with Katherine. 'It was . . . Let me see . . . Yes it was the other side of Castle Hill, where the path swings round to join the river. I saw it just lying on the ground. I called and nobody answered. I don't really know what made me pick it up . . .' William tailed off. He did not want to answer questions about where he'd been and why; didn't really want anyone to know that he'd been riding in a direction that would lead to Katherine and Harry. But, of course, no villager would think it fitting to question their priest about his comings and goings and William realised he was just being oversensitive and his nerves were on edge.

There were murmurs all around as people digested this information and its import and then gradually they lost interest and began to drift away about their business. The mystery was solved, Si Catt had indeed run off and to be honest, few blamed him. Finally it was just James Catt and two of his closest cronies standing by the horse.

'I'm sorry, James, this is worrying news,' said William. 'Will you go after him? Are you sure he's run off? Do you have relatives in that direction perhaps?'

'Waste of time chasing him,' said Josiah Mead, wiping his sleeve across a nose that by its peculiar shape was evidence that he was a man not afraid of a fight. 'Never catch a boy what don't want to be catched.'

William eyed the man and inwardly thought what an unpleasant character he was. A short, thickset man with a shock of dirty ginger hair that stuck out at odd angles making him look as if he'd just risen from his bed and a face that was deeply pitted by smallpox. As always he was accompanied by an evil looking white dog which had long strings of drool hanging from its mouth. It was said that Mead made enough money to keep himself in drink by staging dog fights at the back of the inn.

'Makin' for the coast I reckon. Always wantin' willing lads on the boats,' said the third of the unsavoury trio, Luke Ailwood who had removed his hat and was scratching at his thin greasy hair.

'Well . . .' William hovered uncertainly, unsure what was required of him. 'I will pray that the Holy Virgin will protect him. If you want . . . If you need . . . Well you know where to find me. Good day to you all.' And wheeling his horse in the direction of the vicarage William touched his heels lightly to the willing horse and trotted off.

'Will you go after 'im James?' asked Ailwood. 'Don't reckon you'll catch 'im. You've hit that little sod for the last time I reckon.'

James Catt scowled. Before he had the sympathy of the crowd, now the mystery seemed solved he was just the father of a runaway boy and that put him in a bad light. Without answering he slouched off in the direction of his house, the hat tucked under his arm.

12

For the last two days Ann had found it difficult to concentrate on anything and on several occasions had caught herself standing in the middle of the room, or in the garden wondering what it was that she had been about to do. She couldn't stop thinking of young Simon and wondering what had become of the boy. This really would not do, she told herself. It would be weeks, months even before she had any idea what had happened to him. She thought it possible that he would at least try to send word about himself to his sister Mary, even though he did not want to have anything more to do with his father. And who could blame him, she mused – a violent, uncouth man who had gambled and drunk his way through life making both poor Nell's and the children's lives a misery. 'And now he's after you!' The little voice of fear was persistent. It nagged at her in the darkness of the night and whispered in her ear when she wasn't expecting it.

There had been no other incidents since finding poor Puss on Thursday, although she knew that John and her two sons were quietly looking out for her. Yesterday Nick must have come across to the house half a dozen times on some pretext or other when normally she didn't see him or John from one meal time to the next. Dickon had stayed home yesterday evening too, and hadn't gone into the village as he'd taken to doing lately.

She had wondered recently if there was a girl he was interested in. He was, after all, going on seventeen and there were a number of maids in the village who would be likely catch his eye. Her face softened as she thought of her eldest son and imagined him in years to come with a wife and children. She would enjoy being a grandmother, she thought. Lots of babies to cuddle with none of the responsibility of being a mother. A daughter-in-law would be nice too – if she was the right sort of girl, of course. Ann had always been just slightly disappointed that God had not seen fit to give her a girl. A daughter who would, perhaps, learn from her the secrets of herbs and babies just as she had learned from her Mother. A daughter to grow to womanhood as her closest friend. How strangely The Almighty ordered things, she thought. There was young Lizzie with all little girls and no boys, but it was not for her to question his will.

The day was warm, but a blustery wind was tossing the trees about and adding to Ann's unsettled feeling. She didn't like wind; always hated the way it wrapped her skirts around her legs hampering her movements and flicked the edges of her shawl across her face. It rattled the shutters and snatched washing from the bushes and her beloved bees struggled to fly as it whistled across the garden. Still, she told herself, it was fine and dry and in an indifferent summer that was something to be thankful for.

Her thoughts were interrupted by Nick who had been sent by John to find her.

'It's time for church Mother. Father says are you coming?'

At the sound of his voice she turned from where she had been standing preoccupied with her thoughts, staring unseeing at her two bee skeps. 'I'm coming my son; just give me a moment to change my coif.'

She hurried indoors untying the laces that fastened her coif under her chin as she went. John and Dickon stood ready on the path. 'I'll not be a moment,' she said as she squeezed passed them.

They had always walked to church together as a family and it was a ritual that she had always enjoyed, especially on a summer's day. As they neared the church they would meet other families, often from outlying houses and farms and news would be exchanged and babies admired before they all made their way into the service.

As they walked she continued to be preoccupied with her own thoughts and she was not aware of John and the boys who were arguing good-naturedly about something to do with horses. It was only when she felt a touch on her arm that she looked up at her husband who was smiling down at her and proffering a sprig of honeysuckle.

'Your favourite, I believe - though I think you are away with the sprites.' He lowered his voice slightly. 'You're not still brooding about Catt are you? Don't worry, my love, I'm sure there won't be any more trouble from him.'

'No, no, of course not,' she said hastily. She tucked her arm into his, feeling the firm bulging biceps that were the result of a lifetime's work at the forge. He was her rock, her strength in more ways than one. Her John would never let anything or anyone hurt her, of that she was sure.

As they reached the path leading to the church they drew level with Lizzie who was, once again, very pregnant and breathing heavily as she slowly made her way up the hill to the church, carrying her youngest daughter on one hip, while shepherding the other two in front of her.

Ann turned to John. 'You and the boys go on in. I'll walk with Lizzie and give her a hand poor lass. Hello Lizzie, here let me take the baby for you. You've enough weight to carry without any extra.'

At the sound of Ann's voice Lizzie started and her face flushed scarlet. She clutched the child to her. 'No, no, I'm fine,' she said hastily, pushing the two little girls in front of her.

Ann frowned. 'Are you sure I couldn't—'

'No… no thank you.'

Ann fell into step beside her. 'How are you keeping anyway? Doesn't look as if this one will be long.' She nodded at Lizzie's distended belly 'You'll be sending for me before the week's out I shouldn't wonder.'

'No. Not this time. I'm not to.' She put her hand up to her mouth in a gesture of embarrassment.

'Not this time,' Ann echoed in bewilderment. 'What do you mean? Do you have someone else to help with the birthing? I thought you—'

'I'll be fine. He said . . . he said I'm not to ask you. I'm sorry Goodwife Ashdown, you've always given me courage when it came to having these three, but he said you wasn't to come for this one.'

'By 'he' I suppose you mean your husband? But why has he said such a thing? Why doesn't he want me to help you as I've always done?'

Lizzie looked down at the ground.

'Lizzie?'

She refused to meet Ann's eyes.

'What is it Lizzie, you can tell me, I've known you since you were a little girl and I'll not be offended.

'It's . . . he said . . . he said it were your fault we only had girls. He said he wants a son and he's not taking the chance of you . . . of you bringing us bad luck.'

'Of me bringing bad luck!' Ann was incredulous.

'I'm sorry Goodwife, but I dare not go against him. I don't know what he'd do if you came and it was another girl. Not after what's being said.'

'What's being sai . . .' Ann was aware that she was doing nothing but repeating the other woman's words, but she just did not know how to reply.

'Oy. You leave my family alone.' Both women turned at the strident sound of the man's voice and instinctively Ann backed away as Lizzie's husband, Matthew, strode up the path towards them. He snatched the toddler from his wife's arms and grabbed her roughly by the arm. 'Come on you, what did I tell you? We want no truck with her.' He pulled his wife and she stumbled against him, then he turned to Ann and pointed a finger at her. 'If you've harmed my son with your spells I'll . . . I'll . . . well I shan't forget it. Just you remember. Keep away from my family, you witch.'

Ann put her hands up to her cheeks and then covered her eyes as if to shut out the view of the angry man shoving his family in front of him, then she turned on her heel and ran back the way she'd come. Back to the safety of her home where she slammed the door and flung herself face down on the bed. She lay panting with her arms across her head and her hands in tight fists.

What was happening here? How was it that in just a week she had gone from being Goodwife Ann who helped the sick and suffering as best she could, to Ann the witch, banned from people's houses?

She lay there, her brain whirling and her insides knotted with terror, until the door banged and she could hear heavy footsteps and John calling to her.

'Ann? Ann, are you there, are you . . .?' John's voice broke off as he entered the bedroom. In one stride he was beside her bending over, his hand on her shoulder. 'Ann, love, what is it? Are you ill? We waited, me and the boys, and when you didn't join us ... Are you ill?' he repeated as he gently took her hand and unclenched her fist, lacing his fingers through hers. 'Ann you look . . . well I don't know. No, love, don't cry. You can tell me. Tell me what the matter is.' With his big, blacksmith's hand, work roughened and scarred with burns, he smoothed her cheeks, wiping away the tears. She struggled to sit up and put her arms around him, laying her face against his chest and feeling his shirt dampen as the tears continued to flow. He drew her towards him and patted her gently like a baby, all the while making little 'shushing' noises as he used to with the boys when they were little.

Eventually her sobs lessened and she pulled away from him. 'I don't understand it John. I just don't know what's happening.'

John looked worried. 'Tell me. What do you mean "what's happening"? What is it?'

Ann took a deep breath. 'I said I'd be seeing Lizzie soon for the birthing of her babe and she said—'

'Go on, Ann. What has she said to upset you so?'

'She said Matthew has said I'm not to go near her this time as it was my fault that they only have girls.'

'She said what?' John roared. He threw back his head and laughed. 'Is that all? You silly woman, you had me really worried there. Is that all this is about? I'd have thought—'

'No you don't understand. It's started - just as I feared. Matthew said I had bewitched the babes into girls and that I'd do the same again with this one and he wants a son. He called me a witch John, a witch, same as Goodwife Catt. It's spreading. I knew it would. People are accusing me of witchcraft, John and there's nothing I can do to stop it.'

Her voice rose in panic and John put a hand on each of her arms and held her away from him while he looked intently into her face. 'Look at me Ann and listen well. You must not let them upset you. You have done nothing wrong. It is only a bunch of ignorant men stirring up trouble and it will come to nothing. You must believe that.' He sat silent for a while, thinking, his arms around her as he continued to pat her back comfortingly. 'As soon as Mass is over I will go and see William and ask for his help in stopping these rumours. With his support we can put a stop to this before . . .well, before it gets out of hand.'

Ann fumbled for a cloth to wipe her nose and dry her tears. She nodded mutely, drained of emotion and only aware of a knot of fear that seemed to have been lodged in her belly these last few days and was growing like the lumps she had sometimes seen on people that resisted all her medicines and seemed to eat them up and overwhelm them. Instinctively she folded her arms across her stomach and rocked herself, much as George was wont to do when he was distressed.

True to his word, as soon as Mass was over and the boys were back home, John set off for the vicarage to see William. Ann had heard him having quiet words with her sons and, apart from just putting their heads around the door and giving her rather embarrassed, but consoling smiles, they had kept out of her way, no doubt following instructions from John. For this she was grateful as she couldn't have faced further explanations just now.

As she sat alone in the room that she and John had shared for the whole of her married life, her mind wandered backwards and forwards, thoughts popping into her head in what seemed a totally random way. A picture of John standing tall and smiling in the church porch as she walked towards him with her father on her wedding day; her mother bending down and whispering in her ear when she was a little girl and her kitten had died, 'Tell them Annie, tell the bees. Always tell the bees when something happens. They are part of the family and must be told or they'll leave us. Do you remember the rhyme?' Her lips moved as she repeated the old rhyme about the bees that her Mother had taught her –

"Little bird of Paradise,
She works her work both neat and nice;
She pleases God, she pleases man,
She does the work that no man can."

She loved her bees. Who would look after them if she was found to be a witch and taken away? A sob escaped her. Taken away? She wouldn't just be "taken away", she'd be killed – tortured then hanged or burned.

She forced herself to think of happier things. Of Nick running across from the forge with the first slightly bent horseshoe that he had made all by himself; Dickon clambering onto her lap to look at his new baby brother when Nick was born and frowning with disappointment that the long promised brother was too small to play with; and George, no more than four or five years old, reaching up and gentling Farmer Boscomb's big cart horse as it stood restless outside the forge. She had held her breath, she remembered, sure that her young son would be bowled over by the huge animal, but the horse had calmed and, to the little boy's delight, had dipped its head and had blown at George through his soft, cream coloured nose, ruffling the small boy's hair with its breath.

From outside she could hear a thrush singing from the tall elm tree along the lane and the scent of pinks, warmed by the sun, drifted in through the half open shutters, but these things, which would normally have delighted her, did nothing to lift the feeling of dread that hung over her.

She didn't know how long she had sat alone, but she heard John's voice. Startled out of her reverie, she sprang to her feet just as he entered the room. He was flushed and looked agitated and she could tell he was trying to control himself and speak calmly. She knew her husband so well, there was no way he could conceal his emotions from her.

'Well? You saw William? You told him what was being said about me?' Her voice sounded unnaturally loud and she fought to control herself and speak calmly.

'I did.'

'What did he say?' John hesitated. Despite her efforts, her voice rose again. 'Tell me John. Will he help me? What did he say?'

'He said . . . God's bones! He said there should be a hearing.'

'A hearing? What do you mean? What's that?'

'He said that witchcraft was a serious matter and the church couldn't take it lightly and that those who accuse you should be heard and that you too should be heard speaking your defence.' John spoke the words in a rush and put up his hand as if denying what he was saying.

'A hearing?' Ann was too stunned to gather her wits.

'He says this evening. He will go and see those who make accusation against you and they and you must go to the church this evening to be heard.' John laid his hand on her shoulder looking both distressed and embarrassed that he had to tell her these things. 'I know it sounds frightening, Ann, but he said . . . William was sure that this was the best way of dealing with it. He said if it were just ignored it could get worse. He said that otherwise it could come to an official church hearing and that would be best avoided at all costs.' There were a few moments of silence as they both stood facing each other, considering the import of the priest's words. Then John said, quietly, 'I think it's for the best Ann. We want an end to these accusations. Ignorant people are quick to become hysterical and then there's no knowing what may be said.'

'But what could be said, John?' Ann's voice was tight with stress. 'I haven't done anything. I'm not a witch. No right thinking person could say I was. What am I supposed to have done? I don't understand.' As if listening from a long way away Ann could hear the panic in her voice. She felt as if she was wrapped in a tight shroud and needed to struggle free from the encircling bands.

As she fought to control herself she stretched out her arms to her husband.

'Hold me, John, hold me close and make this go away,' she pleaded, as all the while visions of gibbets and fires danced before her eyes.

Ann grew more and more apprehensive as evening approached. She could neither eat nor settle, but paced restlessly about the room, picking things up only to put them down again without looking at what she was doing. Once she went out into the garden and wandered listlessly around, picking odd leaves and flowers, smelling, then discarding them. She stood for a while staring at the steady stream of bees flying in a straight line over the hedge and into the bee skeps.

Standing by the open shutters John could see her lips moving silently and guessed that she was talking to her bees, telling them her troubles as she often did. He watched as, unconsciously, she fingered the mole that grew on her left cheek. It was a habit she had when deep in thought. It was a dark, brown, beauty spot that he had always loved, but to her fury, he often teased her that when she was old it would become raised and sprout hairs. Despite the seriousness of all that they faced at the moment, he smiled at the thought.

He had known Ann since he was a boy and had fallen in love with her when they were both sixteen. She had been, and still was, in his eyes at least, a beautiful girl - tall and slim with long, corn coloured hair and green eyes that sparked with life. She had a way of throwing back her head when she laughed that made her seem bold and carefree and very different from some of the quiet, simpering girls who had made eyes at him in church. Sometimes, and he smiled now at the thought, when they were courting, he would tickle her and she would laugh until the tears ran down her cheeks. With his fine physique and bulging muscles he could have had his choice of several maids, but he only had eyes for Ann. She had been, and always would be, the love of his life.

His father had died when he was nineteen, kicked in the gut by a huge cart horse, and he had taken over the forge and had provided for his widowed mother. His two brothers – Wills and Robert were old enough to work and provide for themselves and so a year after his father's death, when they were both aged twenty, John and Ann had married. His mother had stayed with them for a while and then had gone to live with an unmarried sister in Tunbridge.

It was nigh on twenty years now that he and Ann had been married and in all that time he had never had cause to regret his choice. Even now the sight of her striding across the meadow towards him made his heart lift, just as it did all those years ago when they had a tryst under the big ash tree at the edge of the forest.

They had been very blessed he thought. She was a wife to be proud of, a good housewife and a caring mother who had given him fine sons. They had much in common and were friends as well as husband and wife, still often talking long into the night as young lovers do.

How those ignorant fools could accuse her of witchcraft he just couldn't fathom. Yes, he had to admit, she was different from many of the women of the village. Her mother had taught her much about the value of plants in treating illness and after her mother died just after Georgie was born, it had seemed natural that, when they were sick or about to give birth, the people of the village had turned to her. She was knowledgeable about herbs and cures and had always been interested in plants, but that didn't make her a witch. She had never willingly hurt anyone and if sometimes she couldn't help them and people died, then surely that was just the will of God and she shouldn't be blamed. He sighed; he just hoped that the priest could sort this mess out.

John had neither liked nor disliked William Collyer, but since Katherine's illness, Ann had become close to both her and the priest in a way that was not usual for someone of their status and, since getting to know him better, John had found the man both pleasant and friendly. But since the priest had changed from Protestant back to Catholic and then denied his wife, Katherine, John had not felt the same towards William. They lived in difficult times – that much he certainly wouldn't deny - but in his view, a man should have principles and stand by them and not blow with the wind.

He thought back to what Dickon had told him recently about a man called Richard Woodman. He was a local man – born in Buxted, but now was an iron master in Warbleton, about ten miles or so from Rotherfield. The local priest at the Church of St Mary the Virgin was one Fairebanke. Like William he was married and, in the reign of Edward was as staunch a Protestant as one could want. However, according to what Dickon had heard, he had now completely changed tack and was preaching for all he was worth according to the laws of the Catholic Church.

Richard Woodman had been incensed by the turncoat attitude of his priest and had publicly admonished him, thereby revealing himself as a Protestant heretic. He'd been arrested and been brought before the justices of the peace. Dickon wasn't sure what had happened to the man, but thought he'd been imprisoned. Was this fair John wondered and wasn't this Fairebanke behaving in exactly the same way as William Collyer?

But then, he reasoned, he was just an ignorant blacksmith and Collyer was a man educated at Oxford. Perhaps education made you see things differently. But his gut feeling told him that education shouldn't make a difference to what was right and what was wrong. John was not entirely happy with the change back to the Catholic Mass and what he saw as William's traitorous attitude, but he also valued his freedom and his family and did not think he would have the courage to act as Richard Woodman had.

He narrowed his eyes as a thought struck him. Perhaps William's eagerness to help Ann today was not simply born of Christian duty, but was a reluctance to have any authority involved in looking too closely at what was going on in the village. Certainly a village claiming to have a witch in their midst would bring attention that William would not want, given that his wife still lived not that far away. John shook his head as if to clear his thoughts. Whatever the man's reasons, there was no doubt that William was their best hope now and he just prayed that he could sort out this mess for them

Recollecting what was to come he leaned out of the window of the room they had shared since they were first wed.

'Ann,' he called. 'Ann, come in and rest, my love.'

She turned at the sound of his voice, her eyes seeming huge in a face that, since this morning, seemed to have aged and grown deathly pale. Obediently, she walked slowly and listlessly up the path, into the house and flopped onto the wooden bench, her head in her hands. 'I can't do this,' she whispered. John knelt on one knee beside her like a suitor, the familiar smell of him warm and comforting. He didn't touch her, but his nearness was balm to her bruised senses.

'You can do this Ann. You will do this, not just for yourself, but for the sake of our family. These ignorant people cannot be allowed to destroy all that we have.'

'I can't—'

'No, don't even think like that. Be strong. If not for yourself or for me, then for Dickon, and Nick and Georgie. Think of them, Ann. Think of the boys. How would it be if their mother was found for a witch? It would mark them for the rest of their lives. No girl would want to marry them. Think Ann and take courage. We'll be there with you. I've sent Nick round to my brother's, to tell him to gather our friends. You won't be alone this evening Ann. There will be plenty there that love you and respect you for all the good you do in this village.'

She put her hand up to his face and caressed his cheek, the dark stubble rasping on her fingers as she looked deep into his eyes. Then she nodded slowly. 'You're right. They mustn't win. They won't win. I am innocent and I will be seen to be so.'

Still pale, but looking more resolute she rose and went to the pail standing in the corner. Wetting a cloth she wiped her face and hands and removing her coif uncoiled her hair and brushed it before replaiting it and covering it once more. She straightened and John thought he had never seen her look lovelier, the soft light of evening shading her features, her green eyes under arched brows, wide and sincere.

'I'm ready,' she said, and hand in hand they went out of the door and headed along the path towards the church where she had walked so light-heartedly only that morning, although already it seemed an age ago.

13

The old yew tree in the churchyard that had already seen a thousand years of history was sending long, dark shadows across the ground as the sun slowly sank in the cloudless, blue sky. Several children were running around it playing tig, but outside the church porch there was already a silent crowd waiting. The morning wind had dropped and it was a beautiful summer evening. The church looked welcoming and familiar and she felt steadied by the feeling that this was her church where she and John had been married and her three boys had been baptised in the solid six sided stone font, but then Ann felt herself flush when, as she walked up the steep path, as one, the people all turned and stared at her. John squeezed her hand and she drew herself up tall and squared her shoulders. 'I can do this,' she promised herself under her breath.

She absorbed rather than looked at who was there. James Catt, of course, and his mother and several of his drinking cronies, but there were also a fair few of her friends. Henry Whetley, the miller, a pleasant, cheery man who had suffered terribly with constipation and whom she had helped by recommending cabbage water taken twice daily; Bridget Taylor who had presented with a breech baby but whom she had safely delivered of a son. Mary Pollard, lurking at the edge of the crowd, trying to be as inconspicuous as possible, bobbed her head in acknowledgement; a nervous woman of late middle years she was afflicted with boils which Ann had treated with some success with a poultice of boiled, mashed onion.

As she and John passed by, Richard Stevenson raised a hand and she recalled how, some years ago she had brought him some relief from a rash on his face with a cream made from chamomile and marigold and finally there was little Elizabeth Wyatt, hopping up and down and clutching at her grateful mother's hand. Elizabeth, aged four, had been struck down last year with a high fever and swollen neck and Ann had used an infusion of willow bark which had lowered the fever and stopped the child's meaningless ranting. To look at her now, you would never know she had ever had anything wrong with her. She waved shyly at Ann and Ann smiled wanly in greeting.

William was waiting by the church door and he came forward as she approached. He nodded to John and greeted her politely and formally. 'Goodwife Ashdown, certain charges have been laid against you and I think it wise that these be answered for all to hear. With God's help the truth will be told.' He lowered his voice slightly, 'I am sure that you have nothing to fear, but this way I believe we can avoid things escalating and ending up with a formal hearing.' He stood to one side. 'Please stand by me in front of the church door.'

As they moved to follow the priest, John couldn't help thinking again about why William was doing this. Of course, as her husband, John knew there was no truth in the accusation, but why was William Collyer going to all this trouble to protect Ann? Was it just that he liked her and also thought she was innocent, or was there another reason?

There was something in his manner that made John uneasy and then he realised what it was. The whole proceeding had an unreal air - almost like a mummers play. Yes that was it - the man was at great pains to put on a show. He was making this so called 'hearing' seem as if it was the normal, legal course of events, and John wasn't convinced that this was actually the case. The more he thought about it, the more John became sure that the priest was very keen that no whiff of scandal about Rotherfield reached higher church authorities. He did not want his bishop turning his attention on him and his parish for any reason, so he wanted this witch accusation nipped in the bud before things got out of hand. John felt partly reassured by this thought, for if he was right, it made it more likely that Ann's problems would be happily resolved this evening – but part of him again disliked the priest's hypocrisy.

The man didn't want it to be found out that he was a practising Catholic priest who still had a wife and child. He may have kept to the letter of the law and sent Katherine away, but from odd things that George had said over the year, John knew that William still visited his wife, and this would not be tolerated by the church. At worst he could lose his living and be excommunicated, and at the very least it would mean that there was no chance of William Collyer getting a more prestigious living. Perhaps that was it, thought John. Perhaps the man had ambition.

With these thoughts whirling in his head, John took his place to one side of Ann and the priest. The crowd pushed forward and several loud voices made themselves heard. William held up his hand. 'I would ask you all to remember that this is holy ground and would remind you all to be respectful of that fact.' Several of the men hastily snatched off their caps and children were hushed into silence.

'I have called you here because I am aware that there are rumours circulating in the village about Goodwife Ann Ashdown. Accusations of a serious nature have been made against her and, as your priest and spiritual advisor it is up to me to decide whether or not there is likely to be any truth in these accusations. If it appears that there is, then it may be that things need to be taken further and referred to the magistrate or to a church council.'

A wave of fear overtook Ann and she swallowed hard.

'If not—' the priest paused and glared round at the crowd, his eyes flashing dark and fierce, '—if not,' he repeated slowly, '—then I expect there to be an end to this matter, with no stain on Goodwife Ashdown's character. Those who have something to say come forward now and you will be heard in turn.'

There was a shuffling and pushing as James Catt, his mother, Josiah Mead and Luke Ailwood moved promptly to the front, closely followed by Matthew Weston who angrily shook off Lizzie's hand as she sought to prevent him.

At the same time, from the other side of the crowd, several villagers whom Ann would count as her friends also stepped forward and smiled at her encouragingly, but she was barely aware of this movement, as her attention was suddenly caught by a tall figure sitting on the wall of the churchyard, half hidden behind a hawthorn bush. She would know that white, blonde hair anywhere and the sight of it made her stomach turn over.

She had been just fourteen when she had met Peter Jones. Of course she didn't know his name then. Knew nothing about the strange man who had so terrified her in the forest.

She had been gathering mushrooms, she remembered. It was very early one summer morning, the ground still wet with the dawn dew. The large, succulent, field mushrooms were a special favourite of her Mother's and thinking to surprise her with a gift, she had let herself quietly out of the cottage, which she shared with her parents and two brothers. She had revelled in the fresh, morning air and been delighted when she saw that there was a good crop just waiting to be picked. Rushing triumphantly from mushroom to mushroom she had not noticed how close she had come to the edge of the forest until suddenly, as she was bending to pluck a large, flat, mushroom a shadow fell across her. She started in surprise and looked up. She had been so busy with her eyes to the ground that she had neither heard, nor seen Jones approach. She'd had no idea who this man was, standing with his hands on his hips insolently staring at her, but the way that he didn't speak, just looked her up and down, made her blush and feel uncomfortable.

He must have been about twenty then – a fine figure of a man with hair that was so blonde it was almost white, pale, pale eyes like the swirl of the river on a cloudy day and a flash of white teeth in a face that seemed too dark for the colour of his hair.

There was no-one else about and with a beat in her stomach she suddenly realised that even her Mother did not know where she was. The terror that had started in her guts seemed to grow up into her chest as the man continued to stare and she swallowed hard as if to stop it becoming a visible thing that would burst out of her mouth and float off into the morning air like a swarm of mad bees. 'Good morning,' she said politely. Her voice had seemed strangled and too quiet and she had cleared her throat nervously.

'It certainly seems as if it is, as you say, a good morning.' He smiled as he spoke; a sardonic smile that sent shivers down her back. His accent was strange and had a lilt to it that made it sound almost like singing.

Still keeping her eyes on his face she bent her knees and felt for her basket which she had set down on the grass. He took a step towards her. 'But, on the other hand, I see that you've been stealing my mushrooms, and that is not so good.'

'Stealing?' She had her basket now and held it in front of her, the flimsy barrier between them giving her some comfort. She tried to make her voice firm. 'I've stolen nothing. These are wild mushrooms and my Mother sent me to collect them for her,' she lied, licking her lips nervously.

'So you say, but then I like a nice mushroom myself. I pick them every morning see and' –he glanced around the field– 'it looks as though there are none left for me today. I think perhaps I deserve some payment for my disappointment don't you?'

Again he stepped forward and she automatically retreated from him, keeping the basket firmly in front of her.

'I'm sorry... I didn't know . . . I . . .'

Each step that she took backwards away from him, he matched with a step towards her until her foot caught on a tuft of grass and she would have toppled had he not suddenly lunged towards her and grabbed her.

His hands were strong and hard on the tops of her arms and as she turned her face to one side away from him, she caught his smell – an acrid, smoky smell that reminded her of bonfires on an autumn eve. Then she realised the truth of the dark skin – it was smoke dirt. He must be one of the charcoal burners who lived solitary lives in the forest, tending their heaps and producing the jet black charcoal from the wood that was stacked in neat piles in sunlit clearings among the trees. She had seen the peculiar smouldering humps of earth once when she and her Father had been travelling through the forest on a visit to an elderly aunt. Strange though - the thought flashed unbidden through her mind - strange that his hair didn't darken too; he must usually wear a hat. Despite her inner fear, at another level, her brain seemed to continue to think ordinary, considered thoughts.

She could feel that the man was laughing softly and she was aware that he knew that there was no way she could break out of that vice like grip. She was caught like those poor rabbits which she had seen, still and limp in the traps set by some of the village boys.

Still holding her, forcing her to walk in step with him in what must have looked like a macabre, slow motion dance, he backed her into the edge of the trees and with a little push tumbled her backwards onto the ground. Her basket fell from her hands as she put out her arms to save herself and then he was on top of her, pressing his mouth to hers. She had kissed Harold Huntley once as they'd sat chatting by the river, a quick shy peck, their mouths barely touching, not like this, his lips moving and sucking, teeth bumping against hers as he tried to force his tongue into her mouth. She tried to turn her head and push him off but, although he pulled away from her mouth, he grabbed her hands and held them pressed to the ground above her head. He looked down at her and grinned, one tooth missing, the rest of his teeth white and even against his darkened skin. 'Well I think perhaps after all this is my lucky day. I think I might be persuaded to swap a tumble with a fair maid for a few mushrooms.'

'No . . . please . . .' She got no further as his mouth covered hers again and one hand loosed her left arm and fumbled at her chest. He squeezed her small breast and then reached down to her skirt which had ridden up as she fell. She felt his hand, cool and dry on her left thigh and the terror in her chest exploded in her with a roar. This mustn't happen. His hand was pushing up between her legs. She couldn't let this happen to her.

Blindly she scrabbled around her with her left arm feeling desperately around for she knew not what and her hand closed on a piece of fallen tree branch. She drew one knee up and arched her back slightly in a superhuman effort to lift the branch. Surprised by what he perhaps thought of as co-operation from her, he shifted his weight slightly and as he did so, with a tremendous heave, she managed to swing the piece of wood in a high arc up from the ground. She didn't even think of the danger to herself, as there was no way she could aim accurately and she risked knocking her own brains out, but she acted purely on instinct and, after all, what other choice was there? Partly under its own momentum and partly by digging in her heels, using all the force she could muster, she brought the branch down with a dull thud onto the back of his head. At the same time she squirmed out from under him and, leaping to her feet, she ran for her life. She had no idea if she had killed him, or just grazed his head and did not dare to look around for she was intent on avoiding tripping over the roots and brambles on the forest floor. With every step she feared that she would feel a tug from behind and he would be on her once more. She ran and ran, her skirts lifted high out of her way. Soon her long, bare legs were scratched and bleeding, as she covered the ground in great leaps like a frightened deer. She neither stopped nor looked back until she reached the lane that lead into the village.

A hasty glance over her shoulder told her that he was not following. Only then did she allow herself to slow down and finally stop. She bent over, her hands on her knees panting heavily. She felt something on her face and as she put up her hand to brush away whatever it was, she realised she was shaking. She took her hand from her face and saw her trembling fingers were streaked with blood. She was aware of no pain, nothing but the furious beating of her heart and the rasp of her breath.

Tentatively she felt her forehead with her fingertips and then winced slightly as her exploration revealed a tender place wet with warm blood. A twig on the branch that she'd hit the man with, must have caught her too. She was lucky it had not taken her eye out. She would have to clean it up and think of some story to explain it to her Mother.

It was at that moment that she realised that she was not going to tell anyone about the attempted rape. Why, she wasn't sure. Perhaps it was because if she never put it into words it couldn't be true. So, in her mind she built a shell around the memory. In it she hid the horror, the shame, the terror and the disgust. She sealed all the feelings up inside the shell and hid it like a secret egg deep within her. So well did she hide it that she had never told anyone – not even her gentle John – and certainly not her parents or her brothers who, she thought, would undoubtedly have wanted to seek out Peter Jones and punish him in some way that she could not imagine.

After the incident she'd dreaded seeing him again and had always been on the lookout for that mane of blonde hair, but it was several months before she came across him once more. She was walking with her Mother to see an old lady who had ulcers on her legs and there he was in the centre of the road, walking towards her. She felt herself go hot as if someone had opened the door of the forge. She had caught up her Mother's hand – something she hadn't done for a long time – and hung on for dear life.

Seeming not to notice her daughter's distress, her Mother had spoken to the man. 'Good day, Peter.'

He'd not looked at Ann nor replied to her Mother, but just dipped his head and carried on striding down the road.

Ann let our her breath, which she realised she'd been holding. 'You know that man? Who is he?'

'Peter Jones,' said her Mother. 'Handsome devil isn't he?' she said with a sideways smile at Ann, totally misunderstanding her daughter's interest. 'Used to work as a burner, but went up to London a few months back so I'm told. Has a cousin hereabouts. Must be visiting I suppose.'

And now he was back again. Why, she thought, has he come here today? Did he still wish her harm? What could he do to her now? She was no longer afraid of him, not with her giant of a husband and sons to protect her and anyway, she thought, I'm no longer a fourteen year old maid ripe for the plucking, but a forty year old woman with greying hair who is thought to be a witch.

Witch, witch . . . Ann came back to the present with a jolt as William turned to James Catt. 'From what I understand,' he said, 'you and your mother, Goodwife Catt, first accused Goodwife Ashdown of witchcraft when your wife died in childbirth.'

Catt thrust himself forward importantly and with something of a swagger half turned towards the crowd. 'That's right,' he nodded. 'She' – and he pointed at Ann– 'came to our house unasked and tried to come in and stop my Nell–' he paused dramatically and said piously, '–God rest her soul– she tried to stop the pains of childbirth, when everyone knows that God told Eve that woman should suffer.'

'Yes and you certainly made her suffer!' said a voice from the crowd.

William held up his hand. 'Go on.'

'Well, my mother was with Nell and sent Goodwife Ashdown packing, but later that night she came back in the dark and she gave Nell, God re—'

'Yes, yes . . . get on man,' said William frowning.

'She gave Nell a potion and then my poor wife bled and died.'

'Were you there when this happened?' asked William.

'No of course I weren't.' Catt looked horrified. 'It wouldn't have been fitting for me to be there with a woman giving birth, but that's what happened. Ask my Mother. That's what happened in't it Mother?'

His Mother took a step forward, almost preening as she found herself the centre of attention. 'Aye, it is. It all happened just as my son says. That wicked woman killed the mother of my grandchildren with a spell and a potion.'

'A spell you say? Catt made no mention of a spell. Pray tell us what was this spell?'

'Err, well, I couldn't rightly hear, but she were muttering words right low, so I'm sure it were . . .' Catt's mother fell silent, but then gathered herself again, 'but she gived her a potion to drink and then Nell cried out and blood came out of her and she died.'

There was a gasp from several in the crowd.

William ignored it and turned to Ann. 'Goodwife Ashdown, would you tell us now how you came to James Catt's house and what befell there.'

Ann lifted her chin and looked round the crowd. Some looked back at her, but others dropped their gaze and would not meet her eye.

'I was walking home from picking wild strawberries and as I passed Nell's house I heard her crying out in sore distress. I have attended enough mothers to know the sound of a woman in travail, so I knocked at the door and asked Goodwife Catt if I could help. Nell heard me and called out to me to help her, but Goodwife Catt would not let me enter. She called me a witch and told me to go away.'

'She called you a witch? Why would she do that?'

'I have no idea.'

'Go on.'

'Later that night we'd been in bed but a short time when young Simon Catt came knocking at the door asking for me to go to his mother, as she still hadn't had the child and was in a bad way.'

'And what did you do?'

'Well, I went of course, as any Christian woman would when asked for help by a neighbour.' As she spoke Ann felt her courage rise. 'When I arrived Goodwife Catt was sitting by the fire drinking—'

'Liar. I never was.' There were a few titters from the crowd hastily smothered as William glared round.

'Nell was lying on a mattress and was in great distress. She had bruises on her and it was obvious she had been beaten recently.'

William looked up sharply. 'Is this so, Catt? Remember you are on holy ground and speaking before God and his priest. Well.'

James Catt looked at his feet and shifted uneasily. 'I . . . I may 'ave given her a slap. She sometimes drove me to distraction with her nagging, but I never—'

'It was more than a slap.' Ann turned to him, indignation against the man who had so mistreated his poor, dead wife, rising in her. 'The poor woman had huge bruises on her face and arms. I think perhaps it was that which had brought on her pains.' She looked back at the priest. 'She wasn't due for some weeks yet and the babe hadn't yet turned for birthing. That was the problem. It was sideways and couldn't be born.'

Several women nodded their heads knowingly and Ann took comfort from their agreement.

'Did you at any time say a spell, or give Nell a potion? You too remember where you are and before whom you speak.'

'No, I did not. I spoke words of comfort to her such as anyone would when tending someone in such pain, and I made her a drink of shepherd's purse and rosemary to give her strength. It is a common enough thing and has no magic in it.'

Matthew Weston took a step forward as he sensed that the mood of the crowd was turning in Ann's favour as she gave her testimony, her voice clear and calm, her bearing dignified. 'That's as may be,' he said loudly. 'But what about our Lizzie? Three girls I've had and each one birthed by that woman.' He pointed at Ann.

'Yes? Your point?' said William coldly, narrowing his eyes at the interruption.

'Well it ain't natural is it? I'm not a gambling man–' more suppressed laughter, '–but three out of three – all girls? T'ain't natural and it's her fault

I say. She put a spell on my babes and turned then all to girls. And look at her,' he added for good measure, pointing an accusing finger. 'Gived herself three sons she did.'

'Rubbish, man,' William waved his hand dismissively. 'Everyone knows that many a man may have a whole family of all girls or all boys and it's nothing to do with witchcraft, rather the will of God.'

'Even the Boleyn witch couldn't give the King a boy like he wanted. 'Tain't possible to change the sex of a babe, man, everyone knows that,' shouted a voice from the crowd.

Like a pricked pig's bladder Matthew subsided in the face of the priest's contempt and the derisive laughter of some of the villagers.

'Does anyone else wish to speak?'

Margaret Bridger, a fat woman with grease stains on her apron stepped forward, wringing her hands nervously. 'I . . .I . . .'

William smiled at her kindly. 'Take your time Margaret,' he said.

'Thank you . . .yes, well I wanted to say that . . . that Ann, er Goodwife Ashdown, that is, is a good woman and not at all a witch. When my Mark were ill she stayed with him day and night for three days. She gave him herb mixtures, but nothing bad, just willow bark and things as she said would bring down his fever and it did and well—'

'Thank you Margaret.' He looked round the assembled villagers. 'Well it seems to me—'

'There's more. You ain't heard all of it yet.' Jame's Catt's voice cut across William's. 'What's the witch done with our Simon? That's what I want to know? She's spirited him off somewhere poor boy.'

'What are you talking about, man? Your Simon ran away. You said so yourself when I gave you his hat that I found.'

'Aye, well that's what we thought at the time,' said Catt with a significant nod of his head. He glanced around the crowd with a triumphant look. 'But if you remember, you also found a piece of blue cloth with the hat and I took it home and . . . Well, tell him Mother . . .'

Goodwife Catt looked as smug as her son as she spoke. 'That cloth. The blue one. Well I know where it came from.' She paused a moment to make sure she had everyone's attention, then said slowly and clearly. 'It belonged to Goodwife Ashdown,' she said dramatically. 'I seed it on top of her basket when she came to the door when Nell were birthing.'

The old woman preened with self-importance and in a rare moment of anger, John felt that he wanted to hit her and wipe the self-satisfied smile from her face.

'Always covered her basket with it she did and it were inside our Simon's hat when my son brought it home.' She turned to face the crowd. 'Inside our Simon's hat,' she repeated loudly.

There were gasps from the crowd and John felt as if he'd been kicked in the stomach. How on earth had Ann's blue cloth got inside Simon's hat? He looked across at her and saw the colour drain out of her face. What had she done?

William turned to Ann. 'Well, Goodwife Ashdown, can you explain this?'

There were loud murmurings from the crowd as they digested and discussed this latest accusation and William had to hold up his hand again for silence.

Ann, who had looked confident, almost defiant in the face of the accusations about Nell suddenly looked crushed and as she started to speak her lip started to tremble. All her fears for young Simon came rushing to the surface. Had she done wrong in helping one so young set out on such an adventure? Why had his hat been found. Did that mean he had taken harm? She didn't know. 'I can't . . . I'm sorry, it's just . . .'

'Look she's crying' said Henry the miller who had always had a cheery word for her. 'That's a good sign that is.' He waved his finger to emphasise his words. 'Witches don't cry - everyone knows that.'

'Aye,' said his neighbour. 'There's truth in that, but how does she explain the cloth if she didn't disappear him?'

Ann wiped her tears away with the back of her hand and sniffed. 'Yes, it was my cloth,' she admitted, 'and I gave it to Simon. He came to me and said how sorry he was that his father had hanged my cat.' William raised his eyebrows and there were more gasps and mutterings from the crowd. 'He said that, when he'd refused to do it, his father had beaten him sorely and that he wasn't going to put up with it anymore; he was going to run away. I tried to talk him out of it – he was, is, so young, but his mind was made up. I couldn't see him go off with nothing, so I gave him some food and wrapped it in the cloth. I . . .I didn't know what else to do. His mother was a good friend and . . . and I wanted to help him – for her sake,' she finished in a low voice as tears overwhelmed her.

'SO SHE SAYS,' said Catt loudly, enunciating each word slowly so that the effect would sink in 'but it's only her word. As I see it, she comes and my Nell dies, she gives our Simon her cloth and puts a spell on him and he disappears. She's a witch and no mistake.'

His friends Josiah Mead and Luke Ailwood slapped him on the back, nodding in agreement with him.

William lifted his head and looked around the crowd. 'Does anyone have more to say?' There was silence while people looked at each other, friend and foe alike stunned by the latest accusation and then slowly, like a wooden puppet coming to life, Peter Jones stood up from his seat on the low wall that surrounded the churchyard. As he did so, the dying sun shone directly behind him and his white, blonde hair blazed like a halo giving him the appearance of an angel.

Someone in the crowd gasped and a small shrivelled woman at the edge of the crowd crossed herself.

'I'd like to say something.'

To Ann, his voice seemed to come from a great distance and from another time. There was that same strange accent with a musical lilt to it that had haunted her nightmares long ago. Now she realised, with the benefit of experience, the man was Welsh. Back then she had never heard a Welshman speak, but over the years several men from the wild lands in the west had come to Ashdown Forest in search of work with the iron.

As he walked across to William, all heads turned to look at the stranger who was intruding on village business,

The priest acknowledged the man with a nod of his head. 'You are welcome. What is you name goodman?'

'My name is Peter Jones and I would just like to say that what this woman is accused of is unjust.' Mutterings and shifting in the crowd. Ignoring the interruptions the man continued. 'Leastways, it is unjust to say that' – he hesitated slightly before pronouncing her name deliberately – 'Goodwife Ashdown, made the boy disappear. He did that of his own accord.'

'What do you mean? You mean you have knowledge of Simon?' William asked.

'If that is the name of the boy with the big hat, sticking out ears and legs as skinny as a twig, then yes I do mean just that.' Several of the villagers grinned at his description and he looked around the crowd, holding the gaze of some in the manner of a story teller, waiting until he was sure that all eyes were on him. 'It were like this, see. I had occasion to be about early myself last Friday,' he glanced at Ann and she looked down at her feet. 'I've recently come back to the burning in these parts after many years away and after a night tending the fires it is my way, as always, to take a walk in the cool, early hours of the dawn.' He paused and Ann could feel the memories in the egg buried deep inside her stir like deformed chicks struggling to hatch. 'As I say, I saw a boy such as I've described, carrying a small bundle tied up with a blue cloth. He was hurrying out of the village as fast as his skinny legs would carry him, heading along the lane that skirts Castle Hill he was; going in such a scurry and with a determined manner like the devil was after him, that he didn't see me, like, standing as I was in the shadow by the trees.'

Lots of people in the crowd all started talking at once. 'That proves it . . .' 'What did I tell you . . .' 'Didn't I say he'd run off?' 'Never seen him before.' 'Why should we believe—?'

'Quiet!' William's voice rang out. 'Quiet, please, good people.' He turned to Peter Jones. 'Are you quite sure that it was this last Friday that you saw the boy and that he was carrying a bundle tied up in a blue cloth? You are sure he was on his own and moving freely of his own will?'

'Saw him clear as day with my own eyes I did and yes, he seemed to me to be running away as fast as he could and he was indeed carrying a bundle wrapped in a blue cloth.'

'Thank you Jones. Your testimony has been of great help. It was good of you to take the trouble to come here this evening and speak out for this woman.'

Peter Jones was now no taller than the adult Ann and he looked across the churchyard straight into her eyes. She held herself erect and proud as she stared straight back at him. To her, the silence seemed to go on for a long time until he said with that strange, musical lilt, 'It has been no trouble. I merely try to right a wrong, see, as all good Christians should.' He nodded his head once at Ann then, without another word, he turned on his heel and loped away down the hill.

After the man had gone, for a few moments nobody spoke as people weighed the importance of his words. Ann put her hands to her cheeks and found they were wet with tears. John looked at her with concern, but mindful of the seriousness of the situation, refrained from touching her out of respect.

James Catt and his supporters looked discomfited and angry while Richard Stevenson beamed round at friends, clearly of the opinion that Ann had been vindicated by the stranger's testimony.

William cleared his throat and stepping forward adopted the earnest and commanding stance he always took up when preaching a sermon. 'I think we have heard enough. We came here this evening to weigh the evidence as to whether or not there was a case to suggest that this woman is guilty of witchcraft.

'We have heard evidence from James Catt and his Mother and from Matthew Weston to suggest that Ann Ashdown is a witch. We have also heard from others who say she is nothing but a woman who has knowledge of herbs and cures and uses them freely to benefit her fellows. What has always been known in the country as a "cunning woman". Finally we had testimony from Peter Jones that disputed that young Simon Catt had been the victim of witchcraft as his father claims.'

William lifted his arms as though in benediction as he addressed the villagers. 'Good people, throughout history there has always been a fear of witches and their evil doings in partnership with the Devil. There are many things in this world which cannot be explained and communities have often sought to lay the blame for unfortunate events on one individual.' Several people shuffled their feet and looked embarrassed, while at the back of the crowd, a mother shushed a babe in arms who had started to wail.

'In 1486 a famous treaty, the Malleus Maleficarum, was written by a man by the name of Heinrich Kramer, an Inquisitor of the Catholic Church. It deemed that midwives, female scholars, priestesses, gypsies, mystics, nature lovers, herb gatherers, and any women, I quote, "suspiciously attuned to the natural world", was guilty of witchcraft and therefore should be put to death.'

The woman clutching the babe in her arms put her hand over its head, as if to ward off evil.

'In this very century, the Witchcraft Act of 1542 was enacted under the reign of King Henry and that too condemned witches and so called cunning women to death. However, in our more enlightened, modern times this law was repealed, as it was deemed that it was better for the Church to deal with such issues in its ecclesiastic courts. That is why I called you together today for, as your priest, it is up to me to make recommendation to the Bishop as to the need for a hearing in the Church Court.'

Ah now we have it, John thought. This is how he justifies his interest, but what do I care for his reasons so long as my Ann is not tainted and we can return to our life untroubled.

'I do not believe that, on the evidence I have heard today, there is such to suggest that Goodwife Ann Ashdown is anything other than a woman with skills that are to be admired and applauded. I have heard nothing which suggests that she has harmed anyone with either spells or potions.'

James Catt kicked in disgust at the ground, spat and folded his arms.

'To make an end to the matter and ensure that there is no further trouble for this woman, I will take oaths from four compurgators, that is,' he explained patiently, 'from four people who are were willing to swear that she isn't a witch. Those willing to take such an oath please step forward before all.'

To Ann's great relief there was a surge as a good dozen people stepped forward on her behalf. As William chose those from whom he would take oath she turned to John and smiled. Almost shyly he stretched out his hand.

'Let there be an end to this,' he said. 'Come now. We will go home.'

14

The sun glinted on the water, temporarily blinding him so that he could no longer see down into the depths, but Simon didn't move. He hadn't eaten since last evening and his stomach ached with emptiness. This fish must not get away.

He closed his eyes then blinked away the dazzle as he peered down into the river. His hand looked pale like the hand of a dead man as it hung in the river water that was the colour of weak beer. The fish was hovering, facing upstream, about a foot below the surface, sheltering under the root of an overhanging alder tree. With infinite patience Simon inched his hand closer so that his upturned fingers made contact with the fish's tail. Holding his breath and trying to ignore the root that was digging uncomfortably into his ribs, he gently began tickling with his forefinger, gradually running his hand along the fish's belly, further and further toward the head until he was just under the gills. Then with a quick grab he clutched at the fish and hurled it up onto the bank where it flapped vigorously, but ineffectively, in the long grass. Simon allowed himself a victorious whoop before hitting it on the head with a stone. The trout was a big one – he would eat well tonight.

Later, after he had finished his meal and licked his fingers clean, he gathered a quantity of long grass and, placing it in the shelter of a bush, lay down on his makeshift bed to sleep. As he gazed up through the branches at the dark, velvet sky he saw a star, like a blazing arrow shoot across the blackness just above him, then another, low on the horizon. Was that a good sign or a bad portent? He wasn't sure, but crossed himself and said a 'Hail Mary' just in case.

It had been over a week now since he had left home and headed out of Rotherfield in the early morning and he wasn't at all sure where he was. Before he set out he had the vague idea that he would try to reach the sea. Once, years ago, one of his mother's brothers had visited them and Simon remembered that he had worked on the fishing boats. He was a fat, jolly man with a bushy beard who had sat Simon on his knee, pinched his cheek and told him stories of smugglers and pirates that had made his hair stand on end. Perhaps, he thought, he might even find his uncle and live with him. He was, after all, the only man who had ever been really nice to him.

He closed his eyes and listened to the night sounds around him. In the distance a barn owl screeched – a fierce, angry sound that would, no doubt strike terror into the heart of any mouse or a vole scampering across the fields. Simon wasn't frightened though. He liked the night time; felt safe in the enclosing, velvet darkness. As he listened he became aware of the gentle chatter of the river nearby. It was so unceasing that he had hardly noticed it, but now its sound seemed to become louder as if it were calling to him. He heard a gentle splash and then a quiet, but high pitched whistle, then another from further along the bank – otters. Perhaps a family of them. Certainly if the fish Simon had caught tonight was anything to go by, the mother would have no difficulty in feeding her young on this river.

His breathing became more regular. The river... fishing... the sea. As he drifted off to sleep a plan was forming at the back of his mind. All he had to do was to follow the river. It was obvious. Why had he not thought of it before? Rivers always led to the sea – his uncle had told him that. His mind made up, he flung an arm across his face and slept.

15

After the hearing in the churchyard Ann often awoke in the night, feeling that she had a tight band around her chest, her breathing rapid and shallow and in order to calm herself she had to force herself to wake fully out of that treacherous land of half-sleep, where terrors seemed so real that sometimes she even cried out.

She dreamed of confinement, of the ducking stool and the choking feeling of drowning, of the horror of a rope chaffing around her neck and worst of all of the sweet, fatty smell of burning flesh – like the smell of pig skin as its bristles were burned off before butchering – and the sudden, sickening awareness that it was not pig, but the smell of her own flesh burning. Sometimes, in her struggle to free herself from the dream-flames she would wind herself in the blanket with John beside her muttering sleepily, confused, wondering what she was about.

But gradually the night-time fears faded and Ann's daily life settled down to a pattern of normality. The weeks passed and, as the summer wore on, the terror of the Catts' accusations faded and she felt happier and calmer. As John had forecast, her neighbours proved to have short memories and almost all treated her normally and seemed to have forgotten the drama of that July evening. As for Catt himself, with no wife to curb him, he and his cronies seemed absorbed in their own activities of poaching, drinking and dog and cock fighting, so blessedly she had seen nothing of them. Nor had she seen Peter Jones again – and nor did she wish too.

It had been strange and unsettling to see him after all these years – a much smaller, quite inoffensive man really. Not at all the creature who had inhabited her youthful nightmares after he had attempted to rape her.

John had blessed him for his intervention that evening in the churchyard, but, although she realised that Peter Jones had spoken as his way of making amends for what had happened between them long ago, she still could not find it in her heart to totally forgive him. Nor could she bring herself to tell John of her involvement with the man and she did not disillusion her husband when he talked gratefully of a stranger being so willing to do his Christian duty and help out a woman wrongly accused. As she had cause to know, John was a kindly man, always willing to see the best in people and why, she asked herself, should she burden him with the unwelcome knowledge that the man was not the Good Samaritan that he seemed?

Ann found peace in the daily round of chores as she busied herself with the task of keeping house, of feeding her family and making sure that there would be plenty to eat in the coming winter.

August proved to be, like the rest of the summer, changeable and inclement. The long days of sunshine needed for the harvest were few and far between and on the farms it was a struggle to harvest and store away the grain. No doubt some would be spoiled with the dreaded mould that the dampness induced and perhaps this year, yet again, famine would visit the Sussex countryside and people would be forced to eat 'horse bread' made from ground, dried peas. The fruit crop, however, was good and from the orchard at the back of the cottage, Ann picked apples and pears, medlars and quince, carefully checking for imperfections and maggots that would send the fruit rotten, then storing it away on wide shelves in the little shed John had built for the purpose at the side of the cottage.

She gathered peas and beans and her hung bunches of her precious herbs from racks near the hearth; she pounded leaves and flowers and turned them into salves and syrups and week after week she continued the backbreaking work of weeding between the rows of turnips and onions that would stay in the ground a few weeks longer. Often, as she paused to straighten her back and rub the soil from her hands, she wished she had George to help in her garden, but he was busy husbanding Katherine's garden and that, she thought ruefully, had been all her own idea.

The days shortened and summer passed into autumn. The wind rustled the trees and leaves of russet, yellow and red shone brightly against the hazy blue of the sky like flags at a fayre. Flocks of birds passed overhead and, as she paused in her hoeing to look up at the dark shapes above the trees, Ann often wondered where it was that they flew to. Was there a large dark cave somewhere in the south where they could rest until the warm days of spring came again, in the same way that the badger and the hedge-pig slept away the winter?

It was a perfect autumn afternoon and Ann had enjoyed her walk along a deeply worn track, its banks covered with arching brambles bearing the last of this season's large, juicy blackberries which, stewed and mixed with her honey, made an excellent remedy for winter coughs. Her hands and arms were scratched and she was vexed to see that it was not just her fingers that were discoloured with the juice; there were several large purple stains on her apron as well. She shivered slightly and became aware that the sun was low and a light evening mist was beginning to form in the hollows. It was time she was heading home.

She picked up her basket that she had carefully lined with leaves so that the juice from the berries did not drip as she carried it home, took up the old shepherd's crook that she kept for hooking those branches that were out of reach and set out for home. She had wandered further than she had intended as she followed the brambles along the hedgerow, the next one and the next always seeming to promise bigger and better bounty. She would need to hurry if she was to have food on the table before John came in from the forge.

As the track ahead of her flattened out, a blackbird sounded its alarm call and, when she rounded a bend, she saw, to her consternation, James Catt and his two friends sprawling on the grass to one side at the edge of a small copse. It was obvious, by the look of them, that they had been drinking for most of the afternoon and she paused, trying to draw back, wondering how she could pass them unseen. But Josiah Mead's dog had already sensed her presence and started to bark, lunging in her direction and pulling on the rope that fastened him to a nearby tree.

Mead swiped at him with a stick. 'Shut up you bugger. Lie down, damn you.' The dog, which had obviously had plenty of practice, nimbly dodged the stick as it swung towards him and took no notice of its master, continuing to strain and bark.

'For God's sake shut that thing up Jo,' said Catt. 'It's doing me 'ed in.'

Luke Ailwood seemed less drunk than the other two and knelt up, peering down the track in the direction of Ann who was trying, unsuccessfully, to push her way unseen through the bushes at the side of the track. 'There's sommat there in the bushes. Aye, look–' he punched Catt on the shoulder. '–it's a woman.'

'A woman!' roared Mead lurching to his feet. 'Me prayers have been answered. Get her boy.' And to Ann's horror he slipped the rope over the dog's head and it came bounding towards her growling and snarling, showing yellow teeth below a curled lip.

She held her basket in front of her and waved her stick. 'No! Get away! Call him off! No . . .' Her voice rose to a high pitched squeal. She had always had a fear of dogs and this one, she knew, had been trained to fight. Already she could imagine its large, yellow teeth grabbing at her flesh.

The dog stopped a couple of feet in front of her its large feet planted apart, the great flat head thrust towards her with bloodshot eyes wild and fierce as it continued to snarl and growl. She could smell its hot, foul breath; terrified she stared at it. After what seemed minutes, but was only a matter of seconds, the three men staggered up behind the animal and stood in a half circle grinning at her.

Catt, ever the leader of the three was the first to speak. 'Well look here lads. Look what Bilzybub's caught us today. If it ain't the witch! No wonder he's making such a fuss. Don't like witches do we boy?'

He hawked and spat a gob of spit which landed on a dock leaf.

'Keep him off me - please,' Ann pleaded in a shaking voice.

'Oh, he won't hurt you,' said Mead grinning. He paused meaningfully. 'Not unless I tells him to.' He picked some food out of his tooth and examined it before popping it back in his mouth and chewing contemplatively. He sucked in his breath through his teeth. 'What d'y think James. Should we let him at her?'

'Might be fun,' replied Catt. 'But I've got a better idea. We never did finish that business in the churchyard did we? I'm not willing to take the judgment of a jumped-up priest. I says she's a witch and I'm going to prove it. Hold her lads.'

To her horror Mead and Ailwood came round behind her and grabbed her arms, pinioning them behind her.

'Now then, my dear,' Catt continued. 'I understands that witches have a mark of the devil. Ain't that right boys? And I intends to find it.' With that he grabbed hold of the front of her blouse and snapped the lacings. 'Often underneath the left breast so I've been told.' He put his face up close to hers and leered at her and she turned her head to one side away from the reek of alcohol on his breath. 'And a fine pair of boobies we have here if I may say so,' he said giving her nipple a tweak.

She gasped and tried to wriggle free, but the two men held her fast as Catt, none too gently, lifted up first one breast then the other and peered closely at her clear white skin. He stood back and looked her up and down and she felt Ailwoods hand creep around from behind and fondle her breast.

'None of that now Lukey Boy – not yet awhile anyhow. Perhaps later,' Catt said pointedly with a grin. 'First we've got to find this mark. Then we've got proof. She's obviously a clever one and has it concealed somewhere, but we'll find it, mark my words.' He stepped closer and started to fumble with her skirt. She tried to kick him and he slapped her hard across her face. She felt her head spinning from the blow and staggered as suddenly, she found herself free.

'Someone's coming Jim. Quick.'

Whistling softly to the dog, the three men disappeared into the trees. She barely had time to retrieve her shawl and cover herself, when a man wearing a hat with a large black feather in it and sitting astride a small donkey, accompanied by three women and half a dozen dirty children, rounded the corner of the track she had just been walking.

The man drew rein just level with her and the little procession behind him stopped too. 'I give you good day, Goodwife,' said the man quaintly, nodding his head at her so that the feather quivered and shook. The donkey drooped its head, seemingly grateful to stop and wait while the man looked at her tumbled basket, blackberries scattered across the grass. No doubt she had a mark across her face too and she put her hand self-consciously up to her cheek. 'Methinks, Goodwife, you have had a mishap here. Would I be correct?'

'Er . . . Yes indeed, I . . . I took a fall and' – she gestured to the berries – 'alas I spilled the berries I'd been collecting.' She drew her shawl tightly across her torn blouse and tied it firmly to conceal the torn lacings.

Without a word, the man clicked his fingers at the children and pointed first at the berries, then at the basket. Immediately they rushed forward and started gathering up the fallen fruit and putting it in her basket, then the tallest of them picked it up and solemnly handed it to her. She looked at the dirty hand holding out the basket now filled again with the squashed fruit, mixed with bits of grass and leaves and smiled at the child.

'That is very kind, child. I thank you.'

The man looked at her with black, twinkling eyes and addressed her again. 'You look upset, goodwife. Your fall has obviously distressed you. If you are going in our direction you are welcome to walk with us.'

'Thank you. That would be good. I do feel a little dizzy after my er . . .fall.'

Gratefully Ann fell in with the women who, she noted, kept a respectful distance behind the slow-moving donkey. It was difficult to be sure of their ages or of their relationship with the man. They wore brightly coloured scarves around their heads and seemed to be loaded with blankets, pans and a large covered basket that two of them carried between them. The man on the donkey carried nothing. What a strange group they were, she mused, but how grateful she was to them for coming along just when they did.

She walked with them to the edge of the village where they turned off down the hill in the direction of Town Row. They didn't speak to her again, but the man doffed his hat to her in farewell. She smiled her thanks and headed gratefully for her cottage hoping that nobody would be home so that she could slip in and tidy herself with no questions asked.

16

It had taken Simon several weeks following the River Rother, to make his way to the coast, but he had been lucky and had found a couple of places where they had been willing to give him work for a few days.

At first, mindful of the law about vagrants Simon had been scared about being seen by anyone as he headed across country. He remembered once seeing a man whipped for coming to the village to beg and so he steered clear of groups of houses. Eventually though, after two days when he'd had no luck with either fishing, or trapping rabbits, he had knocked at the door of an isolated, run-down looking house and been fortunate that the woman was willing to feed him in return for work in the fields. Her husband was sick and not able to maintain their few acres, but he was a surly fellow who obviously resented Simon and the boy was glad to move on after a few days. The second place was an inn where he had earned hot meals and a place to sleep by helping in the stables at the back. He'd been there a couple of nights, glad of a rest from his journey, but then trade slackened and there were no horses stabled, so the inn keeper had sent him on his way.

On some days it seemed that he was hardly making any progress on his way. The river twisted and turned almost back on itself again and again, but having determined to follow it, he felt somehow bereft if he strayed more than a few yards from its banks and its low murmuring voice. He was worried about becoming totally lost and wandering aimlessly in fear of the law and was set firmly on reaching the sea.

Eventually he had arrived at Etchingham where the river seemed to straighten and gradually become wider. Small boats began to appear and by the time he reached Bodiam there were proper barges plying up and down loaded with iron goods.

He stopped to watch a wooden hoist loading goods onto a barge. Was this a ship such as his uncle had told him of? He was so intent on working out exactly what was happening with the ropes and pulleys, that he didn't see the approach of the thickset man with a face like well-tanned brown leather, who appeared in front of him as if from nowhere. His first instinct was to run, but the man stretched out a hand to him and smiled. For such a big man he had a gentle voice with an accent that Simon didn't recognise. 'You want a job, no? You like to work for me?'

Simon was wary. Was the man just trying to find out if he was unemployed and therefore a vagrant, or was it a genuine offer? He squared his shoulders and looked the man boldly in the eye. 'Me'be. Me'be not. What you offering?'

'One of my men is sick and I need 'elp on this barge running down to Rye. You have experience on boats?'

'Er..., not a lot, but I learns quick.'

'I'm sure you do. What is your name?'

'Simon. When would... err... would I start now?'

'Jacques. My name is Jacques.' The man took his hand. 'We shake 'ands, no? If you're willing you could start tonight.' Simon looked puzzled. 'We always load the special cargo at night,' the man explained. 'Be here at dusk Seemon and we'll see how you do.'

The day had passed slowly and he had felt a bubble of excitement in his chest as evening approached. He couldn't believe his luck; he had a job on a boat already, and he hadn't even reached the sea yet. Why the barge was being loaded so late he had no idea, but then he knew nothing about boats or the ways of boatmen, so he made sure that he was waiting near to the river long before the last rays of the sun had faded, leaving the water like a silver ribbon gleaming through a light, evening mist.

Just as it was beginning to be difficult to make out shapes in the gathering gloom and Simon was beginning to think that he had been made a fool of, a cart pulled up beside the barge. Four men jumped down and straightaway, the sacks were unloaded. He could tell immediately what was in them – wool.

They had the warm, earthy, animal smell that he recognised from the fleeces that his mother had carded and spun. She had been well recognised in the village as an excellent spinner and when he was little he had sometimes helped her wind the wool into long hanks ready to be washed and woven. But now he was even more puzzled. Why was wool being loaded onto a barge that earlier seemed to be carrying iron goods?

To Simon's relief, Jacques was as good as his word and Simon was introduced to the three men as the youngest member of the barge crew. He was nervous as the boat rocked beneath him, but he tried not to show it and barely registered that the men were all talking in whispers.

'In there Seemon. Take the sacks and push them in there.' Jacques indicated an area that was, in the dim light, just a black hole. 'Push them well down. It goes back a way, so you will have to crawl through with the first ones, but you are just the right size no?'

Obediently, Simon grabbed a sack and pushing it in front of him, climbed into the opening. It was very dark inside, but the sack was not too heavy and he kept crawling forward until he could go no further. He backed out.

'Good boy. And the next one, quickly now.'

As he crawled forwards and then backed out of the confined space, packing in more and more sacks, he realised that he was, in fact, in a kind of tunnel that ran the length of one side of the barge. It seemed to him an odd way of carrying them and very awkward. He didn't remember seeing the hole in daylight when he had watched the iron goods loaded via the hoist. That was a much more sensible way of doing things, he thought, than all this crawling about in the dark.

Finally all the sacks were loaded and straightway the barge cast off and started its journey silently along the river. There was no moon, but still the river gleamed in the dark. Occasionally a disturbed water bird called, but other than that there was no sound other than the gentle splash of the water.

Twice a week the barge made the trip from Bodiam to Rye and back again, ostensibly carrying iron goods, but actually loaded with a good quantity of wool which was sent across the channel where English wool was highly prized. Simon had no idea about trade restrictions; no idea he was breaking the law; knew nothing about imports and exports and taxes and customs. All he knew was that for four weeks, as summer turned into autumn, he was one of the crew – albeit the smallest and youngest – he had food in his belly and was happy.

17

William pulled his cloak closer against the bitter wind which tossed the bare branches of the trees and flattened the grass. He looked apprehensively at the grey, leaden sky and wondered, not for the first time, if he had been wise to set out on such a morning. However, today, 3rd of November, was the fourth anniversary of Harry's birth and he had promised himself that he would visit with a small gift for the child. If truth be told, he longed to see his son and had found it hard to stay away for so long.

He had not visited either Katherine or Harry for many weeks, sticking resolutely to his decision to give himself completely to the Church in the service of God. This had, in some ways, been made easier for him as he became aware of the persecution of heretics across the country and he was always mindful of the danger that his visits brought with them. He was assured that his kinsman, Thomas Heasman, on whose land his wife's cottage stood, would not betray them - Thomas had no love for Tudor Mary – but these days who could know what men would do for advancement or simply to save their own skin?

His horse tossed its head and pranced as a small branch broke from a tree and tumbled across the track in front of them. At the same time a few small snowflakes whirled down, speckling his dark cloak like blossom in May.

'Easy girl, easy now.' William tightened the rein and patted the horse's neck. 'Not far now,' he said thankfully, as the cottage came in sight.

Katherine was looking out for him, a hot drink ready on the fire, while Harry was like a jack-in-the-box, leaping with excitement and pulling at his cloak as soon as he stepped in the door. Laughing, he swept his young son into the air making the child whoop with delight.

'Hush, Harry; do not be so loud.' Katherine smiled even as she admonished the boy. She caught William's arm and hugged it to her. 'Oh, husband, it is so good to see you. It has been so long.'

William was overcome with guilt as he looked down at her pale face, so trusting and loving and wondered, yet again, what he thought he was doing living this dual life. Setting the child on the floor he drew her to him, but then at the last moment kissed her chastely on the cheek. She looked at him strangely, but then was reassured by his warmer words as he said 'I cannot tell you how I have longed to see you again, but I am fearful—'

'I know—' she interrupted, stilling his words with her finger, '—but you are here now and we have this day for ourselves.'

William looked round. 'George is not here?'

Katherine looked up at him beneath her lashes and she smiled. 'The Lord was on our side and Ann bid him home for a few days. She has seen little enough of him since we came to this remote place and besides, his grandmother was visiting from Tunbridge and would want to see her grandson. So' —she took his hand and led him to the fire— 'we can be together and merry, just the three of us. Come Harry, help me set the meal on the table. Your father will be hungry after his ride.'

'I swear the child has grown, Katherine. And you? You are well? You look lovely,' he said, unable to stop himself from tenderly touching her cheek.

She flushed with pleasure. 'We are both fine are we not, Harry?'

'Yes Mother. I'm nearly as tall as George now, Father - well almost,' the child added as he caught his mother's eye.

'You are indeed grown exceeding tall, Harry, but then four is a very great age is it not Katherine?'

'Oh, certainly it is,' laughed Katherine.

'And I can read now too Father.' He caught his mother's eye. 'Not as well as George 'cos he's older than me, but I know some words. I do, don't I Mother?'

William raised his eyebrows. 'Really, Harry? Is that right? Are you sure my boy?'

'Yes really Father, I know my A,B,C and everything don't I Mother?'

'Indeed you do Harry and later you shall show your Father how well you are doing with your studies.'

'He is young to be reading is he not?'

'Yes, but he is a bright child and willing and it keeps both boys occupied when they needs must be indoors. George is a very able pupil and anything George does, Harry wants to do too.'

'I would not have thought of George as a scholar,' said William as he reached for a piece of bread and bit into it hungrily.

'Oh, but he is very clever. I know he is a strange lad, but for all his odd ways he does not lack intelligence. In fact I have been amazed at how quickly he has learned. It seems he only has to see a word once and he remembers it. When I think of how long it took me to be fluent . . .' she broke off and smiled ruefully.

'And what do you read?'

'The Bible, William; we have nothing else, and what more could we need but the word of God?'

William nodded, but again felt unease at the thought of what would happen if it were known that his wife and child were reading a book now banned by the new church. 'But is that wise? What if George—'

'George will say nothing - you know he barely speaks to strangers. Do not fret so husband. Come, enough of our simple life, tell us news of the village. What has been happening? Since we moved here, I so long for gossip sometimes. Who has had babies and who has married? Who is walking out with whom and who has fallen out with their neighbour?'

'Gossip woman?' William laughed in mock horror. 'I'm not sure a priest should indulge in gossip, but I will see what I can tell you.'

The day passed merrily, young Harry playing happily with his new peg top that William had brought as a birthday gift, while Katherine and William talked and laughed, both delighting in each other's company after weeks of being apart. They had always had that most precious of things as a married couple – friendship. Yes there had been passion and love in abundance too, but above all they were good friends, who could spend hours in each other's company without weariness.

With the shutters closed against the wind neither noticed that it had been snowing steadily since shortly after William's arrival. When, at about three o'clock he was making ready to leave so as to be home before darkness fell, he was taken aback to see that the cottage was an island in a sea of white. Snow lay in drifts across the fields and large flakes were still whirling out of a grey sky making it impossible to see for more than a few feet.

Katherine caught at his sleeve. 'You cannot venture out in this William. The snow is far too deep and getting worse.'

William frowned and looked worried. 'But I'm not—'

'No, William, it would be madness to travel while it is still snowing. You could get lost, or take a fall. You must stay. Likely coming so early in the year the snow will not last and you can leave tomorrow morning if you must. But for now you must stay, mustn't he Harry? You would like your father to stay wouldn't you?'

'Yes, do stay Father. Do stay.' Harry clasped William tightly around the legs making it difficult for him to move.

Patting the child's head William laughed. 'It doesn't seem that I have much choice in the matter with both the weather and you two conspiring against me. Come then, son, help me stoke up the fire; we have chilled the room letting in the wind.'

The evening was spent much as they had spent many evenings together in those happy days at the vicarage that Katherine now felt she had taken for granted. When Harry had finally gone to sleep, excited as he was by a whole day with his father, the couple had sat on either side of the fire for all the world like any normal husband and wife. Only as bedtime approached did the unnaturalness of their position manifest itself as they both felt an embarrassment and a reticence that had never before been part of their life together. Since putting her aside as 'wife' William had kept to his priestly vows and had not slept with Katherine on any of his visits. He looked doubtfully at George's mattress rolled in a corner, but William was over six foot tall and he did not relish the thought of a boy's mattress on the floor. However, after a day in each other's company did he really have the will power to resist the love he saw in his wife's eyes? He said a prayer for strength of mind and spoke gently to her as he followed her into the bedroom.

'Katherine . . .I cannot . . . you understand that it is not that I do not still love you but . . .' He turned away as she loosed her skirt and tried not to look at her as, wearing her linen shift she climbed into bed.

'Hush, my love. I understand and make no demands on you, but hold me William. Do not deny me that comfort. Just put your arms around me and hold me so that I don't feel so alone.' She held out her hand to him and pulled him down onto the bed, winding her arms around him and pulling him close. He smelled the faint, familiar smell of rosemary on her hair as he lay stiff and wooden by her side willing all thoughts of her lovely body from his mind. Gradually her breathing deepened as she relaxed in the warmth and security of his arms, but it was a long time before William slept.

What disturbed them they didn't know. Perhaps Harry cried out in his sleep, or a shutter banged, but in the darkest part of the night, both became aware of the other. In their sleep they had stayed wrapped in each other's arms and as she stirred, William felt her breath on his cheek. He moved his head slightly so that their mouths were almost touching, each breathing the other's breath and then, gently, oh so gently, like a horse muzzling its foal, their lips brushed each other's. As she breathed the scent of him Katherine felt her senses stir. Still half asleep she moved against him and in answer felt his arms tighten around her.

William, his head swimming, tried to resist, but somehow his body would not obey his brain. Unbidden and almost in slow motion, he felt his hands sliding under her shift feeling the warm, heavy weight of her breasts, the answering tightening of her nipples. She arched against him and he knew that he was lost. In that moment, God and his Church seemed very far away and all that William was aware of was the pounding of his pulse and the warm, willing flesh of the woman he loved.

Katherine awoke slowly as if swimming up from a deep pool. Memories of the night sent shafts through the water like golden sunlight. William was here and he still loved her. She stretched out her hand in the grey light of dawn, but instead of finding the firm warmth of her sleeping husband, her fingers found the coldness of an empty bed. He was no longer beside her. Rising silently with a glance at the sleeping child, she limped to the door.

She found William kneeling by the chest in the living room, the small silver cross he always wore laid out on the dark wood as if on an altar. She paused in the doorway watching him. His eyes were tightly closed, but tears slid slowly beneath the dark fan of his eyelashes and his lips moved in prayer. His face was anguished and he rocked slightly as he fervently prayed. As a mother wants to comfort a child in distress she started forward and reached out a hand to his shoulder. As if he'd been stung by a wasp William started up and whirled away from her.

'No! Do not touch me. Can you not see what I have done? I have broken my vows to God and the Church and I am unclean.' He jerked unsteadily to his feet and started to gather his things together – his bag, his hat, his cloak. 'I must go. I have been tested and found wanting and I must try to make amends for my sin.'

'Please William—'

'No, do not try to stop me. Do you not remember the words of St Paul? I do not blame you for what I did, but I cannot stay here. I love you and I am not equal to the task of resisting temptation. For that I need God's help and at the moment I'm not worthy . . .' his voice broke in a sob.

'But when will I see you again? Harry will—'

'I do not know Katherine. Can you not see, I just don't know? I must pray for forgiveness. I do not know what else I can do, but I know that I cannot stay here. I cannot be with you and not love you and, God help me, I do not know if I have the strength to not be with you. I thought I could. I thought I could be strong, but every night I see your face, hear your voice – want to hold you and touch you. It cannot be, Katherine. Oh God what am I to do?'

Still talking to himself like a man possessed he flung open the door and stepped out into a white world glistening and glinting like a sea of diamonds as sunlight streamed from a cloudless blue sky.

She grabbed for her stick and, her feet still bare, she hurried after him into the snow, but he did not look at her as he quickly flung his saddle onto the horse and rode away. She stood like a statue as the fast melting snow made puddles around her red and frozen feet. The black outline of horse and rider grew smaller and smaller in the distance, but she was aware of no discomfort. All she could feel was an ache in her chest that seemed to build and build until she thought she would choke. He was gone. She was alone again. The world seemed to spin as the feelings she had had as a child when her parents died came flooding back to her. She was alone and nobody loved her. He had gone and she was not sure that he would return.

18

Ann tied her shawl more tightly around her shoulders as the wind tugged and threatened to whirl it away into the brook. Her hands were numb with cold and her fingers were clumsy. She would be glad to be back home by the fire, but she still had a way to go. The path wound under tall trees edging the bottom meadow that sloped away from the village and she looked up apprehensively, fearful of falling branches, as the gale roared through the treetops. Already the ground was littered with twigs and, as she made her way towards the houses crouched on the top of the hill, the piles of scattered leaves rose up and danced around her like crazed, brown sprites.

She would not have chosen to go out on such a day and had planned to give the house a thorough clean before the coming Yuletide, but Bridget Taylor had sent word that her labour had started and Ann had felt bound to attend her - especially after the problems the poor woman had last time. Today, however, all had gone smoothly and the baby had arrived with a speed that took both Ann and the young mother by surprise.

As she walked towards home she found herself humming snatches of The Boars Head Carol - a favourite of George's - in time with her steps until the hill became too steep and she needed to save her breath. She wondered again if her son would come home for the twelve days; she hoped that he would, for it would be good to see him, but she also realised that, without his help, Katherine would have a difficult time. Unconsciously she grimaced as she thought of Katherine all alone except for the two boys. It wouldn't be much of a celebration for her, poor woman – nobody to even share a wassail cup.

A few drops of rain spattered around her as, head down against the wind, Ann crossed the bridge over the brook and hurried up the hill as fast as she could. Reaching the road through the village she could see a little group of figures coming towards her. She peered through the gathering gloom and saw that it was Mary, Nell's eldest, with the rest of the children in tow. As they came closer, Ann saw how pale and tired Mary looked. She carried a large bundle of firewood tied onto her back, causing her to stoop like an old woman and was leading the youngest by the hand; she was dragging her feet and snivelling miserably. The other children trailed behind, each carrying a few sticks, their clothes dirty and ragged, offering little protection from the weather. Mary didn't look up as she passed and Ann was reluctant to stop and speak for fear of Catt. Looking down at the straggle of children she was struck by how like Nell one of the little girls looked, but the child had clearly not inherited her mother's kindly nature, for she stuck out her tongue.

Ann walked on deep in thought. Once, she turned and looked back at the little group, now nearly out of sight, and sighed. She would willingly have helped Mary, who must be having a wretched time, caught as she was between her vicious grandmother and no-good father, but the family had obviously been told that they were to have nothing to do with her and Ann was still very fearful of James Catt and his accusations. For Nell's sake, however, she felt she had to do something.

She paused in the middle of the road and was so engrossed in her own thoughts that she was unaware of the hoof beats behind and was startled by the curses of a man on a large dappled horse, who struggled to rein the animal to one side to avoid running her down. She stood for a moment more as the man cantered along the road, her mouth twisted as she chewed the inside of her cheek and then, making up her mind, turned off the main high street down a short path that led to a row of dilapidated cottages, one of which belonged to Tom Wyatt and his wife Maud. The shutters were firmly closed, but that was only to be expected on such a day. She knocked firmly at the door, wincing as her cold fingers struck the wood and it was promptly opened by Maud. Little Elizabeth was dancing around her mother's skirts and, when she saw it was Ann, she ran forward and caught hold of her hand drawing her into the cottage.

'It's Goodwife Ashdown, Mother.'

'So I see, Elizabeth. Hello, Ann, it's good to see you. Come in, do. You must be near blown away.'

Ann entered and Maud struggled to close the door as the wind gusted into the room, extinguishing two of the rush lights that were set on the table. Tutting with dismay, Maud busied herself relighting them, while bidding Ann to sit and make herself comfortable. Thankfully Ann sank down onto a stool by the fire and held out her frozen fingers to the blaze, blinking as the smoke stung her eyes.

'I'm sorry to burst in on you like this, Maud, but I was on my way back from Bridget's – she's had a boy, by the way – and I saw—'

'And is she well?'

'Yes, she's fine, praise be, but—'

'And your family? All well?'

'Yes, thank—'

'And what about George? It's been such a while since we saw him. I was only saying to Tom, he must be getting quite grown up now; they grow so fast don't they?' Maud fondly patted Elizabeth on the head. 'He's working away is he now that Goodwife Collyer's gone? That was an odd to-do and no mistake. Can't think what went on there - her and the child just going away like that—'

'Yes, but—'

'So where is he now?'

'Err . . .' Ever since Katherine had moved to the cottage Ann had been fielding this question from interested neighbours, but it didn't make her any more comfortable with the vague answers that she was obliged to give. She couldn't tell the whole truth as it would compromise Katherine's position, but nor did she wish to tell an outright lie. '. . . oh not far. Just outside Buxted.' she said evasively. 'A good mistress who keeps him busy. He's happy and that's the main thing. But what I came to talk to you about was Nell's children.'

'Oh dear, I know what you're going to say, and it breaks my heart to see them. Our Nell must be turning in her grave. She was poor, but the children were always kept clean and their clothes mended. Poor Mary . . ."
She broke off and shook her head sadly.

'Yes, I've just seen them out collecting firewood, for all the good it'll do them. It'll be so damp this weather that they'll never get a blaze going, but I don't suppose Catt's done anything about providing dry logs for the winter,'

Maud shook her head in disgust. 'That man's a complete wastrel. If only she'd refused to marry him, but her father insisted, you know; threatened to turn her out if she didn't do as she was told. She was my second cousin and we grew up together, so I'd help if I could, but this year's not been easy. All this wet and—'

'No, no, I understand. I didn't mean... I wasn't saying . . .' Ann felt embarrassed as she realised that her words could be taken as criticism. 'What I wondered is – with Christmas coming - well, they won't take anything from me, but if I have a bit to spare and brought it to you, could you pass it on as a gift. Say it was from you? Mary would take that kindly I'm sure as you're family.'

'Of course! If you're sure . . .'

'Oh, I'm sure we'll have something for them. I thank God that we're very lucky compared to some. Unlike farm work, the smithy's always busy and I've a bit of pickled pork I've been saving. I'll perhaps make brawn ready for Yuletide and I always make too much, so I'll bring some over if that's alright.' Ann inwardly laughed at the thought that she could ever make too much for her large, hungry menfolk, but was self-conscious about her role as the bringer of plenty.

Maud put her hand on Ann's arm. 'You're a good woman, my dear. Especially after all that man put you through last summer. He's one to hold a grudge too, unfortunately - always has been - but I trust there's been no more trouble from him?'

Not willing to reveal her lingering fear of Catt, his dark looks and muttered threats and curses when he passed her in the street, Ann shook her head and spoke up more bravely than she felt. 'He's an ignorant fool, but that doesn't mean his children should suffer and Nell was my friend.'

Both women were quiet for a while, each contemplating the sadness of Nell's death until Elizabeth, puzzled by the silence, tugged at Ann's sleeve and held up a rather squashed rag doll for her to admire.

Ann smiled kindly at the child. 'Does your doll have a name?' she asked. Elizabeth shook her head and Ann put her arm around the little girl and gave her a hug. 'Well, you look after her, but I really must be going now, or it will be too dark to see.' She went to the door and turned back to Maud. 'Thank you. Between us I'm sure we can help those poor children and perhaps make Christmas a little happier for them. I'll call in with something for them before the end of the week.' And with a wave at Elizabeth, Ann stepped out into the December chill once more.

19

Christmas was long past by the time Ann visited Katherine's cottage. She had been sad that George had opted to stay with Katherine for the Yuletide celebration and John and her three sons had not all been together as a family but, if George was ever to make his own way in the world, she knew that she had to respect his decisions, no matter how much they might make her own heart ache.

The weather had been foul ever since the early snow of November. For weeks the ground had been flooded and sodden, as it had alternately snowed and rained. People travelled as little as possible as the roads were thick with mud, so the forge had not been busy with passing trade. Instead, John had used the time to make things that he could sell to the villagers, metal hooks for hanging meat up to smoke, tools such as hammers and chisels, as well as hoes and rakes for use in the cottager's gardens. Nick was learning more every day and Ann was happy that he was proving an able assistant to his father.

For Dickon, the weather was a frustration. It was impossible to dig the iron ore from the sodden ground and his carting work was severely curtailed. He had struggled along the roads with the heavy oxcarts loaded with iron and often he wouldn't be home for days as the carts became bogged down and the men were forced to off load the pig iron, dig out the carts and reload. Eventually they had given up, as the roads became totally impassable. He had, though, on one of his last trips, managed to call in and deliver his mother's Christmas gift to George – a new, warm woollen cap that she had woven herself. When he'd finally reached home – wet and cold - he had, at least, assured her that the boy was happy and content with Harry and making himself indispensable to Katherine. So, despite George's absence, Ann had made the best of things and Christmas time had passed pleasantly enough.

In the months since he had left home it was rare for George to visit his home. His brothers thought it strange that he should want to stay in a remote cottage with just a boy and a woman for company - and Nick in particular was not slow to voice his opinion - but Ann understood her youngest son. She knew that for him the best thing in life was continuity – the same thing happening at the same time in the same place day after day. It was change that upset George and people in general were changeable and unpredictable. Visiting, socialising and meeting strangers were situations that brought terror and unhappiness to her son, so she was content for him to bide where he was in the remoteness of the cottage. With Katherine and Harry his days followed a set pattern that to him was security and contentment. After all, she reasoned, all she wanted for all her children was their happiness and, although she knew she should not feel as she did, George would always have a special place in her heart. He would always be her baby, no matter how old he was and she would always feel a protectiveness towards him that with Nick and Dickon had faded as they became men.

Since he visited so rarely it had come as a shock to see George striding up the path early one morning just after John and Nick had gone across to the forge. She had propped open the shutter, as she was hot from the exertions of kneading the bread dough before taking it to the bakehouse for baking, when a movement outside had caught her eye. Dusting the flour from her hands onto her apron, she hurried to the door and smiled a welcome to her son.

'Well, hello Georgie. This is a lovely surprise! What brings you here? Come in out of the cold.' As she looked into his face, she realised with a jolt that he was now almost as tall as she was. There was an anxious frown between his eyes. 'Is all well, my son?'

George did not return her smile, but stood inside the doorway looking worried. She patiently waited while he gathered himself to speak. 'You have to come, Mother. You have to come to Goodwife Collyer's house now.'

'Georgie, what's up? What's happened? Is something wrong? Did Katherine – er, Goodwife Collyer, send you to me?'

'Yes. It's Harry, he's not well. He has a fever and he's not making any sense and Goodwife Collyer bids you come if you can, please.' The words came out in a rush and it was obvious that he had learned them off by heart and probably been reciting the message to himself throughout his long walk home.

'Oh no! Poor Harry.' Ann put her hand to her mouth in consternation. 'How long has he been ill?'

George thought for a moment, 'Two whole days, two nights and half of one morning,' he said, precise as always.

'Oh poor lamb! It sounds serious. Did Goodwife Collyer say he had a fever? How does he look?'

'She did. He just lies in his bed and shivers, but he looks hot. Mistress Collyer wants you to come Mother. She asked me to get you. I had to go the long way round as the river had flooded and I lost count of the steps. That was bad. It might mean that Harry will die. Will he die Mother?'

Ann shook her head. 'If God wills it, my son, but not if I can help it and most assuredly not because you didn't count the steps. Counting steps, or not counting them, can't hurt Harry, George. Now wait here while I go and tell your father what has happened and we'll set off directly.' She peered out of the shutter at the pale sun. 'At least it has stopped raining – for now at any rate. Have you eaten today?' George shook his head. 'Well there's an end of the loaf left and a bit of fish over there so help yourself while I speak to John. It'll be a long walk for both of us and we can't have you faint from lack of food.'

As she spoke Ann was busily gathering herbs from where they hung in small bunches from nails along one of the beams and packing them into her basket. She stopped to think for a moment and then took a small clay pot from the shelf and tucked that safely in between the herbs and covered it all with a cloth. 'There now, that's ready,' she said speaking more to herself than the boy. She looked ruefully at the bread which she had set to prove in front of the fire. 'I'll just put that in the other room where it's cold - it might last - but these things can't be helped and that poor woman, well I just can't leave her on her own. Right, I'll go and speak to your Father, George. Eat up now as I'll be right back.'

John was not happy about the idea of her setting off into the sodden landscape with just George to accompany her, but he couldn't spare Nick from his work at the forge and he knew that his wife was not one to refuse a call from someone in trouble – especially when a child was involved.

He put his arm around her. 'Take care, my love. I'll understand if you feel you must stay, but if you haven't returned by lunchtime tomorrow Nick or I will come and check that all is well. I hope you find the lad better. It must be a terrible worry to his mother – she's suffered enough already, poor woman.

She hugged John and patted Nick on a broadening shoulder. 'We'll be fine. Don't worry about us. It's not so very far and it has stopped raining at least.' She turned for the door. 'I'll be off then. Goodbye, my love. I'll be back as soon as I can, but nothing's going to happen to that child if I can help it.'

John smiled at her determination and watched as she hurried away from the forge back to the cottage where George was waiting in the doorway with her basket over one arm. 'Take my staff,' he called after her. 'It will keep you steady in the mud.'

She turned briefly and waved an acknowledgement of his words and

John nodded to himself as he saw her reach for the stout wooden staff that he kept propped by the door. He stood by the door of the forge watching as his wife gestured to George to move so that she could pull the door closed and then led the way at a brisk pace along the lane from their cottage.

At first the track wasn't too bad as the way led over the higher ground, but as they dipped down towards Treblers Wood they found the streams had overflowed and the ground was spongy and slippery. Ann blessed John for his forethought of the staff as she steadied herself and avoided sliding onto her bottom. The edge of her skirt was already sodden and stained, but that couldn't be helped and she struggled along behind George who was now ahead and setting a fine pace.

It was a good two hours later that the cottage came into view, perched on a slight rise just above the water meadows. At the moment they were living up to their name, the brown, limp grass poking up from sheets of water that sparkled in the watery sun that peeped intermittently from behind drifting, grey clouds.

As they approached she saw the shutters move and realised that Katherine had been looking out for her. How isolated she was here, with no near neighbours, but then that was probably a deliberate move on William's part. Here, she would not be the subject of gossip and he would be able to visit unseen by prying eyes. She returned Katherine's anxious wave from the now open door and not for the first time thanked God for her good steady John who had always been her tower of strength.

The younger woman looked pale and strained and she grasped Ann's hand gratefully as she pulled her into the house.

'Oh thank you so much for coming. I am at my wit's end.' Her voice broke and her eyes filled with tears. 'He looks so small, and I am so feared I will lose him.' She bit her lower lip before continuing in what was only a whisper. 'I couldn't bear it Ann, not if Harry was taken.'

Ann could see the dark shadows under Katherine's eyes. With the child ill, she'd probably had little sleep and, as a mother herself, she knew from experience how draining that could be.

'Sit down my dear and rest a little. I'm here now and promise I'll do all I can and with God's help he will be fine.'

'I'm not sure we can count on God's help.' Katherine's voice was thin and bitter. 'I don't think I understand God anymore. Jesus talks about a kind God, but William's God seems to want nothing but sacrifices. I don't know anymore. I just don't know.'

Ann gave her friend a worried look. 'Don't speak like that Katherine. You cannot mean that.' She reached for her basket and took out a small cloth bag containing leaves. 'Here George, take these and brew them for Goodwife Collyer while I go and see Harry.' She paused before going through the doorway into the bedroom. 'Make sure she drinks it now – it will calm her and give her strength.'

In his small bed the child lay listless and still. His grey-blue eyes huge in his pale little face, his fair curls tousled. Ann walked softly in and stood by the bed.

'Hello, little man. I've come to see how you are and to make you feel better.'

She went across to Harry and laid her hand on his forehead – it was fiery hot. 'Not feeling too well are you?'

She pulled back the covers and could feel the heat of the child coming up from the bed. 'I think we need to get you a bit cooler, young man.'

'No,' Harry pulled feebly at the covers. 'It's cold. Don't take them.' He turned his head away from her. 'I don't know you, I want my Mother.'

Ann stroked his cheek gently. 'Yes you do know me, Harry, it's Ann – George's Mother. I know you feel chilly at the moment, but you have a fever and you are actually very hot inside. Honestly, you will feel better if you are a bit cooler. I'll make you a drink too and that will help. Are you thirsty?'

The child nodded and this time didn't resist as she pulled the covers back from him. She went across to her basket and took out her willow bark and carefully tipped a small amount into her hand. Going to the door, she called to George to bring her some hot water in a mug. She stirred in the bark and added a good spoon of honey to help to disguise the taste.

'Now, Harry, I want you to be a big boy and drink this all up. It may taste a bit funny, but it will make you feel better.' She held the mug to his lips but the child pushed it away, nearly spilling it.

'No, I want George.'

Willing to indulge the sick child Ann made way for George and watched with a proud smile as her son carefully held the drink to Harry's lips and encouraged the child to drink.

She took the empty cup. 'Do you want George to stay with you for a bit while I go and speak to your Mother?'

Harry nodded and George sat on the edge of Katherine's bed.

Katherine gave a start when Ann went through to the other room and Ann suspected that she had dozed a little after drinking the camomile tea George had made for her.

'How is he? I must go to him.' She began to struggle to her feet, but the older woman put a restraining hand on her.

'Be still a while, Katherine. George is with him and I've given him something which should help with the fever. He's very hot and we need to cool him down a bit; then he will feel better.'

'But what's wrong with him? I've been so worried. Apart from that cough he had last spring he's always been such a healthy little boy and then at the beginning of the week he seemed very tired and listless and didn't want to eat. He kept rubbing his eyes and seemed to have a cough again so I thought it was just a winter ague, but then he got hotter and hotter and started to talk such nonsense. I'm sorry. I didn't want to take you away from John and make you come all this way, but I didn't know what to do. I didn't know if I should get William but . . .' She bit her lip, a deep frown furrowing her brow.

Ann nodded reassuringly although she too was worried about the boy. A high fever was not uncommon in small children, but could point to all sorts of illnesses, many of which were fatal. So many young children died before reaching their fifth birthday that Ann had no illusions as to how serious Harry's illness could be. However, she didn't see the point in alarming Katherine further, so tried to be as reassuring as possible.

'Well, at the moment I don't know exactly what is wrong with Harry, but the important thing is to try to keep the fever down. Tell me – I know you are very isolated here, but has Harry been close and spoken to anyone recently?'

Katherine shook her head. 'We hardly see a soul from one week to the next. You see, William thought—'

'Yes, I understand. So no one has come to the house recently?'

Katherine hesitated, thinking. 'No, not for - oh it must be nigh on two weeks. Jane Happley comes once a month from the manor to collect the sewing that I have done for My Lady and to bring me anything else that needs doing. Jane's, well, she's very discreet and an old friend I knew when I was married to my first husband. Last time she came she brought her small grandson with her, a sweet child a little younger than Harry. It was so nice for him to see another child, but they weren't here above a half an hour.'

Ann nodded, twisting her mouth and chewing the inside of her cheek as she often did when deep in thought. 'I don't know how it happens, but sometimes illness seems to pass from one person to another and you and George – praise be – seem well, so I just wondered if . . .'

She paused as George came to the door. 'Harry's asleep now, Mother. I'm going to feed the chickens. I didn't stop this morning.'

'Thank you George, yes, you do what you have to. We will listen out for Harry.'

Ann looked around the cottage and noted the logs neatly stacked ready for burning, the covered pail full of water and the well swept floor – all due to George, she thought. Yes, it had been difficult to let him go, but she was sure that he was gaining an independence that would help him in years to come.

Katherine saw her looking and smiled – the first smile since Ann had entered the cottage. 'George is a good boy, Ann. He has been such a comfort to me since we came here. I would not be able to manage on my own without him - he does all the heavy chores and has managed the garden and the chickens and Harry loves him. He doesn't chatter—'

Ann laughed indulgently. 'No Georgie's always been a lad of few words.'

'But that doesn't mean he doesn't think, Ann. The boy has an amazing understanding. He has learned to read far more easily than I would have thought possible, and he takes such pleasure in it.'

It was Ann's turn to smile with a Mother's pride. 'I'm glad, Katherine, for things have not been easy for you I know.' She hesitated, not wishing to appear to gossip, but concerned for the woman who sat so quietly resigned opposite her. 'Do you . . . do you see much of William? You were reluctant to send for him now with Harry ill?'

Katherine cast her eyes down and fiddled with her wedding ring. 'No,' she said softly. 'I've not seen him since the snow in early November. He came then for Harry's birthday but—'

Ann put her hand on Katherine's knee. 'Oh, Katherine it must be so hard for you. I don't know how I would cope without my John.'

Katherine nodded, looking up – her eyes brimming with tears. 'Sometimes I think . . . I know I shouldn't say it, but sometimes I think it would be better if I were dead. Then there wouldn't be this torment. I love him, Ann, but we cannot be together and sometimes I don't think I can bear it any longer. And it is terrible for him too – I'm sure it is. How did all this happen? How is it that we can have a marriage that isn't a marriage?'

Ann shook her head and for a while the two women sat in silence, neither knowing what to say. It was Katherine who finally spoke

'I don't think he . . .'

She broke off as a cry came from the other room. Rising swiftly to her feet Ann went in to see young Harry. Katherine followed more slowly behind.

The child was flushed still, but his face was damp and his curls darkened with sweat. Holding the bed for support, Katherine hastened to his side.

'Oh Harry, my love, don't fret, Mother's here. Did you wonder where we were? I was just talking to George's Mother.' She smoothed the child's hair back from his face then looked up at Ann in alarm. 'Look,' she mouthed silently. She gestured to the boy's head. As he rolled his head restlessly on the sheet, brownish red spots were clearly visible on his neck. Gently Ann turned his head, first one way then the other, smiling down at him to reassure him as she did so. She looked behind his ears and nodded.

'I've seen this before,' she said quietly. 'My three boys had spots like these and I know it can be serious. Nick was very poorly for a while and I did fear for him.' She put her hand on Katherine's and smiled reassuringly as the younger woman uttered a low moan, 'But then my sons recovered from it with no problems and there's nothing to say Harry won't either. As

I recall Nick said his eyes hurt and could not bide the shutters open, and George had it but mildly – he was a toddler - barely walking - but none took serious harm.'

Katherine looked relieved and sitting on the small bed took both Harry's hands in hers. 'Poor baby, I do so want you to be well.'

'Well it is a good sign that the fever has abated. I will stay here tonight and make sure all is as well as it can be before I return home.'

'Oh it is good of you, Ann. Will John mind? If I wasn't so worried about Harry, I can tell you I would really appreciate the company of another woman. It gets so lonely here sometimes. I do miss village life, for even with my leg so bad, I did see people and hear what was going on when we lived at the vicarage.'

Ann smiled at her and patted her hand. 'Well, we'll have to make sure we catch you up with all the gossip this evening when we've made sure this young man is as comfortable as can be. As I remember he'll feel poorly for a few more days yet and the rash will possibly spread, but if we can keep his fever down I'd say he has every chance of getting well again.'

'It won't mark him, Ann? Not leave him scarred?'

'It's not like the pox, no. I'll go and make him a honey drink to keep his strength up. Nothing like honey to buck you up if you're not eating, I always say.'

The evening was spent pleasantly enough, and despite her worries about her little son, Katherine seemed much more cheerful as she watched with quiet pride as George read from the Bible and then Ann entertained them with tales of the day-to-day goings-on in the village. After another dose of willow bark Harry slept most of the time in relative comfort and Ann was pleased to see that his fever did not seem so bad as when she had first seen him that morning. She hoped that she would feel able to leave the cottage and be home before John or Nick felt anxious and set out to look out for her.

Next morning dawned bright and sunny with a brisk wind that set the shutters rattling. At first Ann thought it was the wind that had woken her and she lay for a moment or two thinking she was in her own house. Then she heard it again – the hoarse, retching sound of someone being sick. Like a door being thrown open, the realisation of where she was streamed into her mind. Her first thought was that Harry had taken a turn for the worse. She threw back the cover of the bed and, rising on her elbow, looked across to where the child lay in his small bed. He was fast asleep; his face now blotched with spots and the cover thrown off where he had tossed in the night. Puzzled, Ann looked back to the other side of the bed she had shared with Katherine and realised that her friend was not there. The sound came again and Ann rose softly so as not to wake the sleeping child and padded barefoot into the other room. Katherine was bent over a pail, wiping her mouth on a cloth and she looked up apologetically as Ann appeared.

'I'm sorry, did I wake you? I think I've eaten something that disagreed with me again.'

Ann looked at her with narrowed eyes. 'Again?'

Katherine nodded. 'I don't know why, but some foods just don't seem to sit well with me at the moment. I used not to be troubled with sickness, but lately . . .' She tailed off. 'I wondered if I had the same thing as Harry, but I don't feel hot or ill – just so tired. I sometimes feel as if I could sleep for a week.' She smiled wanly.

Ann unlatched the shutter and let in a blast of cold air to clear the sour smell of vomit. Outside she could see George scattering grain for the hens as they emerged reluctantly from the warmth of the hen house into the chill of a January morning. The bare branches of the trees at the edge of the wood were tossing in the wind and the surface of the water in the meadows was ruffled and restless, darkening then glinting as white fluffy clouds scudded briskly across a pale blue sky. She stood for a moment watching her son and at the same time thinking before she turned back to Katherine.

'Katherine, I hope you don't mind me asking, but . . . well, I wondered . . . with what you've said about being tired and feeling sick. You don't think you could be with child? I mean, I don't want to pry, but—'

Ann laughed quietly. 'Oh no, Ann, that couldn't be. I mean I haven't seen William since November and . . . well—'

'No, of course, I'm sorry,' Embarrassed, Ann turned her back and looked out of the window again. 'It's none of my business. I shouldn't have asked.'

'No, no, it's alright. I mean we did . . .' Katherine flushed a deep red. 'Well we did . . . but only the once and . . .'

Ann turned and looked directly at Katherine. 'But once is enough isn't it?' she said quietly.

Katherine shook her head. 'Maybe for some, but not me. We'd been wed for several months before I quickened with Harry, so I don't think just—'

'Once is all it takes, my dear. Take it from me. I have seen many a young girl wish it were not so, but there it is. Have you - forgive me - but have you had your courses recently?'

Katherine frowned. 'I'm not sure. I've never been very regular but, well, I suppose, well . . . no. I thought perhaps it was because I was upset when William . . . Oh Ann, you don't really think I could be with child do you? I can't be. But what would I do?' Katherine had gone very pale and her eyes seemed huge. 'It cannot be. Not a baby. William would be so angry.'

'Angry?'

'Oh, Ann, you don't know. He was so angry with himself because we . .

.well, because we—'

'Did what is natural for a husband and wife?' Ann finished for her. 'I can't see what there is to be angry about and I'm sure you're wrong about him being angry if you are having his child. As far as I know he's always been a devoted father to Harry.'

'But things are not the same now. He broke his vows by . . . you know . . . and he was so upset. It was awful to see his anguish.'

'His anguish! What about you?' Ann was like a ruffled hen. 'I'm sorry Katherine, I know William is a devout man, but you are his wife and as I see it he made vows to you too. I'm sure that when he knows—'

'Oh but he can't know. You mustn't tell him Ann. He mustn't know.'

'But, my dear, he has to know. You cannot stay here on your own the way you are and bear his child without him knowing. Anyway, he is bound to visit before long and how do you think he will feel if you haven't told him? I know it is hard, but if I am right and you are expecting a child he will have to know.'

Katherine sat twisting her hands in her lap in her anxiety. 'Promise me Ann, promise me that you won't say anything to William. After all, we may be wrong. I may just be unwell. Yes, I'm sure that's all it is.'

Ann looked troubled. 'Of course I won't say anything if you don't want me to, and true, it is early days yet, but when you are certain you must—'

'When I am certain, if needs be, I will tell him, yes.'

'Mother! Mother!' The cry came from the other room and both women hastened into see what the child wanted, all thoughts of husbands and babies pushed to one side for the moment.

The morning was spent in trying to make Harry more comfortable and nothing more was said about the possibility of a brother or sister for the child. He was still unwell, but today more restless and cross, which Ann took to be a good sign. In her experience it was when a child lay listless and weak that they were more likely to succumb to illness. She persuaded him to eat a few spoons of gruel flavoured with honey and was pleased when, mid-morning, he fell into a restful sleep. The rash was still obvious and would be for a while yet, she thought, but she was happy that the fever seemed to have subsided.

His early chores done, George had come quietly into the house and settled in a corner with a slate and chalk and was concentrating on scribing his letters. It was obvious that he was finding writing so much more difficult than reading, but was determined to master it. Ann gazed at her son, noting that his fingernails were still chewed to the quick. He hadn't grown out of the habit of biting his nails then. He was quite unaware of her gaze – as always in a world of his own. His top teeth were biting down on his bottom lip as he concentrated on his task and she saw the dismay and frustration flash across his face when he failed to form a letter correctly. She watched as Katherine limped over to him and bent to show him how to loop a letter correctly. Noting how Katherine was careful not to touch her son, she was pleased and perhaps just a little jealous to see the easy rapport between them. Despite his increasing size – she'd been surprised by how much he'd grown recently – but he was still her baby and she was as possessive as a cow with a calf.

The peaceful scene was interrupted by a brisk knock at the door which made them all jump. Ann rose to open it and found Nick, windblown and mud-spattered waiting at the entrance.

'Father said I should come and get you as the roads are so bad. There's not so much on at the forge today and he was worried you might take a fall on your own.'

Ann drew him in out of the cold and he nodded respectfully to Katherine and went across to George. 'Good day, little brother.' He peered down at George's writing and the younger boy instinctively put his arm over his slate. 'It's alright, I don't want to look at what you're doing. Haven't seen you in an age though.' He grinned provocatively. 'Is this what you get up to all day?'

Seeing a confrontation looming, Katherine spoke softly from the wooden settle by the fire. 'Good day, Nick. You are welcome. I'm glad that you are here to accompany Ann back home; it is indeed easy to take a tumble in conditions such as these.'

Remembering his manners, Nick enquired after Harry and then turned to his mother.

'Are you ready to set out now Mother? I can't be away too long.'

'Yes, yes, my son. It was kind of you to come and good of your father to spare you. I will be glad of your arm as the way is difficult in places. I'll just sort out a couple of things to leave with Goodwife Collyer and we can be on our way.' She picked up her basket and set it on the table so that she could look more easily through its contents. 'Now, let me see. Ah, yes.' She took out the small pot and handed it to Katherine. 'This is good if his spots become very itchy. Just smooth a little on and it will help to soothe them and this–' she took out a small bag of willow bark, '–this you should have in case his fever returns. Use it sparingly though.' She tipped some into the palm of her hand and held it out to show Katherine. 'No more than this much in some warm, boiled water, and no more than twice in a day. Oh and I'll leave you the rest of this honey as it will help keep his strength up until his appetite returns.'

She went to the door of the bedroom and peered round it, then withdrew quietly. 'He's still sleeping, so I won't disturb him as rest is what he needs. Say farewell to him for me. Remember now, if you are at all concerned or he just doesn't seem to be making good progress send George to fetch me and I'll come straight away.'

'Thank you Ann, it's very good of you.' Katherine rose awkwardly to her feet and went to the door with them. 'Be careful on the way home.' She looked up at the sky. 'At least it's a bright day, so you won't get wet. Perhaps we've done with all that rain and the weather is finally turning,' she added.

Ann turned to George who was still busy with his writing. 'I'm going now, my son. Take care of yourself and be of help to Goodwife Collyer.'

George looked up and nodded acknowledgement of her words, but straightway carried on with his writing. Ann gave a despairing shake of her head, then smiled at Katherine and laid a hand on each of her shoulders. Looking into the younger woman's eyes she said softly, 'And you take good care of yourself Katherine. Lots of rest and nourishing food, remember. I will return before long to make sure all is well with you.'

Nick was already walking down the path, her basket over one arm so, with a final wave, Ann took up her staff and followed him out of the gate.

20

Simon dangled his legs over the edge of the quay and watched as a group of seagulls wheeled and dived into the river below him. No matter if they were English or French, he liked seagulls. They were handsome birds, but they also knew how to look after themselves and he admired that. They were cheeky and brave and would dash in and whip a crust from under your nose if you didn't look out. He listened to their harsh cry of 'Out, out, out, out.' At least that's what he always thought they were saying in English. He wondered idly if these French birds spoke a different language as did the local fishermen here. He couldn't make head nor tail of their strange speech which sounded as if they were constantly clearing their throats. Suddenly he laughed out loud and punched the air with his fist, as two large birds with fearsome yellow beaks both dived at the same time for a fish head floating on the surface and only at the last minute, avoided a collision.

He jumped as a familiar voice roared at him. 'Oi, you. Stop idling and get yourself aboard if you don't want to be left with the Frenchies. Come on, jump to it.'

Guiltily Simon leapt to his feet. The gang plank to the small cargo boat was still down and there were one or two men hurrying aboard. Simon ran nimbly across and jumped down onto the deck. He had grown since he had left home and with hard work and more regular meals his muscles had developed and his arms and legs were less sticklike, while his face and arms were brown and weathered which gave him a healthy look he'd never had before. He ducked under the spars and went to take up his position by the aft rope. He felt the boat sway under him and unconsciously parted his legs and flexed his knees to keep his balance as the bow rope was loosed and the boat started to swing into the channel.

'Stand by aft. Cast off aft.'

He jumped into action and as soon as the rope was released from the bollard on shore he coiled it neatly round like a snake under a woodpile, so that it wouldn't tangle or trip anyone and would be ready when they docked in England. He watched the raucous seagulls now circling overhead as the sails were hoisted and the boat moved slowly away from the quayside.

He'd worked for Jacques on the barge for just over a month, then the regular crew member had returned and he'd found himself without work, but by then he had experience and a good word from Jacques to recommend him and it wasn't long before he was taken on by a cargo boat that plied out of Rye backwards and forwards across the English Channel.

Provided it made money, the Master wasn't fussy what he carried. Sometimes it was wool, smuggled across to the Low Countries, thus avoiding the restrictions on imports to France, but usually it was more regular, legal goods that were swung aboard and run across to small ports along the French coast. Wherever they went, Simon enjoyed the voyage and revelled in the feel of the wind on his face and the taste of the salt spray.

Five months before, Simon had been amazed by his first sight of the sea and had stood awed and wondering as, like a great, grey animal, it pitched and sighed, never still as it whispered its secrets on the shore, clawing at the beach with curled white paws as if trying to heave itself on land. He felt as if he had come home; as if this is where he was meant to be. Unlike some of the regular crew he had never been sea sick and, despite the fact that, like many sailors he was unable to swim, he was fearless and revelled in the excitement as the little ship rolled and bucked, tossed this way and that by the wind.

Even after several months working on the boat and a good number of trips across the Channel, he was still enchanted by the novel idea that he was floating on water. Having spent all his childhood inland, ships and the sea were a whole new world of wonder for Simon. There was so much to see, so much to learn and, because of the changes in the weather, no two days were alike. Sometimes a school of dolphins would follow the boat, diving under the keel, then leaping up and making him laugh as they grinned up at him. Sometimes strange birds could be seen skimming the water, their harsh cries, like drowned ghosts, making his hair stand on end.

The work was hard, and he was often cold and wet, but that was no different from working at home picking stones from the fields and scaring crows. Here on the boat, though, the men were, by and large, a cheery lot and, provided he did as he was told, he wasn't badly treated. He had a place to sleep, curled up under a pile of sacks in the stern and simple, but regular meals. Yes, he thought, as he watched the French coast disappearing into the early morning fog, life was certainly better for him now than it had been at home with his father. Sometimes he missed his brothers and sisters – and he always felt a jolt in his stomach when he thought about his mother – but he was making a life for himself and he was sure that she would be pleased about that.

As the ship passed the headland, the seagulls peeled away and headed back to the line of fishing boats by the quay. The tide was high and the full force of the swell hit them as they headed into the open sea, sending a burst of spray over the bow that all but drenched him. But the wind was in their favour and the sails filled. They'd be back in Rye by nightfall.

21

To Katherine, the winter seemed to have gone on forever. Since the snows of November she had felt imprisoned. She imagined this must be what it would be like on an island far from land or on a ship set adrift on the sea. She was used to not going out much because of her disability, but this was different. She seemed to have no part of the world around her and, sometimes, could almost believe that she and her small household were the only people left alive on earth.

Even the wild animals they often saw around the cottage had disappeared in the wet, cheerless weather. The fox, which had caused George so much worry, had not been seen for weeks and the deer that sometimes lurked at dusk in the shadows at the edge of the trees had moved away. Katherine found that she even missed the ghostly sound of the owl as he hunted across the meadow.

Since Harry's illness Jane Happley had not been to collect Katherine's sewing so perhaps, she thought, Ann had been right and Jane or her grandson had the illness too. For whatever reason, her old friend had not visited and Katherine began to worry that soon she would have no employment and nothing to do with her long, lonely days. She missed, too, hearing the gossip from the big house. She couldn't remember the last time she had had a conversation with an adult – her landlord had been past a couple of times, but was a fairly taciturn soul and not given to idle chatter. Ann was probably the last person with whom she'd had a proper conversation, when she came to look after Harry and that was nearly a month ago.

Harry had gradually recovered from the measles – if that indeed was what it was - his spots faded slowly and a dry cough gradually improved. She was reassured that his energy was returning as he regained his appetite and soon he was restless and pronouncing himself bored. In this never-ending winter there was little to do that would satisfy a four year old's desire for lively activity, although Katherine did her best to devise entertainment for her son.

George, on the other hand, was perfectly content. Provided he was allowed to read and practise his writing every day he went about his tasks with a quiet good cheer that Katherine felt should be a lesson to both her and Harry.

But Katherine couldn't feel cheerful. In fact for weeks she had felt listless and exhausted. The sickness had passed, but as the winter dragged on she felt herself sinking into a blackness that she had not felt since the dark days of her collapse after Harry was born. In her isolation she had time to think and to brood on her situation and day after day, as she watched her boy bouncing around the room pretending to gallop like the knight in the stories she told him, she became certain that things could not go on the way they were. The more she brooded, the more resentful she felt of the way William had behaved. Yes, he was in a difficult situation, but leaving aside her own feelings, she was increasingly aware that Harry was paying too high a price for his Father's conscience. William was out in the world doing a job, but his son, who was bright and energetic and was now at an age when he should be gaining knowledge and experience, was spending all his days shut up with a cripple and a boy. It was not fair on the child, she thought.

And then, in addition to her worries about Harry there was her problem. Old King Henry may have had his 'Great Matter' – should he put aside Queen Catherine and marry Ann Boleyn - but she had 'Her Problem'. Always with her in every waking moment, the conversation she'd had with Ann lurked at the back of her mind and wouldn't be denied. Could she be pregnant? Was she pregnant? If she was, what would become of her? What should she do? Should she tell William and, if she did, what would he say? Round and round went the questions in her head until she thought she would go mad.

Katherine moved nearer to the fire, drawing her shawl close about her shoulders. At last the weather had changed and constant rain had given way to a sharp, easterly wind, bringing clear skies and a bitter frost. She had finished her sewing for the day and was sitting by the fire reading her prayer book, but she would soon welcome the warmth of her bed. Harry was already fast asleep and George was intent on whittling away at a piece of wood he had found. The boy was good at carving and in the long evenings he often made small animals to entertain Harry. The only sounds were the sudden gusts of wind that made the shutters rattle and the soft settling of a log as the fire burned low. Katherine was beginning to feel sleepy and as she laid her book on her lap she felt it – a tumbling sensation in her belly. For a moment she held her breath not believing her senses, then she started to breathe again, slowly and gently. For some moments - 'nothing. She waited. Then it came again – that gentle fluttering that could possibly be mistaken for the natural movement of her gut, except she had already carried a child and knew without doubt that the baby inside her had moved. She was with child!

She put her hand on her belly. Was it more rounded than before? With Harry, her girth had not increased until she was many months pregnant, but then, she'd heard that was often the case with a first baby.

A baby, she thought. A new life there inside her! Was it a girl or a boy? Suddenly, now she knew for certain that she was carrying a child she felt a great calm come over her. All the worry and uncertainty of the last few weeks seemed to drop away as she acknowledged – yes welcomed - the child within her. This would be a summer baby, not like Harry who had entered the world when the frost was white on the ground and the water in the pail had been frozen. This would be a baby - a girl, she suddenly felt sure it was a girl – who, new born, could lie on a blanket in the sunshine and a year hence could take her first tentative steps in a meadow filled with flowers.

She sat for a while watching as the fire died. One by one the glimmers of light on the last log went out as if the fairies had snuffed their miniature candles, and the small wisp of smoke that had been curling upwards faded to a faint, blue-grey haze. A draught stirred the ash slightly making it look like grey, drifting snow. And then all was still. In the silence George looked up from his carving, setting his knife and a small likeness of a fox on the table.

Katherine smiled at him. She felt that she understood the boy now and would be sorry to part with him, but she knew now that she could no longer stay here in the cottage. The time had come; William must make his choice. For Harry's sake and that of her unborn child, he must decide either to be a proper husband to her again or, if he could not, she must go away and make her own way in the world as best she could. No longer could she lead this half-life where she was a wife but not a wife.

Suddenly she felt a new strength. She would not spend her life in waiting – day after day, week after week - for her husband to visit. If she could not be a proper wife, she decided, she would at least be a proper mother, schooling her children in the ways of the world and not shutting them up and condemning them to a life of isolation. Like the sun coming out the realisation came to her. Even without William she was no longer alone – she now had a family; children of her own to love and nurture, who would rely on her and love her and who would be loved in return. Her smile broadened.

'Bed time, George. You have a busy day tomorrow.' He looked at her with a puzzled expression, perhaps sensing the resolution in her voice. She continued, speaking clearly and calmly. 'I need you to take a message to

William for me, oh, and you may go and visit your mother too, provided you are not too long. I will write to my husband in the morning while you are doing your morning chores. Let us hope that the weather holds fair.' She struggled to her feet. 'Good night George. Sleep well.'

As was his way, George just nodded and obediently went to unroll his mattress as she made her way across the room to the bedroom. George, she knew, slept like a puppy, relaxed on his back, arms up by his head, mouth slightly open, his face smooth and tranquil. Tonight, she felt that she too, for the first time in weeks, would have a restful night. She felt serene and almost happy and knew that she and her baby would sleep peacefully and awake refreshed ready to face a new day.

22

William could not believe what he was hearing and the goblet of wine by his side remained untouched. He gripped the arms of his chair and leaned forward in astonishment as he listened to his friend's account of recent events in the city of Cambridge.

He had known Mark Wood when he was at Oxford but, although they had been firm friends as students, it was several years since they had seen each other. Mark was now a successful lawyer and when William had moved to the living in Rotherfield, the two men had rather lost touch. Recently William had received a letter from his old friend saying that he would be in the area in connection with a legal case and would be pleased, if it was convenient, if he could pay William a visit. The priest had been delighted. Living alone, as he now did, the company of his amiable friend to enliven the lonely evenings would be very welcome and William had replied immediately assuring Mark that he could stay for as long as he wanted.

Even though it was Lent, the two men had managed to enjoy an excellent dinner of fish and capon and Mark, who had always been a lively companion, had entertained William with witty tales about the peculiarities of his clients. They were sitting on either side of the fire enjoying the last of the wine, but Mark had now embarked on a tale of a rather different nature; a dark tale that left William speechless with horror.

It seemed that Mark's legal practice often took him away from home and in January he had found himself in Cambridge, where he had witnessed an event which William hardly found credible. According to Mark – and William saw no reason to doubt what he was saying - Cardinal Pole had visited the University of Cambridge, which seemed, apparently, to stand in need of much cleansing from heretical preachers and reformed doctrines. Two men thus accused, by the names of Martin Bucer and Paulus Phagius, who had died and been buried about three or four years earlier, were pronounced excommunicated and anathematized by the Cardinal. Their bodies, which had been buried in holy ground, had been dug up out of their graves and, on February 6, the bodies, enclosed in chests, were carried into the midst of the market place at Cambridge, where a great post was set fast in the ground. The chests were affixed with a large iron chain to the post, and bound round their middles, in the same manner as if the dead bodies had been living persons. The whole had then been set alight. When the fire began to ascend and caught the coffins, a number of condemned books were also launched into the flames, and consumed. All this was watched by a vast crowd of people including Mark, who had been horrified by what was happening.

William shook his head in wonderment. 'Has the world gone mad, that they burn bodies already buried? And books too!'

'It seems to me these Catholics will stop at nothing to . . . Oh, I beg your pardon William, I mean no offence to you and your calling, but I believe myself to be with a friend and so will presume on that friendship and speak freely.'

Unconsciously, Mark affected a position as if addressing a court and continued, rather pompously. 'I know it is now thought heretical, and it may be that in the light of what I say you may feel that you do not wish our friendship to continue, but I find that I am unable to embrace the Catholicism of Queen Mary with all that it entails - the prospect of the Inquisition here in England, the trials and the abomination of these burnings. Do you have any idea, William, of the iniquities that are being committed by Pope Paul – the man to whom you answer as head of the Church? Those whom the Inquisition deem to be heretics for merely selling prohibited books are being burnt in the Campo de Fiori; the Jews are being persecuted again and are made to wear the yellow cap as a badge of servitude, with severest penalties if they do not comply. I can't help it William but, in the light of all that I have learned recently, I have to say that I am, and will continue to be, a Protestant to my dying day.'

William ran his hand through his hair making it stand on end and giving him an alarmed look. 'Your secret is safe with me Mark; although I realise it should not be. The change from protestant to catholic has brought much anguish to my family as you must appreciate. However, I have pledged myself to God and his church and it seems that it is as a Catholic I must serve him.'

'But surely you cannot countenance the abomination of the auto-da-fé? It is not only dead men that they are burning, William. Why, not far from here, in Kent, only a few weeks ago in January, two, good, ordinary men, Nicholas Final and Mathew Bradbridge of Tenterden were burnt together at the stake. You surely must have heard of this?'

Mutely William shook his head. 'No, no . . . God rest their souls. I cannot believe . . .'

Like the good lawyer he was, Mark pressed his point. 'But it is happening everywhere and getting worse, William. I travel around a lot and I can assure you it is everywhere. You are deluding yourself if you think it cannot touch you here. Rotherfield may be a small and insignificant place, but nobody in the land is safe from the accusations and the terrible, unspeakable consequences– neither man, nor woman nor even child. This cannot surely be God's will, no matter what Mary and her Cardinal say, and I fear for you greatly. From what you have told me of your present circumstances, with a wife and a child still living not far away, I very much fear that you too will be exposed as a heretic and made an example of.'

William put down his wine, untouched. Suddenly the evening had soured and he felt the need to escape from the gentle, earnest expression on the face of the man opposite. He had no answers for him. No answers at all to questions that he had been pushing to the back of his mind for a long time as he found himself unwilling to face the alternative – excommunication and a life, or death even, as a heretic.

Abruptly he got to his feet. 'I am sorry Mark,' he mumbled. 'I had forgotten . . . I must . . . I need to go . . . Do not wait up for me old friend. Make yourself comfortable and . . .' he gestured to the jug of wine and gathering up his cloak he let himself out into the darkness of the night.

In his haste he had forgotten to bring a lantern with him, but the night was cold and clear. The moon was a bright face in the dark sky – a necklace of stars looped around it - and he could easily see where he was going provided he kept to the path and steered clear of the shadows of the trees. He strode rapidly down the hill, going nowhere, but feeling the need for activity and movement in his limbs to match the agitated churning of his brain.

The scenes that Mark had painted so clearly with his words had etched themselves into his mind and he could picture only too vividly the terror of those two poor men as the flames consumed them. Yes, he had known that there had been burnings – of course he had. The Bishop of Gloucester for one, but he had told himself that it was just a few people of note who, unwilling to comply with the law, were being made examples of in a brutal, but perhaps necessary way. But, somehow, the burning of two ordinary men who had lived and died not far from here, was much worse. That and the lunacy, the callous insanity, of digging up dead men and making a public spectacle of them was, he thought, beyond the pale. And all this done in the name of God and the Church of which he was a part. The Church for which he had destroyed his marriage. The Church which, he must face it now, was not to prove a path to glory for him and his ambition.

As he walked on, oblivious to the night sounds around him, he felt himself grow calmer, even though he was now fully conscious of the danger in which he had placed himself and his thoughts became more ordered so that, by the time he let himself back into the vicarage some two hours later, he had made a very important decision and felt that now, at last, he would be able to rest.

As he hoped, Mark had already retired for the night, so there would be no need for explanations or small talk. His visitor had considerately left a single candle burning, although the fire was nearly out and the room was growing chill. William was tired after his walk, so didn't linger, but went to his bed strangely happier than he had been for some time.

Next morning, after what had been, perhaps a rather rude and hasty exit the evening before, William felt duty bound to play the good host and, after a hearty breakfast, the two men spent a pleasant morning together looking at some of the books in William's small library. Both were scholarly men and found mutual delight in the beautifully bound volumes that had been left to William by his old tutor at Oxford. So the sun was almost overhead when an urgent knocking on the door disturbed them. With an inward sigh, thinking that it was probably a parishioner needing succour or comfort, William opened the door and was surprised and perturbed to find George standing, shifting uneasily from one foot to the other.

'Good morrow, George. Is all well? Come in lad.'

Ducking his head respectfully George entered the small hallway and pulled out a rather creased letter from a small leather bag tied around his waist.

'For you,' he muttered, thrusting it into William's hands.

He recognised Katherine's writing and hastily broke open the seal. The message was short, to the point and, he thought, strangely formal.

Dear William

I have news of some import of which I think you should be aware. I should, therefore, be glad if you could visit us as soon as possible.

Your loving wife,

Katherine

Slowly William refolded the letter. He stood for a moment holding it in his left hand and tapping it absentmindedly on to his right. Eventually he spoke.

'George, how was your mistress this morning? Do you know the reason for this message? Is she well? Did she seem different from usual? And Harry; how is my son? He is well too?'

George looked down at his feet and picked at his shirt front in an agitated fashion. He was confused by so many questions and had no idea how to answer.

Noting the boy's agitation, William tried to contain his impatience and started again, speaking rather loudly and slowly as if the boy was deaf. 'It's alright George. You did well to bring the letter, but I just want to know. Is Mistress Collyer well?'

George nodded.

'Good. And is Harry well too?'

The boy nodded his head again.

'Do you know what news Mistress Collyer has to tell me?'

This time George shook his head. 'No.'

William sighed. 'Did she say anything else?'

'She said I were to go straight back after I've been to see Mother.'

'Nothing else?'

Again George shook his head.

'Alright George.' William stood thinking. His wife and child were well, and he knew that their material needs were taken care of. This news that Katherine spoke of could not be of such great import. It surely would wait awhile. Besides, in the light of the decision he had made last night he needed more time to think and to lay his plans before he saw his wife once more. 'Just wait while a write a reply – I shan't be a moment – and then you can be off.'

Leaving the boy in the hallway, William went to fetch pen and paper. Quickly he penned a note to Katherine explaining that he had Mark staying with him at the moment, so was unable to come immediately, but would visit her as soon as it was possible. Lighting a taper from the fire he melted wax and dripped it onto the letter before sealing it with a small seal that he took from his desk. He waited a moment for the wax to set then took the letter out to George.

'Here now, boy, give this to your mistress and make sure you don't lose it on the way.'

Without a word George dipped his head again, took the proffered letter and, without a backward glance, went out of the door and down the path in the direction of his mother's house. William remained standing by the door, deep in thought. He wasn't ready to see Katherine just yet. He would go in a few days when Mark had left and he'd made the arrangements.

The ground was still hard with frost underfoot as George made his way from the Vicarage to his parents' house and the air was chill. His mouth watered at the thought of a warm bowl of his mother's pottage as tucked his cold hands under his armpits as he walked. He hadn't gone far when he realised that he was counting his steps. As he passed through the gap in the hedge that led from the field to the lane, he paused. The number was wrong. Last time, he remembered, it had been nine hundred and sixty two and today it was only eight hundred and thirty one. He had taken fewer steps. He stood where he was for a few moments, thinking. Had he miscounted? He didn't think so. And then he realised. Of course – he was much taller now. He had grown a lot in the eighteen months that he'd been away and his legs were longer; therefore he covered more ground with each step. That meant fewer steps. He frowned. But was that a bad or a good sign? He would have to work that out when he knew exactly how many steps he took right up to the door of his Mother's house.

He was so busy puzzling over his problem that he almost didn't notice the man making his way slowly down the lane ahead of him. George stopped; he always tried to avoid meeting people, so drew back slightly as the man glanced over his shoulder before walking on, hugging the shadow of the hedge. When the man had turned, George had recognised him. It was James Catt, Simon's father. George didn't like him. He had a red face and always looked cross and once, when George was younger, he had cuffed him around the ear when George had accidentally bumped into him. The man was moving strangely, as if he didn't want to be seen and George hung back wishing he would hurry. He certainly didn't want to overtake him, yet Katherine had said he wasn't to dawdle.

To his surprise Catt didn't continue along the lane, but stopped and looked cautiously around once more, before quietly opening the gate to the Ashdowns' cottage and treading lightly up the path. George stopped too and watched as, instead of knocking at the closed door, Catt went over to one of the shutters which was partly open and, putting one hand on the wall to steady himself, bent forward and peered inside. George was troubled. Catt shouldn't be doing that. Why was he looking into the cottage?

Suddenly, the door to the forge banged and he saw his father emerge carrying a leather bucket. With amazing speed Catt swung round and headed back down the path, running past George without giving him a second glance. Unaware of the man, his father went straight to the back of the cottage and there was a loud creaking noise as John vigorously cranked the handle of the well. George walked around the side of the house and stood watching his father.

As the bucket emerged from the depths, water sloshing over its side, George stepped forward.

'Hello Father.'

John whirled around. "'Od rabbit it, boy, you gave me a turn. What are you doing here?"

'I came to see Mother. Goodwife Collyer bade me take a message to the vicarage and she said I could say 'hello' to Mother. Where is Mother?'

'Right, yes, I see.' He looked his son up and down and smiled. 'Well it's good to see you, George – it's been a while.' He stepped back a pace. 'And, why lad, you've grown. You've missed your mother, I'm afraid. She's gone to the mill as we're nearly out of flour. She won't be back yet awhile, as no doubt she'll stop for a gossip with Mary.' He grinned at George. 'I don't know what those two find to talk about, but she'll be sorry to have missed you and that's a fact.'

George frowned. 'Why was the man looking in the window, Father?'

'Man? What man, George?'

There was a loud crash from the forge and John whirled around, slopping water from the bucket over his feet. 'Nick?' he called. 'Nick, are you alright? What's happened?'

Nick emerged from the forge looking sheepish. 'Sorry. No harm done, Father, I just dropped . . . Why George, what are you doing here? I thought I heard voices. Haven't seen you in ages.'

'I came to see Mother, but she's not here, so I've got to go now. Goodwife Collyer said I wasn't to be long.'

Nick started towards his brother, but George had already turned away.

'Goodbye,' he said over his shoulder, as he disappeared around the side of the house.

Nick stood staring shook his head. 'I just don't understand my brother. We don't see him for ages and then he disappears again as soon as he's come. What's wrong with him, Father?'

John compressed his lips and shrugged. 'I wish I knew, Nick . . . I just wish I knew.

23

Despite her new found strength, when George returned with William's hastily scribbled message delaying his visit to her, Katherine had felt abandoned all over again. She could not believe that the William she had married - her husband - would have put the visit of a friend before an earnest request from her, his wife. She had made no demands on him since their separation, so surely he should realise that she did not make her request lightly. Did he feel no concern about her and his child? Obviously he did not, she thought.

Katherine had tried to question George about her husband's reaction to her letter, but he was not forthcoming and just said that William had read it, Reverend Collyer had asked if she was well, Reverend Collyer had asked if Harry was well. He, George, had answered yes.

George's speech was always totally literal with no embellishments and sometimes, as now, it drove her to distraction. Her questions about how William looked, how he had received her letter, whether he had looked pleased or concerned had got her nowhere. The boy had just looked anxious and shredded his shirt cuff.

Later that day, she stood by the window and looked around the cottage. Unconsciously, she put her hand over her gently rounded belly and again felt that faint fluttering as if her baby was calling to her. 'Don't worry, little one, I will not fail you,' she murmured. She nodded to herself. It was as she had thought. There was little here that she would need to take with her, just a bag with a change of clothes for herself and Harry and, of course, the small box with the ruby necklace that had been a wedding gift from her first husband, her mother's gold ring and the ring that William had given her on their marriage. They were the most important things, as they and the few coins that she had, would ensure their survival until she could establish some sort of living for them.

She comforted herself with the thought that people always needed a good seamstress and in that respect, she was well able to provide for herself and her children. She tried to make this her dominant thought, but always, underneath, like a worm burrowing through the dark soil, was the fear that they would starve in some unknown place. She was well aware how dangerous was the path on which she was about to embark. There would soon be two children totally dependent on her but, although she was fearful of the future, at least it seemed a future with hope. Here, the cottage had begun to feel like a prison and she would not condemn her children to a life of confinement. No, she thought, she had made the right decision. William's failure to come when she asked was proof of his disregard for his family. She must leave this place and make her own way in the world.

And it was vitally important that she go soon. She did not want to wait until she was big with child; a journey then would be both hard and dangerous. Nor did she now want to wait and see William. It was obvious that he no longer cared for her, but, if she saw him again, could she trust herself to carry out her plan? For all his faults she still loved him and was not sure that she could tell him to his face that she was leaving. She knew just how the corner of his mouth would tighten, how a frown would appear on his brow and she knew that she would not be able to resist if he entreated her to stay. But, in her heart, she also knew that, as a mother, she must be resolute. She would be humiliated no longer. They must leave this place of deceit and loneliness and make their own way in the world.

Her thoughts were interrupted by George as he came in and tumbled a pile of logs in the corner. As she watched him begin to stack them neatly against the wall, an idea came to her. Perhaps George could come with them. She almost thought of him as a second son and he would certainly be useful. True, over the four years since Harry's birth, her leg had strengthened greatly so that she could now walk - albeit with a marked limp and no great distance - with the aid of a crutch, but heavy tasks were still beyond her. With a new baby and a small child to manage a strong lad to aid them would make life a lot easier. But could she afford to pay him, or even provide food for a lad of his age? She had noticed of late how hearty his appetite was and how, now that his voice was deepening, he was shooting up like a bean stalk. No, the sad fact of the matter was that she would be hard put to feed just herself and Harry. Hopefully she would be able to feed the new baby herself with no trouble, as a wet nurse would add considerably to their expenses. She sighed and George looked across at her.

'George, leave that now, I have to talk to you.' She patted the settle next to her. 'Come sit down here for a moment.' She smiled to herself as George obediently left the logs and came to sit where she had bid him, but as far away from her as possible so that their arms did not touch.

'George, I have something to tell you.' He nodded. 'Harry and I are going away. We have to leave this place and I'm very sorry, but I can't take you with us.'

George looked up at her alarm showing in his eyes. 'I don't want to go away,' he said in a matter of fact voice, emphasising his words with a determined shake of his head. 'I'm not going away. When will you be back?'

'No, you don't understand, George, we are not coming back. I . . . I've decided that the time has come for us to move to another place—'

'But I don't have to go. I can stay here; I like it here.'

'No, George, I'm sorry, but you can't stay here. You will have to return to your family. I'm truly sorry as you've been such a help to me and I like to think we've become friends.' Without thinking she laid an affectionate hand over his but he flinched as if she had hit him. 'I'm sorry.' She withdrew her hand and he tucked both of his under his thighs so that he was sitting on them.

'I want to stay here. I like it here,' he repeated in a voice that started at child's pitch and plummeted on the last four words.

'No, George. You can't stay because this cottage belongs to Goodman Heasman. My husband only rents the cottage from him so you see—'

'But how will I read the book?'

'The Bible?'

'Yes.' His voice rose again in his distress. 'How will I read it if we leave this place? Will you take the book too? The book doesn't belong to Goodman Heasman does it?'

'No,' she said gently, an idea forming in her head. 'The book was given to me by William – that and the prayer book. If I can, I will take the prayer book with me for it is a great comfort, but the Bible is too large – too heavy. I cannot take that too. I know how much you enjoy reading it, George. Would you like to have the book and take it with you when you go home?' She wasn't sure she was doing the right thing for the English Bible was, after all, now a forbidden book, but, on the other hand, it meant so much to the boy and wasn't it right that he should read the word of God for himself. She thought so and anyway, who would know that he had it? He was not one to mix freely with other people, let alone volunteer any information about himself or his pursuits.

'I can have it? Truly? I can have the book for my own to keep?' His voice swooped again, so that with his last question he sounded like a man. 'I can take it to my Mother's house?'

She smiled at him. 'Yes, George, you may, but I should warn you – and this is very important, so listen carefully - there are those who do not approve of the book, so you must keep it hidden and not tell that you have it.'

He nodded solemnly. 'I will.' He sat for a moment in silence and then turned to her. 'When will you go?' he asked.

'There is not much to prepare. I need you to go to Heasman and ask for the loan of his cart to take us to Buxted and then there are the chickens . . . so probably the day after tomorrow. We will travel on from Buxted,' she said firmly, trying to convince herself that she had a proper plan. I will give William a day, she thought, her resolve wavering again. I will give him the grace of a day to respond to my message and come here and prove that he still loves us. Perhaps he will come and all will be well. Perhaps the news of another child will make all the difference and he will give up his calling and we can all go away together and be a family again.

But even as the hopes formed hazily in her mind they disappeared like summer clouds on a warm day. He would not come. She must face the fact that her future lay in her own hands. Where she would go she was not yet sure, but in Buxted she would be able to find transport to take her out into the world. In her mind's eye she looked ahead to the future and she shivered.

24

William may have come to a decision regarding his family's future, but as it happened, his plans were completely overturned by an unexpected bout of ague, which seemed to descend on him almost as soon as he had said his farewells and sent his friend, Mark, on his way. Perhaps, he thought, he had taken a chill when he walked in the night air, but whatever the cause, he felt as if someone had thrust a hot poker down into his lungs, his limbs ached and his head was pounding. It was all he could do to crawl into his bed where he lay shivering uncontrollably. He didn't have the strength to make up the fire and despite piling the bed with blankets he was unable to keep warm.

In a lucid moment, he remembered that the woman who now came in to keep house and cook for him had gone to attend the funeral of her mother in Crowborough and wouldn't be back for…. he couldn't hold the thought as the fever overwhelmed him and he saw the buxom figure of the woman floating in the sky high above him. He drifted in and out of sleep where dead men mocked him from burning coffins and a ring of tall skeletons wearing bishop's mitres pushed him around their circle prodding him with their crosiers whenever his legs gave way and he stumbled to the ground.

It felt as if he had lain tossing and turning in his bed for weeks, but in truth it was not more than two days. He awoke on the third, stinking of sweat, his chin rough and dark with beard and his hair matted. He lay in the early light of dawn, increasingly irritated by the constant high pitched cheeping of sparrows as they went about their early morning business and he realised that after all, he was still alive.

Slowly he sat up, resting back on his elbows as the room swam before his eyes. He had no strength and waited some minutes before carefully swinging his feet to the floor. Holding on to first the bed and then the wall, he made his way slowly to the living room. Feeling rather faint, he stumbled across to the shelf where a jug of small beer stood. As he poured it, he noted with dismay that there wasn't much left, and what there was tasted sour and was coated with a thin layer of dust, but he drank greedily, tipping back his cup to catch every drop on his parched tongue. He was suddenly, ravenously hungry, but the bread under the cloth was solid and mould had formed on the crust so he pushed it away in disgust. He looked around for something more palatable, finally cutting himself a large slice from a ham which hung from one of the beams and stuffing it into his mouth.

The early morning sun streamed through the window and warmed him as he stood, his feet bare on the cold stone floor. He felt the strength return to his limbs and slowly he stretched as he stared out at the world. He was greeted by what seemed a sign of hope - the sight of an early primrose, its first flower still rimed with early frost. For a long time he stood staring through the thick pane of glass. Gradually his vision of the outside world blurred as his warm breath condensed on the window, but his eye had turned inward and he was only aware of the plan that had started to take shape in the darkness of his walk several nights ago. A plan which now filled his brain; a plan that felt urgent and all consuming. A plan that called for action with all speed.

25

There was a cold wind blowing from the East, bending the trees and flattening the meadow grass so that it shone like rippled silver cloth in the early morning light. Harry, his blonde curls tossing this way and that, was bubbling with suppressed excitement as he struggled valiantly to help carry their few possessions from the cottage to the wagon that stood before the door of the cottage. He staggered and was nearly bowled over as a particularly strong gust caught at his skirts. George grabbed him before he fell, taking the bag from him and carefully putting it in the wagon.

The driver stood beside the ox's head, taking no part in the loading. He was very tall with a mane of grey hair, a large hooked nose and a slight hump on one shoulder. When he had arrived this morning in response to her request to Heasman for transport, Katherine had felt a tremor of fear when she saw the looming figure of the man filling the doorway. He seemed a surly character. Should she really entrust herself and Harry to this man? Would they be safe? She was also dismayed by the appearance of an ox wagon. Ox wagons were so slow and she had hoped for a good horse and cart, which would have been both more comfortable and a good deal faster. But she had no choice in the matter and, although the wagon was none too clean, having, she suspected, been used for carrying muck to the fields, it was her only means of escape. Possibly, she thought, she would have been capable of riding a docile horse herself, but there was no way that she could also manage Harry and their belongings, so ox wagon it had to be.

She was further put out when the driver told her that he was not going to Buxted, but to Uckfield and although it was not far out of his way, he was adamant that he was not prepared to make a diversion. She supposed that really it did not make a great deal of difference, as she still wasn't entirely clear where she was heading, but Buxted was a place she had visited before and she was not yet entirely ready to relinquish the familiar for the stress of the strange.

They were soon loaded and ready to leave. The driver climbed up and perched on his seat at the front of the wooden wagon, looking for all the world like a large, grey heron ready to pounce on an unwary fish. Katherine would not have been at all surprised if his knees had bent backwards.

She said regretful farewells to George, even shedding a few tears, but as always, he was unemotional and very matter of fact. He listened carefully to her instructions on closing up the cottage and nodded that he understood. She would have hugged him if she had not known that it would upset him, but she noticed that he did not shy away when Harry ran quickly back to him and patted his arm. 'Bye, bye, George. Bye bye.'

As the driver flicked his whip and they pulled slowly away, she looked back, but he did not linger outside the cottage to wave. She shook her head sadly. He was such an odd, silent boy, but she felt that saying farewell to him was like losing one of her family. She hoped that life would be kind to him and that the Bible that she had given to him would bring him joy.

By contrast Harry didn't stop chattering. Where were they going? Was father going to come too? Why wasn't George going with them? Why did the wagon smell so bad? Would the driver let him drive the ox . . .? On and on until she felt her patience was almost at an end. She could understand his excitement, even if she didn't share it. For so long the child had been confined within the cottage and its immediate environs that this was a huge adventure for him. She tried to distract him from his questioning by making a game of seeing which of them could be the first to spot the shy primroses peeping out from the hedgerows, but he soon tired of this and demanded to be set down so that he could walk, but she was fearful that he would stray, or walk too close to the large lumbering beast that pulled them, so she had to say no. After a while, though, she had to ask the driver to stop for her to relieve herself. The baby was growing and pressing uncomfortably on her bladder making this an all too frequent occurrence. She felt embarrassed and was not a little fearful of leaving all her worldly goods in the wagon while she concealed herself behind a bush. There was nothing to stop the driver moving off without her and she was more than a little thankful to find him still sitting where she had left him, flicking the flies from the beast's back with the end of his whip.

Long before dinner time, Harry began complaining that he was hungry and she unwrapped the bread and cheese that she had provided for their midday meal. Her son was delighted with the novel idea of eating as they travelled along, but the smell and constant motion of the cart was making her feel sick, so she contented herself with just a drink from the leather bottle that she had tucked into her bag.

It was a great relief to her when they found themselves on a less bumpy, more frequented road and they were themselves overtaken by several travellers on horseback, all headed in the same direction. Hopefully, she thought, the end of the first part of their journey was in sight.

Indeed it was not long before a line of cottages appeared at the side of the road and three small boys started dashing from one side to the other in front of the plodding ox, obviously playing some sort of game of dare. Harry was enchanted and slid from left to right, watching as the boys disappeared and then reappeared again on the other side, much as a stick does when it floats under a bridge. The driver, though, was not so delighted and flicked his whip at the boys.

'Get out, you varmints. Go on, off with you.'

His whip caught one boy across the back of the legs and he yelped with pain before running off with his mates making rude gestures at the driver as they disappeared between the houses.

Katherine addressed the man, trying to make her voice firm and authoritative. 'Be so good as to stop by the inn, please.'

There was no reply, but she was relieved to see that, as they approached the King's Head, he steered the wagon towards the door and, jumping down, brought the beast to a standstill.

'I should be most grateful if you would help us with our things.' The colour in Katherine's face was high and she felt close to tears. The large, silent man made her nervous. She was not used to ordering men and fending for herself and she felt both vulnerable and alone.

The driver pursed his lips and sucked his teeth, producing a high whistling noise which made Harry giggle. 'Don't want to stay 'ere,' the man said slowly. 'Not the place for a lady.' He pointed with his whip down the street to a small, newish looking house made from bricks that stood near to the bridge over the river. 'She'll take you. Better'n 'ere.' He gestured with his head towards the inn.

Katherine stared at him, surprised by his concern. 'Thank you,' she said gratefully, nodding her head.

The man didn't bother to remount the wagon, but grabbing the rope around the ox's neck, he led it the few yards along the road and guided the beast to a standstill outside the house he had indicated. He knocked on the door with his fist and just when Katherine was beginning to think there was no one at home, it was opened by a small woman, who seemed no bigger than a child. Her greying hair was drawn back tightly from her face which made her long pointed nose look even more prominent. Her coif seemed too small and, perched at an odd angle at the back of her head, looked in danger of falling off as she tipped back her head to look up at the tall figure of the driver who filled her doorway.

'Wants a room,' he said, gesturing with his head towards Katherine.

The woman had a strange way of holding her head on one side and she reminded Katherine of a robin as she looked the travellers slowly up and down. She glanced at the two bags and small box in the cart and then pursing her lips, she narrowed her eyes at Harry. 'I don't take children – not usual like.' The voice made Katherine think of the rusty hinge on the bedroom shutter at the vicarage.

'She can pay.'

If Katherine hadn't felt so nervous she would have been amused by the way the driver seemed to have undertaken negotiations on her behalf, but she was both relieved and grateful when, after a few moments thought, the woman nodded stiffly. 'Provided he's quiet,' she grated. 'I don't hold with noisy children.'

Katherine smiled ingratiatingly. 'Thank you,' she said. 'We will be no trouble.'

Harry tugged at her skirt. 'I don't like her,' he said in a loud whisper.

She squeezed his shoulder to quiet him. 'Hush,' she said through clenched teeth, still smiling at the woman and, before she could change her mind, climbed awkwardly down from the cart, gesturing for Harry to follow her.

The driver tucked their box under one arm and picked up a bag in each of his large hands. Harry watched in admiration as he carried them easily into the house and dumped them on the floor of a room that was surprisingly spacious and smelt of some kind of food that made the small boy's mouth water.

'Oh, it smells good, Mother. I'm hungry. Can we have some?'

'Shhhhhhhhhhh!' The small, birdlike woman pointed a finger at him. 'Shhh,' she said again.

His mother bent down, putting her arm around his shoulders and hugging him to her. 'Hush now, child.' she said softly to him. 'Be good and we'll see what we can do.'

Turning to the woman she said. 'It does, indeed, smell wonderful, Goodwife . . .um?'

'Diplock.'

'Er, Goodwife Diplock.' Suddenly Katherine too felt ravenous. 'We have been travelling all morning and would be grateful for something to eat if that is possible.'

Their landlady smirked a little at the compliment. 'Yes well, I'm famous for my puddings hereabouts. I'll see what I can do.' She led the way to a small, dark room that lead off the main one. 'You can sleep in here if you've a mind, but you'll have to pay in advance. Food's extra.'

Katherine nodded. It seemed that they were accepted and she breathed a sigh of relief that they had found a safe place to stay. She realised that she was going to have to make a proper plan. She had been so concerned with escaping the confinement of the cottage that she had not truly considered what would be their final destination. Having been at first dismayed that the driver was unwilling to take her to Buxted, from what she had seen as they arrived, Uckfield seemed to be a bustling place where she would, hopefully, be able to find transport to take her to . . . She shook her head. Where did she want to go? She wasn't sure. Her knowledge of geography was sketchy and she had little idea of distances.

She had been born in Rotherfield and had never lived more than a few miles from the village. What she knew of the world she had gleaned from her first husband and from William. She knew nothing of large towns and cities and the thought of the strangeness of them made her quail. But she was practical enough to know that if she wanted to earn her living as a seamstress, she stood more chance of doing so in a town where there were plenty of people than in a small village.

Now that money had changed hands and Harry was on his best behaviour, sitting quietly in the corner playing with a little wooden dog that George had carved for him, Goodwife Diplock's manner had softened towards them and Katherine noticed a glimmer of a smile on her face as she laid food for them on the table. Encouraged, Katherine spoke to her.

'Do you often take in lodgers? I mean are there many travellers who pass through Uckfield?'

The woman looked up in surprise. 'Oh, bless you, yes of course. We're on the main route here after all. We get lots of folk so, when my husband died, I decided to offer them a bed for the night. But I'm very particular who I have,' she said glancing across at Harry.

'Of course. Very wise of you, I'm sure. You say the 'main route'. Main route to where—?'

'Why Canterbury, of course.' The woman jerked her head back in surprise, and Katherine wanted to laugh as the goodwife's coif flapped precariously. Their landlady narrowed her eyes again so that they almost disappeared into her round cheeks. 'Isn't that where you're going?' she asked.

'Umm. Well . . . we're not yet sure. But probably,' she said hastily as she saw a suspicious look come over the woman's face.

'How come you don't know? That's a bit peculiar if you don't mind my saying. I took you for an honest pilgrim. Not sure I'd have 'ad you if I'd known you didn't know where you was headed. Call that very peculiar, I do. Don't think you can be stopping here. I don't have people staying permanent.'

'No, what I mean is, we may not go straight there,' Katherine improvised wildly. 'We may . . . we have friends that we may visit on the way.' She felt awkward telling a lie, but she was terrified the woman would ask them to leave.

Goodwife Diplock nodded. 'Oh I see. Well, that's a good thing. If you don't mind my saying so, it's not good for a young woman to be wandering about the country on her own. You're a widow too then, I take it?'

'Er . . . yes.' Another lie, but what could she do? She didn't want to tell the truth as that could endanger both herself and William. What would the woman think about her if she knew she was the wife of a Catholic priest? She surely wouldn't be happy to know she had a heretic under her roof. Lie or no lie, it was better if she styled herself as a widow from now on.

26

As the wagon pulled away, George turned and went back inside the cottage. Before closing the door, he stood just inside the entrance listening to the silence. Heasman had come and taken the chickens the previous evening, so there wasn't even the sound of their contented clucking. He felt sad. Not because Katherine and Harry had gone, but sad because he would have to leave the cottage soon and go back home where there was always confusion – his father and brother hammering away in the forge, his mother wanting to talk to him or expecting him to stop what he was doing and help her. Here he had just been allowed to just get on with his work and read his book. Katherine had always been kind to him, but she did not expect him to chatter with her and was content to sit quietly sewing while he practised his reading.

But then he remembered the book. She had given him the book. That was wonderful and as he remembered it, a warm glow seemed to spread through him and his mood changed. The book was something that made him very happy; made him feel contented and peaceful inside. He went over to the chest and lifted the lid. It creaked and the sound was very loud in the silence. Unconsciously he looked over his shoulder but there was no one there. Then, carefully, he lifted the Bible and set it on the table. He opened it at random and started to read,

'A man was sent from God, to whom the name was John.

This man came into witnessing, that he should bear witnessing of the light, that all men should believe by him.

He was not that light, but that he should bear witnessing of the light.'

George liked to read about John. John was his father's name. True, he didn't always understand what the words meant, but just forming the sounds as they sprang at him from the page gave him a feeling of deep satisfaction and pleasure. He looked up, staring unseeingly at the garden outside as he thought carefully about the passage he had just read. He felt sure that it was saying that John was a good man and that was certainly true of his father.

He had not found his own name in the Bible, nor that of his brothers. He had looked for the name Ann, like his mother, and felt sure that, as his father's was there, her name would be too. Katherine had told him that St. Ann had been mother to the Blessed Virgin Mary. He would keep looking, he thought and when he found it, he would mark the place using something precious. Katherine had a beautifully embroidered bookmark in her prayer book. He must find something equally beautiful to go in his book. He looked around the cottage. He had nothing of his own except for a change of clothes and his knife. The furniture, Katherine had told him, all belonged to their landlord or to William and she had taken her sewing things with her.

Then, as he glanced around he saw on the shelf, the long black crow's feather that he had found at the edge of the forest. At first glance it looked just black, but as the light caught it, it shone with iridescent colours. That surely made it special. Yes, the feather would be his bookmark. He lifted it down and laid it gently on the page about John. He would keep looking until he found another beautiful feather and then, when he found mention of 'Ann', he would use it to mark that page.

Satisfied with his plan, George carefully closed the Bible and laid it back in the chest. It was nearly dinner time and he was hungry, as they had all risen early to prepare for Katherine and Harry's journey. He thought longingly of the hot pottage that Katherine made. He looked in the wooden box. There was still some grain in there and he knew how to make it – he had watched her often enough – but there was the problem of the fire. As she was leaving today she had allowed the fire to go out and he did not like fire, so did not want to light it again himself. They'd had an arrangement – if it had gone out he always laid it ready, placing the heavy logs for her, but he never actually lit it. That was the agreement between them. She knew that he hated the bright, orange glare and the way the flames licked around the wood like the tongues of a dragon that hissed and spat. No, he thought regretfully, a bowl of steaming pottage was not worth braving the fire. He would have to make do with dry bread and the remains of the cheese.

27

The cart jerked as a wheel sank into a pot hole and Harry fell against her giggling and exaggerating the movement. Unconsciously, Katherine put her hand to her belly to protect the baby.

'Careful now Harry. You'll hurt Mother.'

'So - rry.' He almost sang the word on one high, one low note in a rude way that would normally have led to an admonishment from his Mother, but she was, it seemed, past caring.

In the confined space, he shuffled his bottom away from her and leaned over the side holding his nose ostentatiously with one hand and pointing with the other as one of the horses produced large, steaming brown balls of shit from between its fat buttocks. Katherine sighed and grabbed hold of his clothing in case he should fall. There was no doubt her son was bored; they had been travelling for over an hour in this cart and with the couple sitting opposite and all their bags at their feet there was little room for a lively child.

Katherine took a shrivelled apple she had been saving for dinner from the pouch she carried around her waist. 'Would you like this, Harry?'

He beamed at her and settled down to munch his way steadily through last season's fruit while he stared fixedly at the woman sitting opposite him.

She seemed to find the incident amusing and nodded at Harry.

'He's enjoying that, he is.'

'He is,' said the man next to her like a deep echo.

'How old is he – three or four?'

'Four?' Again the echo.

'Yes that's right, he's four, though perhaps small for his age,' Katherine said.

'He takes after you.'

'Yes, after you.'

The couple nodded in unison. They both had long necks and their heads seemed to bob up and down like puppets on strings. They had been in the cart already when she'd joined it but, other than smiling pleasantly and wishing them good morning, she'd been too bound up in her own problems to give a thought to her two travelling companions. She spent the first part of the journey doing sums in her head. It seemed that food and lodgings were more expensive than she'd imagined and she was rather horrified at how much Goodwife Diplock had charged for bed and a meal, so all her thoughts were focused on how she would make her money last.

But looking at them critically now, she saw that they were both very thin with high cheek bones and the same bulging, blue eyes under high, arched brows that gave them a permanently surprised look. They reminded Katherine of a pair of startled hares. She guessed that they must be brother and sister and could almost be twins they were so alike. Well wrapped up in almost identical, warm, russet-brown cloaks, the man wore a high crowned black hat, while the woman had a similar hat worn over a tightly fitting coif. Katherine could almost picture a pair of large, furry, sticking up ears concealed by the high hats. They made a strange pair and she pressed her lips together and looked up at a pair of crows who were passing overhead as she struggled to calm the rising bubble of laughter in her throat.

Finally she thought she had herself under control. 'Are you travelling far?' she asked, trying to make her voice normal.

'Well, yes indeed, we're going all the way,' the woman said.

'All the way,' said the echo.

'To Canterbury?'

'Yes of course. We're going for the burnings, aren't we, Brother?'

'For the burnings . . .yes.'

They can't have seen Katherine's horrified expression, for the woman continued happily. 'Yes, we should be there in good time I think, provided there are no hold ups. We wouldn't want to miss it would we, Brother? They'll probably do all three of them together I should think, so there'll be a proper Mass said first and a procession and everything. Have you been to a burning yet?' the woman asked conversationally and then continued without waiting for an answer. 'Oh it's such a sight and will, we pray, help to bring our country back to the true church.' She crossed herself. 'This will be our fourth. That's right isn't it Brother?

'Our fourth . . . yes.'

'Yes, I thought it was,' She ticked them off on her fingers like a housewife tallying provisions – 'a triple burning at Canterbury nearly two years ago, two in Winchester, one in Lewes. We do like to attend if we can and bear witness and make a day of it. Quite a spectacle it is and in Canterbury it's always that bit special – well, bound to be isn't it with the Archbishop and the cathedral and everything? We might even manage to get a relic if they're not too expensive. There are usually plenty of stalls and you can get all manner of things. I bought this in Winchester.' While she was fishing in her bag Katherine couldn't help thinking what a sheltered life she had led, never travelling more than a few miles from where she'd been born, whereas this couple seemed to be seasoned travellers.

After a few minutes of searching, the woman drew out a small box. 'Oh, I thought I'd lost it,' she gasped, rolling her eyes dramatically and putting one hand on her heart. Opening it reverently she held it towards Katherine. Leaning forward, Katherine could see that it contained a small sliver of dark coloured wood. 'Part of the Holy Cross,' said the woman, touching it to her lips.

'Holy Cross, yes.'

Katherine was totally repelled by the callousness of the macabre pair, but they had given her food for thought. If Canterbury was a place where the burning of heretics took place, she definitely did not want to go there and was grateful that she had been forewarned.

Obviously, as the wife of a priest, she had heard of the city of Canterbury - it was, after all, where the Archbishop lived - and she had thought it as good a place as any to head for, assuming it must be quite large and would, hopefully, be somewhere she could find work. Goodwife Diplock had recommended this particular carter to her as being a reliable fellow who would not take advantage of her position as a woman travelling alone and who regularly made the journey to Canterbury. But now it seemed she had been wrong and must think again. She wondered how long it would be before they would stop and she could find out if there was anywhere that would be a more acceptable place. She addressed the sister.

'It takes two days to get to Canterbury; that's right, isn't it?'

'Bless you, yes, my dear, so the driver assured us; so we should be in plenty of time. Last time we came a different way – up through Tunbridge, but it's good to have a change isn't it? When we get there, we'd be happy for you to join us. Wouldn't we brother? You and your son – as you're on your own. It should be such a good day out.'

'A good day out,' nodded the man.

'But probably not for a woman on her own – so many crowds.' She leant forward and patted Katherine's hand. 'I'm lucky, as Brother and I always go together.'

'You're very kind,' Katherine said insincerely, 'but er . . .unfortunately I'm not actually planning to go all the way to Canterbury. I'm—'

'Oh silly me, I just assumed . . . Just because we are . . .' The woman flung up her hands in an extravagant gesture and raised her eyes to heaven. 'And I'm that excited. You're going to Rye then aren't you? Lovely place Rye isn't it, Brother? Do you remember when we visited Robert there? He's such a dear friend you know and, I must say, a very important man. Has a position at the castle. Oh yes, and it's such a lovely little town. We do love the sea don't we Brother?'

'We love the sea.'

Katherine wondered if the brother had a name and if he ever initiated a thought or a conversation himself. She decided that he probably did not. She didn't want to admit that she had no idea where she was going – she had already learned how peculiar that seemed from Goodwife Diplock's reaction and Rye sounded a nice place. She thought rapidly. It must be quite big if it had a castle and she'd never seen the sea. Why not go there she thought? She had no map to consult and provided she was well away from any burnings, one place was as good as another.

'Yes, that's right, we're on our way to Rye. Do you know where we need to change?'

'Etchingham. That's the half-way point for you then and for us. We'll all stop there for tonight and you should be able to pick up another cart for Rye in the morning. It's about another day's journey – that's right isn't it Brother?'

'Yes, that's right.'

'Good, thank you. That sounds very satisfactory.' Katherine said smiling and ruffled her son's hair affectionately.

For a while they travelled on in silence, each immersed in their own thoughts. Katherine noticed the man scratching repeatedly at the back of his right hand which was covered with red scaly patches and looked sore and inflamed. The figure of Ann and her pots of soothing salve came into Katherine's mind. She wished she had been able to see Ann before she left and wish her goodbye. She felt bad that she had slunk off without a proper farewell and the thought of Ann's kindness to her gave her a further pang as she realised that in a new town she would know nobody - have no friends, no one to confide in, no one with whom to share her fears and hopes. But she would manage. For her children's sake she had to be strong.

As if she had picked up Katherine's thoughts the woman spoke to her again. 'Have friends in Rye do we, dear?'

'Not as yet, but we'll be fine won't we, Harry? We're going to live by the sea.'

Not understanding, but sensing the lift in his mother's spirits, Harry smiled up at her and she hugged him to her. 'A new life in Rye will suit us well.'

28

George had stayed in the cottage on his own for another night. Nobody had come to turn him out, but finally it was hunger that made him pack together his few possessions, wrap the Bible in his jerkin and set off for home.

He walked slowly and looked back several times, the cottage growing smaller and smaller until it was barely visible, surrounded by fields with the dark mass of the forest behind. He sighed and kicked at a tree stump. It wasn't fair. Why did she have to go away and spoil everything?

He had tied up his few clothes into a bundle, which he carried over his right shoulder; the precious Bible, he wrapped carefully in his jerkin to both conceal and protect it and this he tucked under his left arm. Over the last couple of days he'd been thinking of what Katherine had said about not letting anyone know that he had it, but he still hadn't any idea what he would do with it when he reached home. As he walked, he worried and turned the options over in his mind. Their cottage had only two rooms. Each room did have a chest, but he knew that his Mother had things in them already – in fact she was always complaining that they were full, so that was no good. The more he thought, the more he became anxious that there was nowhere in either room that would provide a safe place of concealment.

He shivered without his jerkin and then, just as he came within sight of home, he had an inspiration. Of course! Two years ago his father had built on the small shed at the side, so that his mother had somewhere to store the fruit from the orchard - if left in the house the apples always shrivelled quickly with the heat from the fire. He was sure that he would be able to hide the book there, but he would need to place it in position before he went into the cottage to greet his mother.

He walked warily down the lane and stopped at the bend listening. He could hear the double hammer blows from the forge which meant that his father and Nick were busily engaged and would be unlikely to notice him.

That left his mother. If he opened the gate and went along the path she might see or hear him. She had sharp eyes and good hearing.

He hesitated behind a bush, considering. Carefully, keeping slightly bent so that he was below the line of the bushes, he went around the hedge until eventually he found a gap that he could squeeze through. He was now at the side of the house and so out of sight of the windows. He trod lightly across the neatly dug garden, trying to kick up the dirt and not to leave a neat, tell-tale trail of footprints. When he reached the small lean-to building he quietly unfastened the clasp on the door and let himself in, leaving the door slightly ajar so that he could look around. Even so, the inside was dark and smelled strongly of fruit. On one of the wide shelves there were still two shrivelled apples, which his mother referred to as 'good keepers' that were left over from last autumn's harvest. He froze with one foot in the air as he nearly stepped on a mouse trap containing one small limp corpse. He didn't like dead things. He edged cautiously around it and then peered through the gloom.

He was quite tall now and, without much difficulty, was able to run a hand along the back of the top shelf which was just under the eaves. He reached the corner. This, he thought, would be the best place. In the dim light his mother would be unlikely to notice the book and if she felt it as she placed more fruit on the shelf, she would probably think that it was just a corner of the roof. Still wrapped in his jerkin, George carefully placed the Bible on the shelf, picked up his bundle and let himself out of the shed. He stood for a moment, undecided, then retraced his steps and made his way along the lane to the gate.

Inside the cottage, Ann was busy sewing a new shirt for Nick. He had scorched his second shirt badly the week before and the brown mark had now rubbed into a hole, so she could put off the task no longer. She looked up in surprise as the door opened suddenly and George stood uncertainly in the entrance. He made no attempt to come in, but recited very clearly and precisely, 'Goodwife Collyer says she holds you to your promise, but that what you thought is right, but you are not to be concerned as she is making arrangements and all will be well with her and she thanks you for all your help and kindness to her and says farewell.'

Usually, his earnest expression and the way that he didn't even pause for breath, would have made her smile, but now she frowned.

'Farewell? George what does she mean, 'farewell'? Where has she gone?' She gazed at him in amazement, noticing the bundle clutched under his arm. 'Is this why you're home? Have you come to stay? Is she alright? Has she gone to William? George, answer me.'

As usual when faced with a barrage of questions George hung his head and didn't answer. It was as if his mind could not process so many thoughts all at once. Perhaps, because each of his answers was always so precise and had to be carefully considered, a jumble of questions overwhelmed him. Seeing her son's confusion, Ann made an effort to calm herself.

'I'm sorry George, it's just that I'm worried about Katherine. Come in, lad, come in and close the door.' She took a deep breath and tried to order her thoughts. 'Can you tell me where Mistress Collyer is going.'

George shook his head, standing just in front of her, a frown clouding his face.

She looked up at him. 'Your Father said you took a message to Father William a while ago. Is that right?'

George nodded.

'Ah,' Ann mused aloud. 'So he must know about this. But she still holds me to my promise not to tell him . . . she hasn't told him about . . .' She turned to George again. 'What did Father William say to you before - when you gave him the message?'

'He asked if Goodwife Collyer and Harry were well.'

'What did you say?'

'I said "yes".'

'Well that's a blessing at least.' She paused, lost in her own thoughts. 'Well this is a surprise. I suppose William has finally come to his senses and they are starting afresh somewhere. Yet she still hasn't told him about . . . mm,' she looked puzzled. 'Very strange.' She turned back to George. 'I'd have liked to see her and say goodbye before she went. Goodwife Collyer said that you were to come home then, George.'

'Yes, she said I couldn't stay at the cottage because it belonged to Goodman Heasman.'

'You must have been sad to say goodbye to her and Harry, but it's good to have you home! Your Father will have a surprise when he comes in from the forge.' Ann looked at her son and smiled. 'You're a good boy and I'm proud of you – we both are. I'm sorry Katherine has gone away, but she knows best and I trust God things will work out well for her.'

'I'm hungry, Mother.'

'Now why doesn't that surprise me? If you don't mind it cold, I think there's a scrape of pottage. I must do some more on this shirt now, or Nick will be in rags before it's finished.'

She bent to her sewing again, smiling indulgently as she watched George out of the corner of her eye while he hungrily scraped out the remains of the pottage with a spoon. It would indeed be good to have her youngest home again, although she was not happy at the thought of Katherine setting out on a journey in her condition. She thought, too, how much she would miss her friend. Obviously, though, it was for the best, as the situation could not have continued as it was. William must have made some sort of arrangement for them all, even if Katherine hadn't yet told him of her pregnancy. Perhaps she was keeping it as a surprise for him as they set out on their new life together. Even so, she thought, how strange their marriage was. Each time she had fallen pregnant she couldn't wait to tell John – even before she was certain - and together they had waited anxiously as the months passed and, when her monthly courses still did not come, they had rejoiced. She smiled to herself as she thought of her sons. Yes, it would be good to have all three of them home with her again.

29

For several days after his illness William felt shaky and weak and so it had been over a week before he had made the necessary arrangements and was able to set out on the journey that he hoped was taking him and his family to a better future.

He felt terribly guilty about leaving his parishioners and had thought long and hard about how his plan should be accomplished, but had decided that it was better if no one knew when and where he was going, so he had made his preparations as secretly as possible. He was not a man wedded to possessions and, apart from his books, he had little of value.

Regretfully he had taken his precious volumes from the chest in which he always kept them and laid them on the table. Although no more than half a dozen, there was no way that he could take them all with him. Running his hand lovingly over the smooth leather bindings, he had made his choice. He would allow himself two – but which two? His hand had hovered over a book of sermons but then moved on and alighted on Virgil's *Aeneid*. The cover was shiny with use and had been a constant companion since his student days. He could not leave that behind. His second choice was Erasmus' *'Novum Testamentum omne'*. And that must be it, he thought with a sigh. He would leave a letter instructing his housekeeper that the remaining four books should be sent to his friend, Mark, who could have joy of them and, perhaps, keep them safe until such time as William could take them back.

So it was that William packed his two precious books into his saddle bags along with a change of clothes, some gold coins and food for the journey. He rode his tall white horse and led behind him a docile brown mare which, he trusted, would provide safe transport for Katherine. Harry, he thought, could ride with him. The thought of seeing his son again gave him a deep sense of pleasure and the corners of William's mouth curvèd in a smile as he guided the horses along the grass in the rapidly falling darkness.

He had left it as late as he dared to set out, thinking it better if nobody saw him go so that no questions were asked. He was fortunate as, by taking the back ways, he did not see a soul. The horses' hooves made hardly any sound on the soft ground for the frost of a few days ago had given way to mist and light drizzle and this, he felt, was a blessing, as it helped further to conceal his departure.

He arrived at the cottage when it was becoming almost too dark to see where he was going and he was becoming anxious that the horses would stumble and perhaps damage a leg, which would make an end of his plans. He was not surprised that there was no light from behind the shutters, as he expected that the little household would have taken to their beds long ago. He walked the horses around to the back to the drinking trough and tied them on a long rein so that they could graze if they wanted to. He would unsaddle them, he thought, when he had spoken with Katherine. He did not want her to hear noises and to be alarmed into thinking that there were strangers outside the cottage in the dead of night. Not expecting to find it unbolted, he none the less tried the latch and was surprised when the door swung open. Strangely, here was no glow of fire in the grate and it was pitch dark.

'Katherine?' he called. 'Katherine, my love, it is I, William.' With his left hand he felt his way along the wall to the door of the bedroom, only to find that it was already open, the blackness beyond even more dense than that of the living room. He stood listening. Something felt wrong; the silence was complete. No sound of breathing, no slight stirring at his call. 'Katherine,' he called again, his voice more hushed this time as if he was afraid of disturbing the shadows.

He stumbled as he entered the bedroom and nearly fell. Putting his hands out to save himself he encountered the softness of the mattress cover. Bewildered he patted his hand across the bed, all the time calling to his wife. There was no reassuring warmth, no soft, gentle hump of his sleeping wife. The mattress was flat and cold. Why was she not in her bed? Why was she not answering? Where was she?

Stumbling out into the living room once more he flung open the shutters so that the last grey glimmers of light from the darkening sky penetrated the gloom of the cottage. He could just make out the regular shape of the straw palette in the corner where George always slept. He went across and kicked it gently with his foot. There was no movement. They had all gone and he had no idea when or where.

30

For George, who had been away from home for almost eighteen months it was strange to be back with his family. The rooms were cramped with four of them living permanently in the cottage and when Dickon was there as well, he felt as if he wanted to gasp for lack of air.

His brothers treated him warily at first, unsure of this new, rather capable George, who was as withdrawn as ever and who did not seem to want to enter into the banter of family life. As Nick remarked to Dickon, George as a small child had always been odd, but somehow, now that he was that much older his behaviour was downright peculiar. Whoever heard of someone who was afraid of fire? To Nick, whose hands already bore the scars of burns from the blacksmith's forge, it was inconceivable. As always, Dickon was more charitable towards his youngest brother.

'Well everyone's frightened of something,' he said philosophically. Look at Mother – she's terrified of dogs. I don't like bats and you . . .,' he poked Nick in the chest, none too gently. 'You, brother, are scared of thunder. I mean how daft is that? '

'No I'm not, so shut up.'

'You are too. I've seen you hiding under the bedcovers, so don't try to deny it.'

Nick looked discomfited, but then nodded sagely. 'Ah, but there's the difference. I *used* to be afraid of thunder when I was little, but not any more now I'm grown up.'

'As of a couple of weeks ago you mean,' Dickon grinned and ducked in anticipation of the swipe that Nick took at him.

'Leave it you two, for heaven's sake.' Ann had just come into the room and was nearly bowled over by the two young men who were dancing around like boxers sparring at each other. She looked around. 'Where's George? Has he disappeared again? I don't know where that boy gets to. Since he came back from Katherine's he's forever dodging off; he's like a wood sprite – here one minute and gone the next. I don't know what I'm going to do with him I really don't.'

'Get him a job like the rest of us and make him earn his keep,' said Nick rather bitterly.

'That's enough, Nick. It's not that easy and you know it.' Ann found it hard to conceal her irritation as she tried to keep the peace between her children. It really was too bad that George kept disappearing to heaven knows where. How did he do it? One minute he was there and she was just about to ask him to help in the garden, or to get water from the well, and the next minute he'd gone. Leaving the two boys to their arguments, she went out of the cottage and looked around and was just in time to see George slipping out of the little lean-to at the side of the cottage.

'George,' she called. 'George, where have you been? I've been looking for you. What have you been doing?'

Instantly the boy's face coloured up in a way that she recognised as his guilty look.

'Nothing,' he mumbled, looking forlorn as he stood with his arms straight and slightly in front of him, his hands hanging limply. Immediately, Ann's heart softened as she looked at the boy. He was as tall as she was now, but he still had about him a fragility and vulnerability that aroused all her mothering instincts. She found it hard to be cross with him and yet she knew that this couldn't go on. He had to realise that he would alienate his brothers if he didn't start making himself useful and it wouldn't be easy now with another mouth to feed – and she had noticed since his return that George certainly had a hearty appetite. There was much that he could do that would help and surely, she thought, when he had been living with Katherine he had been expected to work hard. After all, she wouldn't have kept him if he hadn't been useful. So why was it that he kept disappearing, and what did he do? She had never thought he was lazy. She determined that she would keep a closer eye on him, for it was no good expecting a sensible explanation from the boy.

Since he'd returned Ann hadn't been able to help herself asking George about Katherine and Harry and how they had seemed as they set off on their journey. So many questions - when exactly had they left? How did they travel? Where were they going? Had they seemed excited, happy, apprehensive? So many questions had made George's head ache and sent his brain in a whirl, so that, as usual, his replies were minimal and his mother had to be content, for she could soon see that she was going to gain little satisfaction from his answers.

'Well if it's nothing George, you'd better come in and give me a hand. Come along now,' she said, making her voice brisk. 'There's plenty to do.'

31

The gale had been blowing for three days and the Master and crew were getting more and more irritable as they found themselves stranded in the port of Boulogne-sur-Mer. Few of the crew seemed to like the town, complaining that the locals weren't friendly and most had taken themselves off to drown their sorrows while they waited for the wind to drop. Simon and Walter, however, were still aboard, sitting on the deck mending sails, sheltering from the wind in the lea of the cargo. The old man was telling him the tale of how he'd been in the town when the French had besieged it and Simon's eyes were alight with excitement.

'And you remember all this, Walter?' Simon asked.

'Aye lad, it weren't that long ago – only seven or eight years I reckon. Them Frenchies they came creeping at dead of night you sees, but we was ready for 'em. They thought we'd be caught napping in our beds, but at around two after midnight the alarm sounds and we was at 'em. They didn't stand a chance. Bloody fools – even their ladders was too short.'

'Yes, but, why were the French attacking their own town?'

'Weren't theirs then were it? Belonged to us then it did. At one time a deal of France belonged to the English, but over time we lost it.' Walter paused, his mouth turned down as if he felt the loss personally. Simon waited patiently. 'Lost this'n,' Walter said eventually, nodding towards the town, 'the year after the siege.'

'Why? Did the Frenchies attack again?'

'Not really. Was talked away it was, in some treaty or other. They got Boulogne – damned if I know what we got.' The old man scratched his bald head then hawked and spat over the side in disgust. 'But heard tell how their king came to visit the town, strutting around like a puffed up cockerel, while our poor little Edward was tucked up at home in London. Not much of a king he weren't, poor lad. Not like his father. Now he was what you'd call a king. I remember him when he were at Portsmouth when the Mary Rose went down.'

'What sunk you mean?'

'Aye, like a stone, and all hands on her.'

Simon's eyes were round with astonishment. 'And you saw it – and the King?'

'I did.' The old man's clear, green eyes took on a faraway look. 'Amazing sight it were, with all the fleet lined up in the Solent and the king riding up and down in velvets and gold with banners flying.'

'And did . . .'

'No, no more lad. This 'ere's done now. Can't sit 'ere jawing all day. Fancy a walk up to the church? I always likes to pay my respects to Our Lady of the Sea while I'm here. She's good for miracles so they say so p'raps we should go and ask her to make this bleedin' wind drop so we can all get back to England.' His knees creaking like the timbers of a ship, Walter got to his feet. 'You coming or not?'

Simon jumped up, happy to follow the old man with his fund of tales. They made an odd pair, Simon wiry and slim wearing breeches that were too large for him and were held up with a piece of thin rope and the old man with short legs and wide shoulders, his head shiny like a polished apple, and a face creased and brown like the bark of a tree. The two of them walked companionably side by side up the steep slope from the waterside – Simon all gangly like a young horse and Walter with one hand on the boy's shoulder, rolling from side to side as if still experiencing the swell of the tide. It was obvious that Walter took pleasure in the youngster's company. Perhaps he reminded him of his own son who had been lost at sea many years before; perhaps it was just that they were two people like a pair of book ends, at either end of their lives and this gave them a fellow feeling.

Simon now had a new question. 'Why's she called 'Our Lady of the Sea,' Walter?'

'Holy Cross, don't you ever stop asking 'why' lad? Because she sailed into port 'ere all on her own, a thousand years ago, glowing like a firefly, that's why.'

It may have been their visit to the church of Notre-Dame or perhaps it was just chance, but later that day the wind suddenly dropped and there was a last minute scramble by the crew to get back on board and ready the ship for sea. One or two of the men were rather the worse for drink and the captain was not in a good mood as he steered a course for their home port of Rye, but the wind was still brisk and they made good time.

As always Simon felt a sense of homecoming as the castle came into view. They sailed up the river to their usual berth in the shadow of a much larger ship that plied regularly between Rye and the Low Countries. As usual, there was a last minute flurry of activity; commands rang out and men hurried to and fro as sails were lowered and ropes made ready. It had been a long day and there were already lights glowing a welcome from the houses that ran up from the quayside. It was too late to unload the boat tonight, so Simon would be free until morning and he was looking forward to treating himself to a hot pie at Ma Coulson's.

He walked along the dockside and was just about to turn up the road into the town when he saw a man talking to the skipper of the larger *Mary Jane* which was berthed alongside them. There was something about the man that was familiar. The clothes were different, but there was something about his stance that made Simon pause. The light was poor now and his features were not clear but, as he drew level with the pair, Simon heard the man's voice and it made the hairs on his neck stand up. He would know that voice anywhere, an educated voice with the beginnings and endings of words clearly enunciated, a voice that carried clearly through the evening air, a voice he had heard every Sunday of his life until he had left Rotherfield. It was the voice of William Collyer, the priest.

Simon's first thought was that he had come to take him back to his father and in a panic he slipped into the shadow of a stack of large boxes that were waiting to be loaded onto the ships next morning. As he grew calmer, he realised that it was unlikely after all this time, but he was curious to hear exactly what was being said. Still fearful of drawing attention to himself he moved cautiously closer, keeping in the darkest shadows.

' . . . no problem with the passage money – it's just for myself. How soon do you sail?' He just caught the end of William's sentence.

'Not til the day after tomorrow on the noon tide. Have to get her unloaded and then this lot aboard. Won't be ready 'afore then.' The skipper gestured to the boxes where Simon was lurking and he sank further into the gloom.

William was speaking again. 'And how long will the voyage take?'

The skipper's reply was lost as three men headed up the road singing raucously.

Another priest fleeing abroad thought Simon. There had been others he'd heard of in the last few months. The voice and bearing of a priest always meant that they stood out from ordinary travellers and the sailors laughed at the way many thought that a change of dress was sufficient disguise. He, like his mother, was a staunch Catholic, so was glad to see them go, but he had never thought of William Collyer as a heretic. Ever since Mary had come to the throne the priest had been saying Mass in the village church. Had that all been a sham? Well if so, good riddance he thought, but he wondered what had become of young Harry and Goodwife Collyer. She was pretty and had often smiled kindly at him in church.

The singers passed through the town gate and Simon watched the two men draw closer together. There was the chink of coins changing hands. William moved away and as the skipper shoved the money into the bag at his belt he called after the priest. 'Don't be late. We won't miss the tide for you.'

'Rest assured I'll be here. I shall seek lodgings in the town and will be ready to leave the day after tomorrow,' William replied and he strode off up the hill, through the gate and into the town.

32

It had been a beautiful spring. After the dismal wetness of the winter it seemed like a miracle as clouds of blackthorn blossom burst forth from the bare, black branches, and a profusion of primroses starred the banks. As the blackthorn flowers faded, a pale green haze washed over the hedgerows. Gradually, day by day the colour intensified until, suddenly, everywhere was draped in bright, yellow-green leaves. Birds were busy gathering twigs, moss and anything soft with which to make their nests and the fragrance of bluebells and hawthorn drifted on the breeze. Ann watched happily as her bees plied to and fro, almost weighed down with bright, yellow pollen clinging to their hairy bodies. As she drew near to the skep one of the insects landed on her bare hand, but she was unafraid. She lifted her hand up to level with her face and watched curiously as the tiny insect pattered across her skin, then stopped and seemed to wash its antennae almost like a cat washing its whiskers. Then it was still and seemed to be looking straight at her. She whispered gently to it.

'Where does he go then? What is the lad up to?'

As if in answer to her question, she heard a slight creak behind her and turning, watched George let himself quietly out of the lean-to shed at the side of the cottage. Under his arm he had a bundle. He glanced around cautiously, a rather furtive expression on his face, but failed to see his mother, standing as she was under the shadow of a crab apple tree. She remained quite still, almost holding her breath as, with a last look behind him at the cottage, George set off along the lane. Where was he off to and what was he carrying?

Stealthily she crept after him, holding her skirt close to her so that it didn't swish through the long grass and give her away. He didn't go far. She ducked back as she saw him stop by the old oak at the side of the lane. It was huge, with a wide gnarled trunk and branches that dipped almost to the ground where the hill sloped up behind it. She watched as he went to the far side, scrambled up the slope and despite the bundle still firmly clasped under his arm, easily lifted himself onto a branch. She held her breath as he walked along it, one hand out for balance; she knew where he was going. Ever since he'd been a young child, when he'd been so small she had had to lift him up herself, his favourite place had been the fork where the huge trunk split into two massive branches. It was so wide that it made a perfect seat and George had spent hours up there sometimes playing his own solitary games, sometimes just sitting, motionless and silent, watching the wildlife that went about its business.

From where she stood now, she watched as he settled himself comfortably. Despite the new leaves, she could still see his face; his lips were moving. He was talking to someone, but there was nobody around and he did not pause for an answer. She frowned, puzzled, then she realised where she had seen him doing just the same thing – when he had read to her from Katherine's great Bible when Harry had been ill. He was reading to himself now, of that she was sure.

That is what must have been in the bundle he was carrying – a book. But books were precious and valuable. How would he have got hold of a book unless . . .? It had to be that Katherine had given him the book before she left. But was that likely? The more Ann thought about it the more improbable it seemed. Surely William would want to take it with them? And then the dread idea came to her with a jolt. Perhaps her son had stolen it. She put her hand to her mouth to stop herself making a sound. Surely he wouldn't do that? He may be strange, but he had always been a good, honest child. She turned and silently made her way back to the cottage. She couldn't leave the matter there; she needed to find out the truth.

Ann did not have chance to question George the next day as his father had sent him on an errand to his Uncle Wills, but she did take advantage of his absence to search the shed thoroughly. As she had feared, she found, on the top shelf tucked right at the back so that she had never noticed it, the large Bible written in English that used to be in Rotherfield Church until Queen Mary had come to the throne. The same Bible that George had, so proudly, read to her when she visited Katherine. The same Bible that was now not allowed in church. She felt a hollow feeling in her stomach. If the book was now forbidden, did that mean that George was committing a sin? But how could that be when, not long ago it had been in church for all to read, if they knew how? It was William's book so it couldn't be bad could it? How had George come to be in possession of it and, if he'd been given it honestly, why was he hiding it and being so furtive? She felt sick with worry. There was nothing for it, she would have to question him and find the truth, but she knew that questioning George about anything was never easy.

The opportunity presented itself the following afternoon when she and

George were setting out young cabbage plants to grow on and provide food for later in the season. She noticed how he worked along the rows with a rhythm of dig, plant, firm that came of practice and she thought again how well he had coped with the garden at Katherine's cottage. While still feeling anxious about the coming confrontation, part of her mind wondered if it would be possible for him to find work as a gardener at the Manor.

As she drew level with him she straightened and put a hand to her back. 'You must have been sorry to leave the garden at Goodwife Collyer's, George, but it's good to have your help here,' she said, forcing a smile.

He grunted and carried on along the row, back bent, feet apart.

'They must have had a lot of luggage with them when they went. Did you have to help pack up?'

He shook his head, barely breaking his planting rhythm.

'So William did it all himself did he?'

George finally stopped and also straightened. He looked at her. 'He weren't there.'

'William weren't, er, wasn't there? What do you mean?'

'He weren't there,' George repeated and went back to his planting.

'George, leave that a minute. What do you mean? Are you saying that William wasn't there when they left? Katherine can't have done all the packing up herself surely?' She realised she was talking almost to herself as George was developing the shuttered look that always came over him when questioned about anything. She was getting side-tracked and going about this the wrong way, but she had to know. She took a deep breath.

'George, I know about the book; I know you have William's Bible.'

He looked up, alarm showing in his face. 'You're not supposed to know.'

'Why, Georgie?' She deliberately softened her voice so as not to alarm him. 'Why mustn't I know? Did you steal the book? The truth now lad.'

'No, I never stealed it.'

'Stole,' she corrected automatically. 'Then how . . .'

'Goodwife Collyer gave it to me. She said she couldn't take it 'cos it was too heavy. She said I could have it as I'd done so well with my reading. But she said not to tell; she said it was dangerous.' After such a long speech the boy seemed breathless and a flush spread over his cheeks.

Ann shook her head in confusion. 'She *gave* it to you? Are you sure lad? Because it was heavy? I don't understand. Surely William could have . . .'

'I told you, Mother. He weren't there. Only her and Harry.'

'Then where on earth was William? He's not been seen these last few days. Why wasn't he there to help?' said Ann - again asking the question more of herself than her son.

There had been much talk among the people in the village about the unexpected disappearance of their priest. It was extraordinary, they thought, that he had not said anything about a journey, but perhaps he had urgent church business somewhere. They had waited, fully expecting that William would return, but when he did not, they had cast around for a reason. There had always been speculation about what had happened to the priest's wife and child – they'd not been seen for almost a year – but none, other than the blacksmith and his family, knew the truth and they kept the secret as they had promised. Some wondered about an accident, others, less charitably speculated that he'd run off abroad with the church silver, but a look in the church soon quashed that rumour.

'Well, I just don't understand. I suppose they were going to meet up somewhere, but I can't understand a man leaving his crippled wife and son to pack up and set off on a journey on their own. How many bags did they take George?'

'Two.'

'Only two? Is that all? Nothing else?'

'And a box.'

'A small or a large box?' Heavens above thought Ann, getting information out of George was like pulling turnips out of frozen ground.

'Small.'

So that explained why Katherine could not take the Bible, but it was strange that William did not pick it up later.

'So you didn't see William at all before you left for home?'

'No. You won't take it Mother will you? You won't take my book away?' His voice rose in agitation. 'She said I wasn't to tell anyone I had the Bible. She said I was to keep it hidden. She said some people don't approve of the book, but you don't mind me having it do you Mother?'

Ann frowned. She still wasn't sure how she felt about the book. There had been so many changes of religion, backwards and forwards, first one thing was right then another, that she was confused. She had trusted William, even though he had taken away the Virgin, and when he'd put the great book in the church for all to read she had not questioned it. Then suddenly the book had been removed and the holy saints and Mother Mary had been restored to the church. They said it was the Queen. That Queen Mary wanted the country to be Catholic again to please her Spanish husband, but was it up to the Queen to decide? What about God? Katherine chewed her lip. She didn't want George to be reading something that was wrong, but then she looked at his earnest, bewildered face.

'Do you mind, Mother?' he repeated, anxiety making his voice swoop down in a way that ordinarily would have made her smile.

Slowly she shook her head. 'No, George, if it was given freely and you didn't steal it I don't mind but . . .' Katherine was right, Ann thought. There were plenty of people who would not approve of an English Bible, but it obviously meant so much to the boy she couldn't see the harm in him having it. Whether his father would agree, she wasn't sure; they never really talked about religion. Best he didn't know about it she thought. He'd only worry. John might feel that the boy was running a risk by keeping it. She didn't agree though. It had taken her several weeks to discover it right under her nose, so how would strangers come to know of it? 'You may keep it, George, but, like Goodwife Collyer said, it must be a secret and you must tell no one nor show it to anyone. Understood?'

Relief flooded over the boy's face. 'Yes, Mother. It's a secret.'

33

Almost without anyone noticing, Spring passed into early Summer. Buttercups spangled the fields like drops of fallen sunshine and the early morning mist was echoed by the drifts of white cow parsley that billowed along the edge of the lanes.

Travellers took advantage of the good weather, so the forge was busy and Ann, too, was kept occupied, not only in the house and garden and but also in the village. There were several births that she attended - no doubt the result of merrymaking at harvest time, when the drink flowed freely and couples had time to relax after toiling for long hours trying to salvage what crops they could after an indifferent summer. A few of the village children developed summer colds and her mixtures for sore throats and coughs were in great demand. Others were afflicted with sneezing fits and itchy eyes, and for those sufferers she made up a syrup of elderflowers which gave them some relief. The accusations of witchcraft that had loomed so large last year seemed forgotten and, as she went about the village, people generally were grateful for her help and she was greeted with a ready smile. Catt was rarely seen in the village and seemed to live a twilight life of poaching and stealing with never a thought for his family. How they survived she wasn't sure, but sorry as she was for them, she did not feel able to risk a confrontation with their father again.

Nick and George had come to some sort of an understanding and Nick no longer tormented his younger brother, so there was peace at home. She knew that George continued to slip away and read his precious book, but he was very discreet and she rarely saw him go or return. She would just be aware that he was missing for a while and when he returned there was a stillness about him that made her glad that she had not interfered and taken the book from him, or mentioned it to John, who might have felt differently. After all, what harm could it do?

Wearily, Simon sank down on a fallen tree trunk at the side of the road, resting his arms on his knees and letting his head sink down. He seemed to ache all over and sighed as he slipped the small bundle he carried off his shoulder onto the ground. Unknotting the top, he took out the last of his bread, making sure that not so much as a crumb dropped onto the damp ground. With a whirr of wings a robin landed at his feet and looked up at him.

'Sorry mate. Can't spare you none,' the boy said as he put the bread into the side of his mouth and wrenched at the hard crust with his teeth.

The robin hopped forward and cocked it's head on one side before pouncing on a small worm that ventured out from under a leaf.

'Been a bloody long walk,' Simon continued addressing the small bird as he chewed. Raising his head he looked up and saw the mass of a hill in front of him. He nodded to himself. 'But not long now, eh?'

When he'd left his ship, it had taken Simon a while to feel steady on his feet as, after nearly a year at sea, he'd become used to the rolling and tossing of the deck, but once he'd got into his stride he'd made good progress towards home. It had been a fair while, he reflected, since he'd seen his brothers and sisters and it would be good to know how they fared. His expression darkened as he thought about his father. Simon didn't much want to bump into him, as he was sure he would not have forgiven him for leaving.

'But these things can be managed, can't they?' he said to the bird, who seemed to dip its head in agreement. That had been a favourite phrase of Walter's and Simon had taken to using it too. Whenever there seemed to be a problem Walter would calm tempers and take the heat out of a dispute with a gentle 'It's alright lads, these things can be managed'. Simon pressed his lips together and sat quietly thinking about the old man. He'd been more of a father to Simon than James Catt ever had and now he was dead. One moment he was hale and hearty and the next moment he'd dropped on the deck like a stone. It had been a great blow to Simon and the death of his friend had added impetus to Simon's desire to see his brothers and sisters.

It was encountering William on the quayside that had started him thinking about them again. Hearing the priest's voice again had brought home back to Simon with such a rush that it almost took his breath away. He hadn't been aware of feeling homesick, but the tone of the voice that had spoken to him every Sunday for as long as he could remember had made him long to see Rotherfield and his family again. Then Walter had died and there seemed no good reason not to leave, so he'd set out for home almost at once.

He wiped his hand across his mouth and the robin took fright at the sudden movement and flitted away. He was sure that his mother would want him to see his brothers and sisters were alright and, buoyed up with the idea that he was doing the right thing, he got to his feet and set off again in the direction of the village.

He was wary of meeting neighbours who might tell his father he was around, so kept a careful look out and ducked back behind bushes when he heard, or saw, the odd person plodding home after a day's work. True, Simon was a very different person from the scared boy who had scuttled away from home nearly a year ago but, he thought to himself, there was no point in taking chances. He was still thin, but with regular food and exercise on board ship he'd shot up and was now strong and fit. There was a new confidence; he'd made his way in the world, been to foreign places and had money of his own. Not a lot, he reflected ruefully, as he trudged along, but perhaps just enough to help his eldest sister a little. He was sure she'd be having a hard time feeding the young'ns.

By the time Simon reached the outskirts of the village he was tired and hungry and hoped that, as usual, rather than coming home, his father had gone off with his mates either poaching or to drink himself into his usual stupor. Even so, as he approached the family cottage he kept low behind the hedge and then crept around the side of the house. There was no point in inviting trouble. Strange, though, that the shutters were closed on such a fine evening. Looking cautiously round he peered through a crack in the shutter.

Inside, the room looked even more dismal than he remembered it. A single candle on a table, littered with dirty wooden platters, guttered and smoked and he could make out the figure of a girl sitting on a stool. She held a bundle of rags cradled in her thin white arms and her shoulders were shaking.

'Mary?' Simon could not prevent the sound escaping from his lips, but his whisper was carried away on the breeze and the girl did not look up. Senses alert, Simon walked slowly to the door and lifted the latch quietly. As he pushed the door open he could hear muffled sobbing and with a hasty glance around, he moved quickly to his sister's side. At his entrance she jumped up in alarm, clutching the bundle to her chest and exposing a third, small arm even thinner and paler than her own.

'Who? What? Oh Sweet Jesus is it….?' She took a step back and stared at him wide eyed. 'It is you - Si,' she breathed. 'Oh Si, you've come back. Oh, thank God.' She put out her hand to him and he took it in his.

'Mary, I—'

She withdrew her hand and put it to her mouth as she turned away. 'But you're too late, brother. Too late for little Ruth….' And the girl's voice caught in her throat as a sob overtook her.

Simon reached out and gently moved the ragged blanket that he now realised was wrapped around his youngest sister. 'Ruthie?' his voice was just a whisper as he exposed the small face, gaunt, flushed and streaked with dirt and dried tear marks. 'What's wrong with 'er? Where's Grandmother?' He looked around the single room and saw more ragged bundles stirring in the two far corners – his brothers and sisters.

Mary shook her head. 'Grandmother never comes here. She's gone a bit strange in the head I reckon and says she's washed her hands of us. And Father....pa!' Mary spat the contemptuous sound from her lips and a small speck of her saliva landed on Ruth's cheek.

'But what's wrong with Ruth? How long's she been like this? Why 'aven't you sent for anyone?' He reached forward and gently stroked away the moisture on the child's cheek, but she did not stir.

'Who? Who'd I send for? With that drunk for a father, who'd want to help us?' Mary's voice was hard and Simon looked up, shocked by how bitter she sounded.

'But surely—'

'It's alright for you, brother.' She looked him up and down. 'You look as if you've done alright – wherever you've been. You've no idea what this last year's been like for us - Mother gone and Father drinking himself silly whenever he has money and taking it out on us when he don't.' Her voice rose and a child called out sleepily from the corner.

'Mary? Wha'ss up Mary?'

But Mary was in full flow and didn't pause for breath. 'We're slowly starving to death and he doesn't give a damn,' she hissed. 'Says I could always make a few pence if I was to go round the back of the inn with one of his disgusting cronies, but I can't... I won't... it's not Christian and Ma would...' Mary's rant finally petered out and she sank once more onto the stool sobbing quietly.

Tentatively Simon put out a hand and squeezed his sister's shoulder. ' S'alright Mary. I'm here now. I'll 'elp you. I'm sorry I went, but... Look, I have money. It's for you. For you and the little ones.' He put a small pile of coins on the table. 'Oh Mary...' Unconsciously he patted Mary's shoulder as he'd seen his mother do when comforting the little ones. 'It's alright now,' he murmured over and over while staring down at his two sisters.

Eventually Mary's sobs subsided and she sniffed loudly which seemed to bring Simon to his senses. 'How long's Ruth been ...? What's the matter with 'er?'

Mary sniffed again. 'Three days. She got sick on Sunday after she got wet in all that rain and she's so hot and she won't eat and now she doesn't even speak anymore. I don't know what to do with her.' She rocked back and forth in her distress. 'I think... I think...' Her voice sank to a whisper. 'Oh Si, I think she might die and then I'll have failed Ma.'

'No, no don't say that. We won't let 'er die. Why ain't you fetched Goodwife Ashdown?'

Mary laughed - a harsh mirthless sound. 'Goodwife Ashdown? You think she'd help us after what Father done to 'er?'

'What do you mean? What did 'e do?'

'You don't know do you? Oh yes, you was out of it – gallivanting around when it happened.'

'Don't be like that Mary. I weren't gallivanting. You knows I had to go.' Simon frowned. 'But what did 'e do to Goodwife Ashdown. Didn't 'urt 'er did he?'

'Accused her of being a witch, didn't he?'

'A witch? No! You can't mean it! Why—'

'Said she'd killed Mother with her witchcraft and spirited you away. Had her tried by the priest, but Father Collyer didn't agree did he?'

'Blessed Virgin! 'e's stark mad. Goodwife Ashdown's a good woman. I'm sure she'll 'elp our Ruth. I'll go fetch 'er now.' He turned, but Mary caught at his clothing and held him fast.

'No Simon, you mustn't. He'll kill you if you bring that woman here – even supposing she'll come. He won't have her in the house. We can't even speak to her.' Mary looked terrified.

Simon shook his head in bewilderment. 'We 'ave to, Mary. You said yourself little Ruthie might die. We got to try an' help her for Ma's sake. I'll go now. She'll come – you'll see.'

'She won't come. There's no one as will help us now. It's too late and I've tried and tried, Simon. I really have. I didn't want to fail Mother, but it's been so hard.'

A pang of guilt shot through Simon as he heard the desperation in his sister's voice. He hadn't really thought of how difficult things would be for her after he'd left. He'd been so caught up in his new life; so amazed by all the new things he was seeing and learning that he'd only given his family the odd passing thought. Until, that is, that he'd heard William Collyer on the quayside.

'Well we can't leave Ruth like this. We gotta try. I'm going to Goodwife Ashdown's house. If Father comes, don't tell him I'm back.'

Mary gave a mirthless laugh. 'Oh, no fear of that. He won't be back ....'

With a loud crash the door opened and the figure of James Catt stood silhouetted against the evening sun. He came forward - straight towards Simon.

'You!' Catt pointed an unsteady finger at his son. 'So they were right. You're back then – you little piece o'shit! I 'eard as how you'd come sneakin' into the village. Thinks you're all growd up don' 'ee. Thought nobody seed you didn't you? Well you needn't think you're stoppin'. You ain't no son o' mine.'

Catt's voice was slurred with drink and he stank of stale alcohol. He staggered slightly and Mary gasped as he nearly fell.

Simon stood tall in front of her and faced his father. 'No,' he said. 'I'm not stoppin'. I'm doing what you shoulda done. I'm going to fetch 'elp for our Ruth. I'm going for Goodwife Ashdown.'

Catt waived his hand wildly. 'You'll do not such bloody thing. That woman'll never set foot in this house again.'

He lurched across the room pushing past Simon and flicked back the blanket that Mary had wrapped around Ruth.

'Nothin' wrong with 'er. Just asleep that's all. And so she should be. 'slate. At this hour all little childer should be ashleep.'

Mary clutched Ruth closer and shrank away. 'She's ill, father. She has a fever. She's all hot. Please—'

'Don't you argue with me girl.' He glared round the room. 'Where's me supper?'

'Supper!' Simon cried. 'Is that all you can think off? You never cared about any of us did you? I don't know why our mother married you. You're worthless. Well I ain't frightened of you anymore. I'm gonna get Goodwife Ashdown.'

'Like 'ell you are! Don't even say her name.' he crossed himself. 'That woman's evil and I'll not have 'ere with 'er spells. Fucking witch she is. Should be strung up.' He leant on the table for support and breathed heavily. 'We'd have got 'er too, if it hadn't been for that interfering busybody of a priest. The bitch. She killed our Nell.'

Simon took a step towards Catt. 'I ain't listening to you, Father. You're mad. She didn't kill Mother. You killed with your beatings.'

'Why you little—' Catt lunged at Simon and grabbed his arm, swinging him around. For a moment they struggled with each other then broke apart as Mary let out a high keening cry. Both men looked towards the girl and saw her struggling to hold her little sister who was violently twitching and shaking. They all stood as if rooted to the spot. Then suddenly the child was still.

'There. What I tell you? She's spelled our Ruth an all. I told 'ee.'

'No! Dear God no – please – not our Ruthie,' Mary's voice was hoarse and strained and she began to sob uncontrollably.

Swiftly Simon was at her side, but he could see that there was no life in the child who hung limply in Mary's arms. He looked at his little sister and was suddenly filled with an all engulfing rage. He turned to his father who stood carelessly examining the pickings from his nose.

'You've done this,' Simon shouted, jabbing Catt with an accusing finger. 'It's all your fault our Ruth's dead. You've killed 'er just like you killed Mother.'

'Nonsense. She ain't dead. 'ere, I'll wake her up.' Catt grabbed at the small figure cradled in Mary's arms; but Mary was not going to let him take her sister and tried to fend him off with one arm while still holding onto the small body.

'Leave them. Don't you touch 'em you… you no good bastard.'

Catt ceased pulling at the child and rounded on Simon. 'Don't you speak to me like that. I'm your fuckin' father. You show res…res…pah!' He shook his head as if to clear it. 'I'll bloody teach you a lesson you won't forget.'

He lunged towards Simon, but the boy was too quick for him and dodged to the side.

'Come 'ere you piece a shit,' Catt roared grabbing for Simon again. Unsteady on his feet, he crashed into Mary who was still clutching Ruth's body and she cried out.

The blood roared in Simon's ears and his eyes were wide. 'Get off. Don't you touch my sisters. Never again! Never again!' he yelled, punching at his father to emphasise his words. The second blow landed squarely on Catt's chin. The man staggered, then fell, crashing into the table as he went down. He lay still, his mouth sagging open, a pool of blood gathering on the floor under his head.

Mary stopped sobbing and clutched at her brother in horror. 'Sweet Jesus, Simon, you've killed him.'

'No. No I ain't,' Simon's voice was uncertain. 'Didn't 'it 'im that hard.' He shook his head in disbelief – 'I ain't done for 'im Mary.'

He crouched down and shook his father, but the man just lay there seemingly lifeless.

'You have Simon. Look at the blood.'

The pool beneath Catt's head was steadily growing.

Mary's face was bleak and shuttered. Still clutching her dead sister she looked at her father and then at Simon. 'You must get away Si,' she said urgently. 'Quickly. This family is cursed because of him. Go now, while you can and don't come back. If he is dead there'll hang you, and if he ain't and he wakes and finds you here, he'll kill you, brother, so go. Either way, at least you can escape from him and for that,' she raised her eyes to heaven, 'me and Ma up there,'ll be grateful.'

'I can't leave you Mary, not now.'

'Yes, you can, Simon. You went before because he near killed you and you must go now.'

'But—'

Mary seemed calm and her voice was steady. 'Please. Please go and then I can have hope that someday you'll come back and everything will be alright, but if you stay then what hope is left for me and the kids?'

34

With the weather at last clear and fair, Dickon was brimming with excitement that he was to be travelling with the iron wagons once again and that this time he was being sent with a special consignment all the way to London. He had never been to the city before and he was greatly looking forward to seeing the wonderful sights that up until now he'd only heard about from travellers passing through their small village.

'They say that there are so many houses altogether, that you could jump from roof to roof and go for a mile and never touch the ground,' he told his Mother, his face alight with enthusiasm, as they sat down to their meal.

'That's as may be,' she said as she spooned out the pottage, 'but I'd keep your feet firmly on the ground if I were you, lad.'

'And the streets are so crowded with people and coaches and carts and wagons that sometimes it's hard to make progress. I hope we'll have time to explore a bit. Sometimes the gang has a whole day and night in London before they return so I might even get to see the Queen.'

'I'd steer well clear of Her Majesty, if I were you,' said John, coming in from the forge. 'That woman's been nothing but trouble ever since she came to the throne.'

'Hush,' although they were in their own home, Ann automatically glanced around. 'Don't say such things, John, if they were repeated,' she nodded towards her three sons, 'who knows what trouble we'd be in?'

John took his place next to her and put his arm around her. 'Don't fuss woman,' he said giving her a quick hug, 'there's only the mice in the thatch to hear us here and they won't talk.'

'No,' said George looking up. 'Mice can't talk Father.'

'Quite right my son,' John nodded kindly at the boy. He turned back to his wife. 'But you can't get away from the fact that Mary has brought misery to this country with her Spanish husband and their damned religion and now all this trouble with France. You mark my words – it'll be all out war before much longer.' He helped himself to a chunk of bread. 'Even the weather's been bad since she came to the throne. D'you know, Old Jack Phipps was only saying the other day that when he was a boy, they brought in twice the harvest we get now? Look at last winter with all the rain and floods . . .'

'But it's not raining now. It's been really fine lately Father, so cheer up,' said Nick cheekily.

'That's enough from you. But you know what I mean. These days things seem to go from crisis to crisis. After all,' John sat back, 'even in a little place like ours things aren't right. Whoever heard of a village with a church and no priest? Last time there was a burying they had to get one over from Crowborough to come and do him. It's not right. And now, of course there's another to be done, so who'll do that I wonder?'

'Another burying, John?' Ann looked puzzled. 'I hadn't heard. Who is it? Who's died?'

'Only heard myself this morning. Peter Dibbler put his head round the door of the forge not an hour ago with the news. Josiah Mead. Last night it was.'

'Josiah Mead!' Ann's eyes widened with astonishment. 'Why whatever happened?'

'Seems he was drunk as usual and whether he hit, or kicked that dog of his, nobody knows, but it turned on him. He went down apparently and the dog went crazy. No one dare get near it. Just tore into him. He was covered in blood and died soon after.' John paused. 'Ann? Are you alright? You've gone very pale. It's not like you to go faint at talk of blood – you've seen enough in your time.'

'No, no, I'm fine – really. It's hot in here,' she said, fanning herself with her hand in exaggerated fashion and taking a tiny sip of her small beer. Her insides seemed to quiver and she felt sick as she remembered the slavering jaws and hot, reeking breath of Mead's dog as it stood facing her in the lane last autumn, the three men in a leering circle behind it. The idea of being torn to pieces by that animal was just too dreadful to contemplate. John was still speaking and she forced her thoughts away from what could, she felt, so nearly have happened to her, to listen to him.

'What happened to the dog Father?' As always George was far more interested in the dog than the man.

'A group of men finally cornered it and they killed it. Had to, George,' he said as he saw George frown. 'Once a dog has gone for a man like that it could never be trusted again. Not fair on the dog, I know. After all, Mead had trained it as a fighter and that's all it knew; probably never been shown any kindness in all its life, poor devil. Had one kick too many I reckon. Anyway, that's all by the by. My point is, there's now another burying to be done and there's still no priest to do it.'

There was silence for a few moments broken only by the scraping of spoons as the boys hungrily shovelled the pottage into their mouths. Talk of dogs tearing their owners to pieces was not going to put them off their meal.

It was Ann who finally spoke.

'I wonder where they went?'

'Who, Mother?' said Nick.

'Katherine and William. It was your Father saying about the lack of a priest reminded me. I'd have thought, well, with George working there and all. Well . . . I was just a bit hurt that William didn't even say 'goodbye'. They just disappeared - just like that.'

'Very sensible too, if you ask me, with all this persecution of heretics. Getting worse it is too, by all accounts' said John with a sigh. 'They should have gone a long time ago when it all started. I can't believe what he put that poor woman through. I mean it's all very well having a belief in something, but when it comes to abandoning your wife and child,' John shook his head. 'But I think . . .' He broke off and frowned at the two eldest boys. Bored with their father's pontificating, they'd been whispering together and now Nick kicked Dickon under the table and the board jerked on its trestle. 'What are you two about? Stop it before you have our meal on the floor.'

Nick was flushed and looking embarrassed and Dickon was grinning. 'She does,' he said quietly out of the corner of his mouth.

'No, she doesn't.' Nick's hands were on the table and he clenched his fists 'Now shut up.'

Ann smiled to herself realising that the fracas was over a girl. She had to face the fact that her sons were fast growing and would soon leave her to have families of their own, but for Nick girls were, just at present, both a source of fascination and embarrassment – something that his older brother was only too delighted to tease him about.

She looked across at George who was steadily spooning his food into his mouth and taking no part in the conversation. Would he ever find a girl willing to put up with his ways, she wondered? He was a handsome boy and was growing fast, but she somehow could not imagine him being interested enough in another person to want to marry. He really did live in a world of his own. What would become of him when she and John were not here to shield him from things he seemed not to understand?

She shivered and John put his hand on her arm, making her start.

'Cold?' he asked.

'No,' she answered. 'Someone just walked over my grave. Did you say something? I'm sorry, I was miles away.'

'I was just saying I promised my brother, Will, I'd go over and lend him a hand with fixing his roof before it gets dark. This fine weather can't last and the timbers at the west end of his house have quite rotted through, so it'd be good to get it fixed up before the rain comes again. You lads can come too. The more hands we have the better.'

Ann rose from her seat and began collecting the bowls from the table. 'Dickon, you'd best take the rest of this bread and some cheese when you leave in the morning.'

Dickon rose too and picked up the remains of the loaf. 'Thanks that would be good. I don't know the route, so I'm not sure where we'll stop to eat.'

'Yes, and I know how starving you get.' She looked up at her tall son and put a hand up to his cheek, feeling the rasp of bristles under her fingers. 'I know you're a man now, but you will take care going up to London, won't you, my son? The city'll be a very different place from here.'

He smiled down at her. 'Oh, don't worry about me, Mother. I've been wanting to see London for a long time, but I always seemed to get the coast runs before now. Perhaps I'll bring you back a present,' he said, his eyes alight with excitement.

'That's very kind, Dickon, but you save your money. After all, you might need it soon if Margaret's daughter says 'yes',' she added naughtily.

It was Dickon's turn to flush and Nick let out a whoop that caused George to drop his spoon with a clatter.

After the men had gone Ann found it difficult to settle to her usual tasks. She picked up some wool to card and put it down again. She scooped grain into the cleaned pot ready for the morning, but paused and looked out into the garden. She went to the door. The evening air was fresh and sweet after the stuffiness of the cottages and she drew in big breaths, trying to calm her anxiety about Dickon's coming trip.

For a while she wandered around her garden, taking pleasure as she always did in the miracle of new growth from the tiny seeds she had planted earlier in the season. Now and again she bent to remove the odd weed or to crush a sprig of thyme or rosemary between her fingers, inhaling the fresh, sharp smell. Inevitably her feet took her towards her bees, but there was now a slight chill in the air and the last few latecomers were hurrying into the shelter of the hive.

The loud cawing of a crow caught her attention and she followed its flight as it swooped over the church, seeming to suggest a course of action to her. With a shrug and a glance back at the silent house, she made her way to the church. Inside it was shadowed and still and there was a calmness and a sense of peace that Ann felt she needed. She crossed to the statue of the Virgin and sank to her knees. Her thoughts were not formed. Her mind was a jumble of hopes, fears and worries and she tried to order her thoughts. Her son was a grown man now; she could not tie him to her apron strings for ever. This trip to London was an adventure such as every young man should have at least once in his life. She should be glad for him. Why then, did she feel this sense of foreboding and worry?

She looked up at the calm face of the Virgin above her. 'Blessed Mary, keep my son sa…'

The loud and unexpected thud of the church door closing made her pause and turn around. Somebody tall and thin was hurrying towards her. The rapid, bandy-legged gait seemed familiar somehow, but she didn't recognise who it was and rose uncertainly to her feet.

'I knewed it was you.' The stranger blurted out. 'I saw you comin' in.'.

Ann started. 'Si?' Her voice seemed to croak as she caught her breath. She cleared her throat. 'Simon, is that you?' As Simon walked towards her he was caught in a sunbeam coming in through a side window and for the first time she saw him clearly. 'Why Simon, whatever is the matter, you look as if you've seen a ghost.'

Simon rushed up to her babbling incoherently. 'I ain't killed 'im. I didn't' it'im that hard. 'E can't be dead.' He looked up at the statue of the Virgin and sank to his knees, his hands clasped in front of him.

'Simon? Calm down, lad. Who have you hit? What do you mean?' Ann put her hand on his shoulder and bent towards him. 'Who've you killed? I mean what…' She tailed off.

There were tears in the boy's eyes. 'Father. I 'it father. He came back 'n when Ruthie died I 'it 'im. There's so much blood and Mary says I've got to go or I'll be strung up. I didn't mean to kill 'im – I'm sorry Mother.'

Ann wasn't sure if he was talking to his dead Mother or the Virgin and shook her head in disbelief at what she was hearing 'Ruth? Dead? Oh Simon you can't mean that? And your father's…? How? Simon what have you done? I mean… I'd better come, but—'

Simon leapt up and grabbed her arm. 'No, you mustn't. If he ain't dead he'll… well he won't have you in the 'ouse.'

'Yes, I mean…' she twisted her hands in anxiety. 'But if he's badly hurt we can't just leave him. And Ruth? Poor lamb! She's dead? How? Poor Mary.' Ann was talking more to herself as she hurried towards the door, Simon trailing uncertainly behind her.

It was only a short distance to the Catt's house and, as they approached, Ann's apprehension grew. She certainly didn't want to confront Catt, but then again could she just leave someone who needed help? And what of Mary and poor little Ruth? Was the child really dead? She was so engrossed in her thoughts that she would have fallen as she stumbled over a tree root had not Simon put out a hand to steady her. She nodded her thanks and took a deep breath. There was no turning back now. She gestured for Simon to go ahead of her and he cautiously pushed open the door. Immediately Ann could hear the sound of quiet sobbing and the sound of someone in need of help had a strangely calming effect on her. Without hesitating she stepped inside.

The last time she had been in this cottage was when poor Nell had died and Goodwife Catt had screamed her accusation of witchcraft. But that was then, and this was now, she told herself as she looked around in the dim light. There were people here who needed her and she was not one to refuse a cry for help.

It was even dirtier and more squalid than when she'd been here last time and stank of a mix of drink and unwashed linen, but her attention was focussed on the girl who sat clutching a pathetic bundle of rags in her thin arms. In the gloom, as she went forward towards Mary, her foot kicked against the prone body of James Catt who was sprawled on the floor.

Ann gasped. 'Mother of God!' she exclaimed and bent down to peer at the man. Immediately she could see the pool of sticky red blood under his head and feared the worst.

'See. I knewed I'd killed him.' Simon's voice was shrill with fear. 'Oh God forgive me I didn't mean—'

Ann looked up at him reassuringly. She shook her head. 'Hush now, lad. You haven't killed him. He's not dead; see he's breathing. Here, help me turn him.'

With Simon's help she rolled Catt onto his side so that she could see the side of his head where the blood was. She let out her breath. 'Praise be. It's not his head that's bleeding; it's his ear, look.' She pointed to the left ear which had a ragged tear in it. 'Ears always bleed something terrible, but it won't kill him. See the blood's beginning to thicken, but if you've any flour in the house shake a bit on it Mary and 'twill hasten it.'

She looked up at Mary who shook her head miserably. 'No? Well, never mind.' Ann wrinkled her nose and sniffed. 'He'll be fine, I'm sure, when he's slept off the drink.'

'Is our father dead?'

A voice from the corner made Simon turn. 'No 'enry. He ain't dead. Go back to sleep now.'

'I wish he were dead.' Mary's voice was low and harsh. 'Him instead of Ruth. What did she ever do that was wrong? Why should she be dead and he be alive?'

'We mustn't question God's will.' Ann said quietly. 'Are you...' she gestured towards the child Mary was holding, 'sure?'

Miserably Mary nodded and wiped her sleeve across her nose. 'Yes. She's dead. Took a fever didn't she and I've failed me Ma. Always promised I'd take care of them if anything.... It's like she knew she'd go. Asked me to look after them - and I've failed. All due to him.' And she poked her father with her foot. He gave a grunt and Ann stepped back.

Mary seemed to rouse herself. 'But he mustn't find you here when he wakes, Simon – or you Goodwife, come to that.'

'I can't leave you Mary. Not—' Simon's voice was anguished.

Ann interrupted him. 'Mary's right Simon. You can't stay here. He's a violent, vengeful man and it's not safe to stay.' She looked into his face and raised her eyebrows in a questioning way. 'Have you got something to go back to? You look well, lad. You must have prospered in the year since you left.'

Simon nodded. 'Went to sea. And it's good.' He took a shuddering breath. 'I loves it. Better 'n 'ere. It's not hard to get a job now I knows what I'm doing.'

'Then go and, if you can make a life for yourself, there is hope for your brothers and sisters. With you dead or injured there is none.'

Tears started to stream down his face as silently Simon hugged his brothers and sisters who rose like wraiths from their bundles in the corner. He tried to stutter his thanks to Ann, but she pushed him gently towards the door. 'Go. Hurry. You have the night ahead of you. I doubt he'll stir before morning and a good thing too.'

'Where will you go Si?' Mary asked in a quiet voice.

Simon shook his head. 'Dunno…um… guess I'll make for Lewes and pick up a boat going downriver from there. The sea's good. Clean and sort of free, but it don't seem right runnin' out on you like this.'

'Yes it do, brother. Go now while you can and make your fortune for us.' Mary managed a shaky smile as she gave her brother's arm a final squeeze. 'God go with you, Si'

She turned her back as if she could not bear to see her brother walk away down the path. He turned back once and seemed to hesitate, but then strode off into the setting sun.

35

The sky was only just glimmering light and the birds had barely started their early morning chorus when Ann heard the door close softly. He was away then.

She slipped out of bed and, squinting through a gap in the shutters, watched as Dickon strode away on his adventure. 'God and Blessed Mary keep you, my son,' she murmured as he turned the corner and disappeared from sight. Protestant or Catholic – she cared not what they called themselves – she did believe in a caring God who, as her mother used to say, helped those who helped themselves. As she whispered the words, she had faith that he would respond to a mother's prayer and keep her son safe.

It was a relief to be up as she'd not slept at all in the night, but had gone over and over the events of the previous evening in her mind. She had been back home from Catt's house some time before John and the boys returned from helping John's brother and she hadn't said anything to them about Simon or little Ruth's death. Whatever the repercussions in the future, there was nothing to be done about it and besides, the men were tired and wanted nothing more than a good night's rest - especially Dickon who was setting off early this morning on his big adventure.

She padded silently into the other room and, taking care not to wake either George or Nick, she drew her shawl around her shoulders and slipped quietly out into the soft shadowed garden.

A flock of rooks flew overhead, their raucous calling making Dickon look up at the reddening sky. Not a good sign in the morning; the weather might break today. Just my luck he thought, as he strode purposefully along the road. But soon all gloom and apprehension was dispelled as he was hailed by Joseph Baker who was tramping up the hill from Town Row. He had formed a friendship with Joseph a couple of years ago when they were both employed digging the ore. Like him, Joseph had a taste for adventure and had been only too glad to swap a shovel for the promise of places new and so, whenever they could, they tried to be on the same wagon gang.

In looks, Joseph was the opposite of Dickon. He was short and stocky – almost a head shorter - with broad shoulders and a mop of light-brown, curly hair that refused to be tamed. He was immensely strong with legs that in width, made up for what they lacked in length. Unlike Dickon he didn't speak much, as he was afflicted with a stammer that would have made him the butt of jokes if he'd not had such a sturdy physique. However, as his family said that Dickon talked enough for two, this was not a problem between them and, sharing as they did, the same sense of humour, the two young men made a good team. Despite the long haul ahead of them, both were fizzing with excitement and full of what they hoped they'd see in London.

As they came within sight of the wagon they recognised the figures of Peter Tabury and Rufus Smith, the other two members of the gang who had arrived before them and were waiting at the roadside. The two youngsters looked at each other and grinned with satisfaction. They'd all worked together before and got on well.

Dickon slung his bundle up on the wagon 'Looks like it'll be a good run if the weather holds,' he said as he went to take the head of the ox on the outside. 'Steady you,' he said soothingly and scratched the animal's nose. He liked oxen – felt that they had a quiet dignity about them that the more skittish horses lacked. The animal looped its long drooling tongue over its nostrils leaving a wet streak on Dickon's shirt. 'Get off,' he said laughing and wiping it down his jerkin.

'Oi! Don't stand there petting that beast, come and give us an 'and,' called Rufus. As the oldest man at just over forty years of age, he was in charge of the wagon and was known among the men as a fair master. Provided you did your share, you could expect to be treated well. Unlike some of the bosses, he did not believe in driving men and animals until they nearly dropped, but he always made sure that there was time for proper food and rest stops and he was a fund of tales that kept them amused for hours. Yes, Dickon thought - this definitely promised to be a good trip.

36

It had been raining steadily now for nearly forty eight hours. With the sky covered with thick, dark clouds, the light was fading much earlier than was usual for mid-June. Ann turned from the window. She couldn't put it off any longer she thought with a sigh. The men would be in soon so she would need to light the candles. She didn't expect to have to use them in summer and hated the smell of the burning fat in the closed room. Even though she kept her own bees, wax candles were still a luxury that they kept for special occasions.

The door banged as John and Nick came in shaking off their wet clothes. The candles sputtered in the draught sending a curl of smoke into the air. Ann wrinkled her nose in distaste. 'Oh this rain,' she said. 'Can you ever remember a summer like it? Poor Dickon, I wonder how he's getting on? They should nearly have reached the city by now, I think, but it can't be much fun in this; the roads will be awash and they're bound to be delayed.'

'Oh stop worrying about the boy – he can take care of himself, and he's used to the wet. We all are just recently.'

'Mm . . . Whatever happened to those lovely hot summers when we were young? Do you remember the summer when we were walking out? It didn't . . .'

'Don't you remember, Mother? Father told us the other night; it's all the fault of the Queen.'

'Nick, that's enough now, and for heaven's sake stand still. You're worse than a dog spattering wet everywhere! Here, dry your hair with this,' she tossed him a cloth.

John had just poured himself a mug of beer from the jug that always stood ready on the table, when there was the thud of hoof beats that stopped outside. John and Ann looked at each other frowning.

Ann pulled a face. 'Not someone wanting shoeing at this time of night surely? You've only just come in.'

John went towards the door, but had barely gone three paces when

191

there was a banging on the outside.

'What the hell . . .'

He flung open the door. A tall, well-built man, his cloak dripping with water stood outside. 'Ashdown?' he said.

'I am John Ashdown, yes. Who wants to know?'

'Stephen Burges. News of Richard - Dickon Ashdown – your son?'

'Dickon?' Ann came up behind John, craning her head, trying to see past him. 'Did you say you have news of Dickon?' Her voice had the edge of panic to it. 'Is something wrong?'

John stepped back, bumping into Ann, treading on her foot and making her cry out. 'Come in, man, come into the dry. Ann, a drink for our visitor. You have news of our son?'

The man nodded. 'Bad news, I'm afraid.'

Ann put her hand to her mouth and gave a little cry. 'He's not . . .?'

'No, no.' The man shook his head and put out a reassuring hand. 'Your son - an accident. Broken leg.

'Oh God! Where is he?'

The man looked exhausted; he gratefully accepted a mug of ale and slumped down onto the wooden bench. He pulled off his hat, sending a shower of drops across the room, but nobody stepped back or protested. Rather they pressed closer, eager to hear what he had to say. The man gulped down the ale eagerly draining the mug in one go. Wiping the back of his hand across of his mouth he continued. 'An inn - Farmhouse Inn - north of Sevenoaks. Road was bad. Wagon bogged down. Tried to free it. Son slipped.'

Despite her anxiety about Dickon, Ann couldn't help noticing how words seemed to shoot out of the man in short bursts, like air from the bellows. He had obviously ridden hard, or perhaps was just not used to making long speeches. 'Wheel caught his leg – broken.'

John burst in. 'Is he hurt elsewhere? It is just his leg?'

'Lucky - but a bad break.'

'We are indebted to you. How come . . . You were travelling this way? '

'At the inn. On my way to Lewes. Not far out of the way. Sorry to bring bad news.' The man subsided like an empty sack, as if he was now drained of words.

'We must go to him, John. Oh, Dickon, Dickon . . . I knew something would happen. I've been waiting – ever since the bees swarmed onto that dead branch last week. I knew it was a bad sign. I said so at the time. Bees always know. They say it means a death or a tragedy, but please God – not Dickon.' She twisted her hands in anxiety.

'Not *we* my love. You cannot come. You must bide here.'

'But John I must. I know about—'

'No Ann. Listen. We need to get him home quickly and with the roads mired as they are it'll take two strong men to keep a cart going. The more people there are the slower the cart. It's best if Nick and I go and you make ready for him here.' He turned to his son. 'Nick go now to Will's and tell him we need to borrow his horse and cart tomorrow. First thing – soon as it's light. Tell him his nephew is in a bad way and we must get there as soon as possible. Hurry now lad.'

'But John—'

John's voice was firm. 'No, Ann. Tell me what to do to make him comfortable and you can see to him when we get him here. Trust me, it's the best way.'

Although she was not happy about being left behind, Ann knew that her husband was right. With all his work at the forge, Nick was much stronger than she was and together the two men could heave a cart out of the mire if necessary and reach Dickon in the shortest possible time. Even so, it would take them a day to get to him and another day to get home. She turned to the stranger who was gratefully spooning up the remains of the pottage she'd put in front of him.

'When did this happen – how long has he been waiting?'

'Early this morning. They'd only just left. Good thing. Inn to hand. I set out straight away. Good horse.'

Ann laid a hand on his arm. 'We are so grateful Goodman Burges. It's so kind of you, and so lucky that you were travelling this way. To think of him lying there. He must be in such pain . . .' Her voice broke, but she gathered herself. 'Yes, pain . . .' she repeated, half to herself and went over to her basket that was always set ready in the corner. She looked inside, but seeming not to find what she was looking for she crossed to the shelf and ran her finger along the line of jars and potions. She selected two and put them on the table, then went to her bedroom and came back with a bundle of cloths. 'George, come here. Go and find two straight sticks about this long and this thick.' She indicated with her hands. 'They must be straight now. Take the lantern – here.'

The man stood up. 'I'll be off then,' he said.

'Indeed not,' John put his hand on the man's shoulder and pressed him back in his seat. 'After your kindness the least we can do is provide you with a bed for the night. You must be exhausted. That's quite a ride in weather like this. You rest. I'll go and see to your horse. It'll be fine in the stall by the forge for the night.'

37

Just after midnight the rain had stopped so that the morning sky was a clear, pearlescent grey, but it was barely light, when Ann woke from a deep sleep and heard the rattle of the cart on the lane outside. John and Nick were already astir and the door creaked as John slipped out for a word with his brother, Will. He was a good man and it was lucky that he was prepared to let them borrow his horse and cart to bring Dickon home. Reluctantly Ann swung her legs out of bed and stifled a yawn. She hadn't slept until nearly dawn, worried as she was about Dickon. Broken legs could be hard to mend and could lead to all sorts of complications. She had successfully splinted the arms of a couple of the village children when they had taken a tumble, but a man's leg was altogether a different matter. She couldn't bear the thought of her handsome, energetic son becoming a helpless cripple and had tried to put the image from her mind as she fought back the tears and prayed that he wouldn't take a fever as so many did after an injury. She had tossed and turned for most of the night but, tired out by the events of the last few days had finally fallen asleep, only to be woken what had seemed just minutes later by the noise of the cart.

All was prepared, and even before the sun peeped over the horizon, Ann was standing at the gate waving goodbye to Goodman Burges who was continuing his way west and to John and Nick setting out at a brisk pace north. She stood motionless, long after they were out of sight, until the last rattle of the cart, the last hoof beat, died away in the clear stillness of early morning. She shivered slightly. Suddenly feeling very alone. Drawing her shawl closer about her shoulders, she looked over at the bee skeps and felt a prickle of unease. Had it been a warning when the bees swarmed on the dead branch of the old pear tree last week? Was the old saying right? Pray God it was not.

A few early morning risers were already moving about at the entrance of the neatly woven skeps, but she knew that the main worker bees would not be about their business until the sun had properly risen and warmed the air.

Even so, she paused for a few moments watching the tiny, furry brown creatures.

'They've gone,' she murmured. 'John and Nick. They've gone to get Dickon. He's hurt, but you'll see. They'll bring him home safely - I know they will.'

Back indoors, she looked around the neat room and sighed. Without the two men to cook for, the day seemed to stretch endlessly ahead. She certainly wouldn't see them again before tomorrow night, for they would have to go carefully with Dickon in the cart, 'And I must keep busy,' she said aloud to herself.

It was still early, but George, too, had been roused by the movement in the house and, after cutting himself a hunk of bread, he took the scythe from the corner and disappeared into the orchard. Ann nodded to herself. He seemed much more contented these days; had finally settled back into the routine of family life and was making himself useful without being asked.

'Now, what to do?' she asked herself, frowning. 'Ah . . .' She took up the basket containing part of a fleece and settled herself on a stool in the doorway where the early sunshine warmed her. After first spreading a cloth across her lap to catch the debris, she set about carding the wool ready for spinning. Using a small bunch of teasels she kept for the purpose, she stroked the long strands of wool with the spiky heads, so that the fibres all ran in the same direction, picking out bits of grass and dirt as she did so. As her skin became soft and oily with lanolin from the wool, she put her hands up to her nose and sniffed the warm, earthy smell appreciatively. Carding and spinning was a soothing task, which she hoped would calm the turmoil in her brain but, although she was absorbed in what she was doing, she was still aware of an uneasy fluttering like a trapped bird at the edge of her mind.

After an hour or so there was a mound of neat rolls of wool ready for spinning, but that was a job that she could not do until she had paid a visit to Alex Fermor. Last week she had accidentally knocked her spindle from the table and as it fell, it struck the leg of the trestle and the end had snapped off. She picked it up and compressed her lips ruefully. She had used the same spindle for a long time and it was like an old friend, but it was no use now; she would have to buy a new one from Alex. Anyway, she thought, a visit to the Fermors' was perhaps what she needed to take her out of herself and stop this nagging worry that kept clouding her day.

The sun was well up and she was suddenly aware of how hot she was; there was certainly no need for a shawl. After taking some coins from a wooden box on the shelf and slipping them into a small leather pouch tied at her waist, she paused in the doorway. From the orchard came the steady swish of the scythe as George cut the grass; he was obviously still busy and would not miss her.

Alex was the local wood turner and he and his wife Margery lived on the other side of the village at the edge of a small copse where the ground sloped quite steeply down towards Jarvis Brook. Ann made her way along the main street and then turned right down the hill past the church, several times being stopped by neighbours who had already heard about Dickon's accident and wanted to wish him well. It certainly wasn't easy to keep secrets in a village Ann mused and wondered yet again how Katherine and William were faring.

She could hear the rasp of Alex's lathe long before she came within sight of his cottage, but the sound was nearly drowned by the barking of two large, lumbering dogs announcing her presence. She hesitated, viewing them warily and was relieved when Margery appeared at the door, wiping her hands on her apron. She was a large, jolly woman who always reminded Ann of a soft, round pin cushion. Several years older than Ann, she and Alex were childless, but she seemed very content with her dogs and her many cats, several of which were lying luxuriating in the sunshine by the open door.

'Why, Ann, it's been a long time since we saw you. When I heard the dogs I thought it was those men coming back?' Hearing their Mistress's friendly greeting the animals wagged their tails in unison and flopped down with a thump next to the cats.

Ann smiled. 'Hello Margery. Men? What men?'

'Oh quite fierce they looked – and they were very unpleasant about the dogs. I was quite frightened. Came by about an hour ago, heading for the village. Lucky you missed them; don't want to get mixed up with the likes of them. But come in do and I'll fetch you some ale, you must be thirsty after a walk in this heat.'

Ann accepted the invitation gratefully and followed Margery into the house. It was pleasant to be out of the hot sun and soon the two women were exchanging news and Margery was sympathetically commiserating with Ann over poor Dickon's accident. Relieved to have someone to listen to her worries and fears, it was with a lighter heart that Ann realised nearly an hour had passed and she had still not fulfilled her errand.

She rose from her stool and stretched. 'I really must be going Margery, I've kept you far too long, but I have to say it's been so good to chat.'

'Well, my dear, "a trouble shared . . ." as they say. Now come along into the workshop and choose yourself a spindle. I know Alex was making some only last week, so you should have a good choice.'

Following closely behind Margery, Ann walked across to the workshop that stood behind the house. As she ducked her head and entered, she was struck by the smell of fresh wood shavings that curled over the floor like a child's blonde ringlets – a clean, aromatic smell that had a soothing, calming effect on her.

Alex didn't look up as they stood watching him, his eyes fixed in concentration on the wooden bowl that was taking shape in front of him. The long pole above him dipped and rose like a nodding horse as the leather strap whirled the block of wood around and his foot bounced rhythmically up and down on the pedal. Both women were content to watch as slowly the bowl took shape until at last, just when Ann felt herself becoming mesmerized by the constant whirling, Alex seemed satisfied with his work and ceased pedalling. A tall, thin man of few words with a sad, rather dour expression Ann could never understand how he and his jolly wife could be such a contented couple.

'Ann has come for a spindle, husband. I told her that it was lucky as you made some only last week.'

Without speaking Alex nodded slowly and pointed to a bench on one side of the workshop.

The sun was almost overhead as Ann walked home and the village looked strangely empty for most families were at dinner. George would be hungry, she thought guiltily, but, nonetheless, she crossed the road to speak to Mother Birdy who was, as usual, sitting on a stool outside her door. Ann hadn't had time to offer a greeting before the old woman was bobbing and beckoning to her.

'Have you seen them?' the old woman wheezed in excitement. 'Came right past here they did, then stopped and asked me for directions.'

'Seen who?' Ann shook her head. 'I've seen hardly anyone, I've been to fetch a—'

'You mean you haven't seen the strangers? Three of them. Big fellows with swords at their belts. Never seen the like. When they came over to me I was that feared, but they were pleasant enough. Wanted to know where Hosman's place was.'

Ann frowned. 'They must be the men Margery was telling me about. But who were they? What did they want with—'

'Can't say, but they said they were on the Queen's business' The old woman nodded importantly. She put her hand on Ann's arm. 'They had a cart too - and horses. I heard horses, so p'raps there was more of them.'

'Were they soldiers? P'raps there is to be a war with the French. John did hear something . . . but why would they want—'

'Couldn't say, my dear, but I've never seen the like.' The old woman gesticulated with excitement seemingly buoyed up by her encounter with the newcomers

'Oh well, no doubt we'll hear soon enough. But I must be going – George will wonder where I am.' And raising a hand in farewell Ann continued on her way home.

Ann and George had shared a simple meal of plain barley pottage before he'd taken himself back to the orchard. Usually she liked to add something to flavour the gruel, but today she didn't have the heart and, anyway, despite her walk, she had little appetite. Keeping busy all morning she had managed not to dwell too much on the problems that John and Nick might encounter.

Before John had left they had put a thick layer of straw in the cart and she had added some blankets, so that Dickon might travel more comfortably and not take a chill. She had given John the poppy syrup that she hoped would ease her son's pain, with strict instructions not to give more than she said, but she was, in fact, loath to trust anyone with the administering of her potions. She knew, however, that without it, Dickon would face a long and difficult journey on the deeply rutted roads.

She couldn't stop herself worrying and going over and over their journey in her mind. She glanced around the empty cottage, almost feeling the silence. She was uneasy with John and Nick away as, always at the back of her mind, like a worm borrowing through her brain, was the anxiety that Catt would cause trouble for her again. That somehow he knew she'd been to his cottage again when poor Ruthie had died.

Suddenly, whether from anxiety or a sudden chill, Ann shivered. As if reflecting her mood, the morning sun had gone, blotted out by large white clouds blown over the forest on a rising North West wind. She drew her shawl off the peg behind the door and, draping it over her shoulders she picked up her new spindle, looped a length of thread around it and twirled experimentally. It was well balanced and felt good.

She plucked a roll of wool from the pile she had made earlier. The rhythmic twirl and twist of her hands calmed her and she felt the spindle grow heavy as the spun wool looped around it. It was always a job she enjoyed and she remembered how, when she was a small girl, her grandmother had taught her how to spin, telling stories to pass the time as the two sat companionably side by side. She had almost filled her spindle when there was a crash at the side of the house followed by shouting. Alarmed, she jumped to her feet.

'George?' she called. 'George, is that you?' But even as she cried out there was a thumping on the door.

Her heart racing she went to open it. Her shawl dropped to the floor, but she still clutched the spindle in her hand as she found herself facing two men who were crowding the doorway.

'Ann Ashdown?' The man was very tall and well built, with a black beard that had been cut to a sharp point.

Instinctively she drew away from him, though still kept a firm grip on the door, holding it partly closed. 'Er…Yes…Who are you? Why do you want to know?' She looked more closely at the men and noticed, fearfully, that they were both wearing short swords at their belts. Were these the men that Margery and Mother Birdy had told her about? What could they want with her? Did they have horses that needed shoeing? John wasn't here. He couldn't help. They'd have to go somewhere else. Thoughts raced through her mind.

'I'm sorry my hus—'

The second man, who was only slightly shorter, turned and, as he did so, Ann felt as if the world was tipping. Standing at the end of the garden path, was James Catt.

'Is this her?' the man said, addressing Catt.

'Yea – that's her what I told you about.' Catt pointed a finger at her. 'That's Ann Ashdown,' he said with a barely concealed smirk.

A third man came around the side of the house. In his hand he held George's English Bible. 'It was there. Just as he said it would be.' He flicked his head in Catt's direction. 'Hidden on a shelf in the corner.'

'Yea.' Catt grinned. 'Thought she could keep it hid in that shed – the witch. Thought nobody knowed. But I found it. I was on to her. Lucky I seed you fellows this morning. She's a witch and no mistake. Something needs to be done about 'er.' Catt crossed himself with exaggerated piety. 'Witch and an 'eretic - that's what she is, reading the Holy Book in English.'

'But I can't...' Ann stopped herself just in time as, holding herself rigid, she resisted the temptation to look towards the orchard.

The tall man took the book and held it out towards her. 'Ann Ashdown, is this your book?'

Ann raised her chin and looked him straight in the eye. 'It is,' she said. 'It's my Bible.'

'Then under the law against heresy, I arrest you. Take her.'

Ann found herself grabbed by the shorter of the two men and pushed roughly along her path to the gate. As she passed him, Ann noticed the still bloody, ragged tear in his ear, then Catt thrust his face forward and leered at her. 'Witch,' he hissed. 'Now you'll get what you deserve!' and she felt his spittle on her cheek.

As they forced her along Ann desperately twisted her head this way and that, looking frantically around, looking for anyone who could help her. Oh, if only John and Nick were here.

As they reached the lane a cart came around the corner pulled by two horses, one black, one brown. Standing in the cart, Ann was astonished to see Alexander Hosmer, a young man, not much older than Dickon, who had inherited much of the land around Rotherfield when his father died. As the cart drew closer Ann could see that he was dishevelled as if he'd been in a struggle and his hands were tied behind his back.

With a rising sense of disbelief, she felt her own hands dragged behind her. Her new spindle dropped to the ground, the last twist of wool trailing in the mud, as her wrists were tied with rough rope. Then, with no more courtesy than they would give to a sack of vegetables, the two men hoisted her into the cart, where she was further fastened to a chain that ran along the length of the cart - just like a beast being tethered in a stall.

'Stop! What are you doing? Where are you taking me?' Panic washed over Ann and she thought she was going to be sick. 'You can't do this,' she screamed.

The driver flicked his whip and the cart started with a jolt. Ann lost her balance and was thrown against Hosmer. She could feel that he was shaking although his voice was steady.

'Stay calm, Goodwife,' said the young man softly, as if he were twice his age, 'and make your peace with God. There's no hope for us now in this sad world. Pray that our reward will be in heaven.'

George sat huddled in the fork of the oak tree, the thick summer canopy concealing him from the strangers. He peered down as the cart rattled slowly along the lane underneath him and frowned as he saw that Alexander Hosmer and his mother were both fastened to a chain. Then he saw something that made him rise to his feet. On the floor next to the two strangers was his book.

Steadying himself with arms outstretched, his hands against the rough bark, he leant down from the tree. 'NO!' he bellowed.

But his voice was caught on the rising wind and drowned by the rumble of wheels as the cart passed out of sight.

38

Tuesday 22nd June 1557

'The white wings of Angels! Look above us. He comes! Our Saviour comes for the righteous.'

The ranting voice of the man continued and like waves breaking on the shore, the crowd swayed and moved everyone craning for a better view of the huge pile of faggots heaped in the middle of the square. The boy drew himself up and peered this way and that until suddenly there was gap that gave him a clear view. His eyes widened. He caught his breath. 'No, no – it can't be. Not 'er,' he closed his eyes then opened them again. 'No, no,' he moaned, hunching his back and folding his arms across his stomach. The bearded man standing on his right looked at him curiously.

'You knows one of the 'eretics boy?'

Silently Simon nodded. 'She i'nt a heretic; she's my friend. I can't.... I can't.' Simon turned away putting a hand over his mouth as the chanting of the faithful rose in a crescendo, drowning the voice shouting verses from the English Bible. People gasped as a man dressed all in black stepped forward to the thrust a flaming torch into the faggots piled around the ten men and women roped to a central post.

For a moment it seemed as if all held their breath. The wood would not catch. Then a curl of smoke rose up, followed by a spurt of orange and a cheer went up from the crowd, almost - but not quite - drowning out the screams from some of the condemned as flames licked around them. Simon could stand it no longer and lunged towards the fire. 'Goodwife,' he called in despair, but the man next to him grabbed his arm. 'Goodwife Ashdown!'

'No. No you don't lad,' the man said urgently, holding Simon in a strong grip. 'Easy now. Don't you call attention to yourself, not unless you want to be took too. You can do no good there, it's too late.'

Tears streamed down the boy's face and he cuffed the snot from his nose and sniffed.

'But she's my friend, she helped us and now…'

'I know, lad, I know, but there's nowt you can do for her or any of them now, 'cept pray their suffering will be short.'

'They can't do this to her,' he gasped. 'They've made a mistake – she i'nt an 'eretic. I knows her. She prays to the Virgin. I've seen 'er.' Simon shuddered and retched.

'Aye, that don't surprise me,' the man said in a low voice. 'I hear that there are several that was only took yesterday or the day before. Not time for a proper 'earing or nothing. Probably didn't have a writ from London for your friend there, but it don't make no difference and you certainly don't want to get mixed up with them lot.' The man jerked his head towards the crowd of people holding crosses and chanting prayers. 'Not if you knows what's good for you, you don't.'

Suddenly the crowd and the condemned fell silent. The only sound was the spitting and crackling of the fire as it rose up like a roaring beast in the freshening breeze. Sparks drifted high up into the sky dancing like fireflies above the hushed crowd and thick black smoke billowed above the town, filling the air with the smell of scorched flesh and blotting out the summer sun.

AUTHOR'S NOTE

Ann Ashdown was burned at the stake in the town of Lewes on 22nd June 1557. The event is recorded in John Foxe's Book of Martyrs.

Execution of ten martyrs at Lewes. -

"Again we have to record the wholesale sacrifice of Christ's little flock, of whom five were women. On the 22d of June, 1557, the town of Lewes beheld ten persons doomed to perish by fire and persecution. The names of these worthies were,

Richard Woodman; G. Stephens, W. Mainard, Alex. Hosman, and Thomasin Wood, servants; Margery Morris, and James Morris, her son; Dennis Burges, **Ashdown's wife,** and Grove's wife.

These persons were taken a few days only before their judgement, and suffered at Lewes, in Sussex, June 22, 1557. Of these, eight were prematurely executed, inasmuch as the writ from London could not have arrived for their burning."

It was while researching my family history that I came across Ann and felt I wanted to write a story about her. According to parish records, Ann did live in Rotherfield with her husband, John and three sons, Richard, Nicholas and George. Historically, nothing else is known about Ann other than that she was one of the so called Marian martyrs, so my novel is total fiction. While writing this book, however, she has become very real to me and I like to think that I may possibly be related to her. My maternal great-grandmother was Sophia Ashdown who came from the same area of Sussex and several generations of men in the Ashdown family were blacksmiths.

Church records for this time show that one, William Collyer, was the priest at the Church of St Denys in Rotherfield. He was deprived of his living in 1556 – a year earlier than in my story - although I am not aware that the reason for this is known. His character and family are totally fictitious and entirely my own invention. Interestingly, no entries are made in the registers from April 1556 to 1559 and it is probable that the parish was unserved by a priest throughout that time. This was not unusual; there were many such parishes, due to the difficulty the Catholic Church faced in finding enough suitable priests to serve all parishes.

I should like to thank Chris Morgan for making me believe that I could write a novel, Alison Fuggle for her helpful criticism and my family for all their help and encouragement.

Thank you too, Reader, for reading Sacrifice. If you have enjoyed it, please consider leaving a brief review on Amazon.

ABOUT THE AUTHOR

Rosalind Fox has had a number of stories broadcast on BBC radio and was recently long listed in a Radio 4 Short Story Competition. Her monologue, Justice, was performed by Laurence Saunders at the Midland Arts Centre, Birmingham. She has written articles on commission for various magazines and had several poems published. Sacrifice is her first novel.

Printed in Great Britain
by Amazon.co.uk, Ltd.,
Marston Gate.